A DISTANCE OF GROUND

Buck Clegg has twenty years of horse racing behind him, beginning at the age of fourteen on bush tracks in Oklahoma and Texas. But he's had to give up the saddle, and is now a jockey's agent. Whilst working in New Mexico, he receives a call from his old employer Charlie Vann with shocking news: Jim Ned, Charlie's champion bay stallion and Buck's old mount, has been stolen — and Charlie wants Buck's help to track him down. But the underworld of illegal horse-trafficking is a dangerous place. A fraudulent attempt at claiming the $50,000 reward ends with bullets flying. Then Tom Shelby, the ranch manager who blames himself for the horse's loss, is found dead in an apparent suicide — although Buck suspects there is more to the tragedy than meets the eye. Will Jim Ned ever see his home pasture again?

A Distance
of Ground

Fred Grove

SAGEBRUSH
Large Print Westerns

First published in Great Britain by Gunsmoke
First published in the United States by Five Star

First Isis Edition
published 2015
by arrangement with
Golden West Literary Agency

A catalogue record for this book is available
from the British Library.

ISBN 978–1–78541–017–8 (pb)

Published by
F. A. Thorpe (Publishing)
Anstey, Leicestershire

Set by Words & Graphics Ltd.
Anstey, Leicestershire
Printed and bound in Great Britain by
T. J. International Ltd., Padstow, Cornwall

This book is printed on acid-free paper

CHAPTER
ONE

I'm still asked why I don't ride racehorses any more. Kinda preens the old ego a little. I can give you a list of solid reasons: seven busted ribs, left collar bone broken twice, right collar bone once, broken left arm, compressed vertebrae, right leg broken in two places, broken left knee, torn ligaments right knee, eight broken fingers, nose broken three times, which is why some people take me for an ex-pug. I've lost count of the concussions. That's the tally in twenty years of race ridin'. All I can remember. I left out some.

I started at fourteen on the bush tracks in Oklahoma and Texas. That's all I wanted to do, and about all I did, besides a little bull ridin' in rodeos. Never went past the eighth grade. They said I was a natural. Today they say Buck Clegg is lucky to be able to walk, even luckier to be alive. I agree. I could be training racehorses, but, if I did, I know I couldn't stay out of the saddle. That's a no-no, the docs say. One more bad fall and I could be paralyzed from the waist down, a jockey's greatest fear.

I'm also asked if Lori Beth, who sings top country songs as Margo Drake, is another reason I quit — because she wanted me to. I'd like to say that now, but it wouldn't be true. I don't have a wife any more. That's

1

another story, one I'm not proud of, including a big question which I guess will remain unanswered the rest of my life. A man can make some awful mistakes when he's flushed with money and too much pride, sometimes with whiskey and amphetamines to keep going, and he's known from coast to coast as the hottest quarter horse jockey in the country.

So now I'm a jockey's agent, and I can't say the pickin's have been like a bird nest on the ground. But it's a living most of the time, except when my riders are out with injuries, or set down for rough ridin', or banned for drugs. That's why, when the girl on the desk at the Amigo Motel, where I stay when I'm in Ruidoso, New Mexico for the race season, said I had a long-distance call, I had hoped it was Chip Romero to tell me he was able to ride again for some fresh stakes money.

But I figured it was trouble when a familiar voice, high-pitched and urgent, came on the line. "Buck, it's me . . . Charlie."

"Yeah. What is it, Charlie?"

Charlie Vann was not only born with a silver spoon in his mouth, he was born with oil wells all over the family's red-dirt farm back in Oklahoma. I used to ride for him. A good fellow, but as tight with money as the bark on a blackjack. He seldom called unless he had horse problems. He still campaigned a string of quarter horses, and I advised him when he asked for it.

"You won't believe this," he went on, and stopped. I could hear him choking as he tried to get out the words. "Jim Ned's gone," he said at last.

2

I jerked. "You mean he's dead?"

He choked again. "No . . . but almost as bad . . . stolen."

"My God, Charlie! How?"

"When I went out to his barn this morning, he was gone. I figured he'd broken out. But a bull elephant couldn't bust outta there and the paddock . . . and the gate was closed. I followed his tracks out to the highway. They must've put him in a horse trailer . . . That's all we know. Oh, I called the sheriff and the Highway Patrol. But there's no trace yet. I'm offering a reward."

I was stunned into silence. That horse meant a lot to me.

"Buck, you still there?"

"Yeah. I'm just in a state of shock . . . and sick and mad."

"Listen, I want you to catch a plane up here *pronto*."

"I'd like to help, but I don't know how right now. Besides, I've got a livin' to make. I'll look out here and pass the word."

"I need you up here, Buck. This is like losing a member of the family." The more he talked, the more miserable he sounded.

"I know. I feel the same way. But what can I do? I never figured I was cut out to be a detective. I ain't the type."

"But you know the horse and you know horse people. Maybe you'll think of something nobody has here. I need you, Buck."

A jockey's agent can have only two riders at a given time — this rule is to keep an agent from cornering the market on top reinsmen. At the moment, both my boys were convalescing. But, no matter, how could I refuse an old friend? "I'll be there," I told him.

You've probably read all about Jim Ned. How he won the Triple Crown for two-year-old quarter horses at Ruidoso, the Kansas and the Rainbow and the All-American futurities, and then next year took the All-American Derby, setting records in both All-Americans. If you follow speed horses, you'll remember how he could go short and how, stretched out, he could go long. The modern quarter horse also packs Thoroughbred blood, which enables him to reach out there and cover a distance of ground, as folks in the game say of a long-running horse with speed left for the stretch drive. He had the breeding — by Easy Jet, called the "iron horse" because of his durability, Easy Jet by the great Jet Deck, Jim Ned's dam the stretch-running Della Mae, another Derby winner at Ruidoso — and he had the heart. You don't always get the two together. I've seen super bred horses that couldn't outrun a fat man on a hot day because they didn't have the heart, or couldn't stand mud in their faces on a heavy track; and then I've seen not-so-fancy breeds that could burn a hole in the wind, though back there somewhere there had to be runnin' blood. Yet, more often, good breeding pays off. In the short horse world, the idea is to breed speed to speed, heart to heart, and look for good conformation and soundness.

As I drove to El Paso to catch a plane to Oklahoma City, Jim Ned's image came back to me like a walkin' picture. He carried the name of an old-time Texas

4

runner that Charlie had read about and admired. Charlie's Jim Ned was a mahogany bay stallion that stood sixteen hands and weighed twelve hundred pounds in training, with black points from the middle joints of the legs to the hoofs, and black mane and tail. A proud head. Fox ears pricked. A small star on his fore-head. Straight forelegs. That sloping shoulder and powerful forearm that horsemen like. Good hips, good back, good bones, and long barrel. Furthermore, something extra special you see in an exceptional horse: style, speed, intelligence, toughness. When he moved, it was like a piece of silk. And what my father said the great ones have: "The look of an eagle and the step of a deer."

Reckon I should know all this, because I broke Jim Ned and rode him in all them big stakes races. In the All-American Futurity, he won by daylight over a field of fast horses. I was just a passenger along for the ride. That was the day he ran the quarter-mile classic in twenty-one seconds flat, which broke the record set by Truckle Feature in 1973 by two-hundredths of a second. For the past two years, Jim Ned had been standing at Charlie's Valley View Ranch near Norman, Oklahoma, for $20,000 per leap, live foal guaranteed. Charlie, hungry for big stud fees, had retired Jim Ned too early in my opinion. But lately Charlie had put him back in training, planning to campaign him again, now that Remington Park was going big in Oklahoma City.

Charlie Vann met me at the airport. He was almost as downcast as a kid who'd just lost his most prized plaything. He owned car dealerships in Oklahoma City, Tulsa, and Dallas, three or four banks, and was as cagey

5

as a treeful of owls when it came to making money on the stock market — but he was still a kid at heart about some things. Overweight, ruddy-faced, always in need of a haircut, with doleful brown eyes, clad in run-down cowboy boots, a shirt frayed at the collar, jeans that bagged at the knees, a sweat-stained Western hat, his paunch overlapping a bronze belt buckle with a racehorse on it, he would never be taken for a millionaire. He'd passed up college — business school was far enough. All he needed with his native know-how, acquired in part, he admitted, from his horse-trader father.

I guess you would call Charlie a conservative conservative. If you stopped for coffee, you'd likely have to pick up the check. He seldom carried much cash, yet no credit cards, because he hated to pay interest. Tight as he was, when I rode for him, I always liked Charlie. He always saw that I got my ten percent jockey's fee, which is no small item when you win the All-American Futurity. The winner gets one fat million. First thing I did was buy me a new four-wheel-drive pickup. Charlie didn't even buy himself a new hat that I could see.

From the airport we drove off in a Ford pickup well into its dotage, now a faded green, with banged-up sides and an ominous clanking in the motor.

"Charlie," I said, while trying to close the hanging door on the passenger's side, "I believe it's about time you bought yourself a new pickup."

"Oh, there's still plenty miles left in this ol' baby," he said, and drove the speed limit to show me.

As we headed for the ranch, Charlie asked the question that had been nagging me ever since I got

6

the news. "Why would anybody want to steal Jim Ned? I just can't figure it."

"Maybe to save that fancy stud fee."

"Naw. I'd give a good man credit if he had to have it."

"You have any real bad enemies? Maybe somebody the bank foreclosed on and swore revenge?" His bank in Norman was one of the few in town that hadn't gone under when the bottom fell out of the oil market.

"No threats of any kind." He grew thoughtful. "I've closed out some good ol' boys that hurt me as much as it did them. In turn, some so-called good ol' boys flew the coop and left me holdin' the bag, and they didn't seem to mind a bit. Only way a man can get a sizable loan now would be to put up his wife and kids."

"Look back. Say somebody that holds an old grudge."

He shook it off. "If they did and wanted to hurt me even worse, they could've shot Jim Ned from the road. He runs in his paddock during the day. Be a fairly easy shot."

"I think he was stolen for his blood," I said. "The fastest quarter horse in America. Cross him on some fast mares, fake the breeding and registration, man could come up with a passel of track burners. How much reward are you offering?"

"Ten thousand," he said gloomily.

"You may have to raise it. How much is Jim Ned insured for?"

"Three million. Of course, he's worth far more than that."

"Sure he is. Couldn't be you hated to pay more high premiums?" I had to call him on that. With today's inflated prices on good horses, a man has to protect his investment, particularly if he has the fastest blood to breed at top fees. Charlie didn't answer, though I knew I'd hit home. "Have you notified the insurance company?"

"Did right after I called the law. Scared hell out of 'em. Sent an adjuster down from Tulsa right away. College type. Y'know . . . Brooks Brothers suit . . . Gucci loafers . . . brief case . . . camera. Took a batch of notes and asked more questions than a country boy at his first county fair. Did I have a night watchman? Never needed one before . . . Had I fired anybody lately? Never had to . . . How old is Jim Ned? What did I feed him? Who handled him? On and on . . . He acted suspicious of me. Told me there's only two ways the company will pay off. After a long period, say some years, if the horse isn't found . . . or soon, if we find Jim Ned's body. Like a homicide, y'know. No *corpus delicti*, no case. I reminded him right there that my horse meant more to me alive than dead for three million. Made me think of what happened to Jet Deck."

Every short horse man in the game knows the story of Jet Deck, Jim Ned's grandsire. Retired to stud, he was found dead in his paddock at a ranch near Perry, Oklahoma. His body was taken to Oklahoma State University's veterinary school for a *post mortem*, where the doctors noticed a peculiar odor. Examination of the jugular vein indicated evidence of a foreign substance. Tests showed the stallion had died of a massive overdose of barbiturates. His killer or killers were never

8

found. Tire and boot tracks marked the road leading to the paddock . . . that was all. A ball of fire on the track with a great finishing kick, Jet Deck was gentle by nature, easy to handle. That very gentleness had led to his death. Jim Ned had the same disposition.

Charlie's Valley View Ranch drew the eye like a scene on a postcard as we turned off the main road onto a graveled lane that wound up to a two-story, Spanish-style house. A silent house most of the time — Charlie's wife, Elizabeth, deceased some four years and his two teen-aged sons in school back East nine months of the year, now on distant summer jobs. Charlie believed in work, the same way he was brought up on that red-dirt farm. An elderly housekeeper looked after the house and fixed his meals. Not far beyond the house stood barns and corrals and a breeding shed, all structures painted red. Mares with their leggy spring foals grazed pastures of bluestem behind white-washed fences against a backdrop of towering cottonwoods along the South Canadian River. A circular track that joined a long straight-away completed the lay-out. Nothing was too good for Charlie Vann's horses, now the main interest of his life.

We stopped, and he took me to a small paddock and barn near the house. "I always look in on my horse before I turn in. It's the last thing I do. Usually about ten-thirty, after I've watched the news and weather. So I stepped out and looked. He was standing right over there, head turned into the wind." Charlie almost choked up then. "Maybe I made it easier for 'em. I always let him run loose unless the weather looks bad.

I'm afraid of lightning. Well, a little after ten-thirty the wind came up and thunder started rumblin', so I shut him up in the barn. He was haltered, like always . . . That was the last time I saw him."

"Did you hear any ruckus later?"

"You won't believe the traffic this river road carries at night. And you ought to see the beer cans in the bar ditches come morning. I judge the grass around here by how high the cans are. No . . . I didn't hear a thing that sounded different . . . no ruckus, no horse clatter."

I stared at him, then looked all around. Something was missing. "Wait a minute," I said. "Where's old Shep? He always barked when anybody came up to the house."

"Died a month ago. Got old and tired. Haven't had the heart to look for another dog." He faced away from the corral. "This took more than one person. These were professional horsemen. Although Jim Ned's easy for you and me to handle, I don't believe a total stranger could come into his stall, put a lead shank on him, lead him out, and not make a racket. Too, I figure they had to tranquilize him a little to load him. You remember, he never liked trailers?"

"I remember."

Charlie balled up a fist and beat the air. "If I'd just got another dog! If I'd just put a big lock on that paddock gate!"

I felt for him. "Don't blame yourself. Nobody would expect this to happen."

He was showing me the tracks outside the paddock that led to the road, when Tom Shelby, Charlie's long-time ranch manager, walked up from the lower barns. We shook hands.

"Glad you're here," he drawled. A tobacco-stained Buffalo Bill mustache dominated rugged features weathered by wind and sun. His gray eyes were the eyes of a horseman. A soft-spoken man in his early fifties, somewhat reserved. Like me, I remembered, he didn't believe in rushing young horses and spoke out against yearling futurities.

"I blame myself," Shelby said right out. "If a ranch manager is worth a damn, he should be responsible for whatever happens on the ranch."

Charlie cut him a look. "Tom, I don't want to hear any more of that. Who was the last to check on Jim Ned? Me. It wasn't your responsibility at all. Now I want to show Buck where they took him."

The three of us walked out to the highway, tracing the hoof prints as we went, prints that became more visible in the soft, grassy turf of the shoulder among the scattered beer cans.

"You'd think," Charlie said, "there'd be some kind of ruckus when strangers loaded a big stud like Jim Ned into a trailer he didn't like."

Shelby, apparently reliving the scene, stared hard at the ground. At Charlie's suggestion we ambled back to the house for a drink. Shelby excused himself, and Charlie called after him: "Take it easy now, Tom."

"Tom keeps blaming himself," Charlie said, pouring double jiggers of Maker's Mark on ice. "I hope you can stay a while?"

"I will. Maybe I can do something. Maybe not."

11

"I appreciate that, Buck." He handed me my drink, and I sipped it. Charlie might be tight in certain areas, but he's no cheapskate who, to impress a guest, serves common whiskey from a bottle that had once held good whiskey.

"There had to be some indication trouble was coming," I said.

He held his glass. "You'd think so, but there wasn't any."

"I mean any unusual visitors come to see the horse?"

"You always have people wanting to see a champion race-horse. Some strangers. Some just like horses. But mostly horsemen from over the state or down in Texas. Many I know. Despite that twenty thousand dollar stud fee, Jim Ned had a full book."

"Somebody would've had to get a good idea of the lay-out here. Where you stalled the horse, and if there was a watchdog, say."

"If old Shep had been alive, this wouldn't have happened."

"They could've fed him a bait of poisoned meat, say the night before. So it wouldn't have done any good if you'd got another dog. They'd have got him, too. Sure, these were professional horsemen . . . I mean professional horse thieves . . . and there had to be a jackleg vet in the bunch to quiet the horse down." I started to say what I feared most, but checked myself.

"What is it? Don't hold back."

"They might plan to take him to Mexico, like what happened to Town Policy. Remember?"

"I don't remember the horse. What happened?"

"Town Policy was the fast gelding that ran second to Hot Idea in the 'Seventy-Seven All-American Futurity. Not long after that he was stolen from his paddock in California. At first, the owner couldn't find out a thing. 'Sorry, *señor*, there is no trace of your horse.' Six months went by. When the owner started passing some money around . . . they call it *mordida* in Mexico, or the payoff . . . officials became mighty co-operative. They located the horse in Durango. He'd been run in match races . . . that was evident. But he was OK, and the owner paid a twenty-five-thousand reward." I didn't have the heart to tell Charlie that Town Policy had lost several hundred pounds, was down to skin and bones, and the owner stood there and wept when he saw him.

"I'd pay a lot more than that to get my horse back."

Charlie was growing gloomier by the second, and I eased off about Mexico. "Maybe he's close by. Maybe you'll get a call for ransom."

"Ransom!" He almost spilled his drink. "I never thought of that."

Sitting there in Charlie's oak-walled den, I found myself looking at a blown-up photo of Jim Ned winning the All-American Futurity by two lengths over a fine filly called Silver Belle. In fact, Silver Belle's nose was barely in the picture.

"You syndicated Jim Ned," I said. "How did it work out?"

"All right, in one way. I sold a hundred shares for a hundred thousand each . . . good for one breeding per season, syndicate members not to share in the colt's winnings, if I put him back on the track, which I'd aimed to do."

"Sounds like you made a good deal."

He made a face. "Except at times I've had a hundred people to please, and there's a rumor that shareholders are complaining about lack of security. You see, I've never had a man on guard at night. Why have one, when I kept the horse close to the house? I'm home every night."

We chatted on, our talk ranging far and wide. It wasn't logical that the thieves would run Jim Ned soon under another name, though he had no distinguishing marks except that small white star, which could be painted over. Easy to pass one solid bay horse for another. Somebody expert with a brush could paint on a white stripe, or even a blaze. Lip tattoos were still the main means of identifying a horse; yet not all tracks required them, and they wear off in time and can be changed. Blood type was another thing, but who would call for a blood-type check at most quarter horse tracks?

The phone rang, and Charlie talked a short while, then hung up frowning. "That was the Associated Press. They just checked with the Highway Patrol and the sheriff's office. No news there, so they called me. What can I do, Buck?"

"Just sit steady in the saddle and wait. If nothing pops in a few days, raise the reward."

"You'd think ten thousand dollars would loosen some tongues."

"It may yet."

14

"You should've been here yesterday. Newspaper and TV reporters thicker'n fleas on a hound dog. It looked like the Fourth of July. Phone rang and rang. Finally had to take it off the hook."

He handed me a copy of the morning *Daily Oklahoman* sports section. There was a three-column photo of Jim Ned, me in the saddle, on the happy ground of the winner's circle after the All-American Futurity, when he had set the quarter-mile record. Grouped in front of us Charlie and Lori Beth and the trainer, Mike Peterson, and the usual overbearing outsiders who manage to slip in and get their pictures taken with a winner. I looked younger then. Much had passed under the bridge in two years, and it wasn't all water. Just the sight of her gave me a pang. Lori in tailored jeans with turquoise belt buckle, an open-neck shirt with a pretty floral pattern, a slim-look Western hat on her dark head. The wide eyes, the sun-scrubbed look of a model, which she also is when she can spare the time. The sweet smile to go with the sweet voice that had taken her to the top. Maybe I'd been wrong. Why hadn't I believed her? If I was right, whatever happened to forgiveness? Guess I was too damned proud, too macho. A man can get like that when he's ridin' high on winners, and people bet the jockey about as often as they do the horse. Now I'd never know the truth. Where was she? Nashville, Vegas? I wondered, and I still cared. In a way, our life together had been like a big stakes race — over before you realized it. When the gates open, you run. You can't go back and start over if you've made a mistake. I'd read somewhere that Lori was supposed to marry some TV producer. Well, I wished her happiness.

Charlie's voice broke across my guilty thoughts. "Glad to see that picture in there. I'll ask the quarter horse magazines to do the same. A side view might be better." He forced a dry smile. "Maybe I need to have me some reward posters printed and stuck around the post offices . . . I do have one piece of good news, however. Forgot to tell you the FBI called. They're involved under interstate transportation of stolen property . . . anything that has a five-thousand-dollar minimum. All their offices have a detailed description of the horse. Now they're watching the airports. They also notified the Border Patrol." He made a gesture of despair. "All this hucklety-buck and not one lead."

"Something has to break," I said. I felt sorry for him because his loss was mine as well, and was equally sorry that I had mentioned Mexico, though I still felt that was the strongest possibility.

When Charlie said he had some business calls to make, I strolled down to the barns, hoping to see Shelby. He wasn't in sight. With Jim Ned gone, a depressing blanket of silence seemed to hang over the ranch. Its pulse was gone, its very life.

I was idling back when a stringy young man dressed in work shirt, jeans, boots, and baseball cap crossed from the tack room toward the main barn. Head down, he hadn't noticed me. He jerked around, startled at the sound of my foot-steps. "Oh . . . ," he said with a quick grin.

"Howdy," I said, and held out my hand. "My name's Buck Clegg."

His eyes bugged. "Buck Clegg!" His tone would have stroked my ego as my proper due when I was leading rider at Ruidoso Downs and Sunland Park, and there seemed no end to the big stakes money. It felt good to be remembered. "Mister Vann said you's comin'." He pumped my hand. "I'm Rick Hinton, Mister Clegg."

I had to smile at his formality. "Since I'll be around here for a while, you might as well call me Buck."

"You bet, Mister Clegg."

"It's Buck, remember?"

Behind his uncropped brown beard I saw hangdog eyes, like maybe he'd been kicked around when he was growing up, and a hard-bitten mouth in a slim, dark face, that made him look older than he was. Hair hung to droopy shoulders. In all, Rick Hinton had the stamp of hard times. Still, there was a durable toughness about him and an obliging way that would help him survive.

"I wanted to be a jockey," he said. "Rode in some match races, but couldn't keep my weight down." He grinned a crooked-tooth grin. "Too much beer, too many burgers and fries. Mister Vann gave me a job, muckin' out stables and feedin'. Whatever needs to be done for Mister Shelby. Mister Vann, he's a right fair man."

"I'll second that. You'll be a lot healthier, if you don't race ride. No mounts to go down with you. No busted bones, maybe, unless you get kicked feedin'."

"You look like you're in good shape."

"Sometime I'll show you my x-rays."

We had drifted over to the shade by the barn. "Rick, were you here the night they took Jim Ned? I say *they*, because it took more than one horse thief to do it."

17

"I didn't hear anything. I sleep in the bunkhouse." He pointed past the barn to a low, frame building.

"Of the many horsemen who came to see Jim Ned," I said, "do you remember anybody who seemed to ask more than the usual questions or seemed extra interested in the lay-out here?"

He gave me a sidelong grin. "A stable boy don't get a chance to talk much to visitors, and he sure don't show 'em around. Mister Vann and Mister Shelby do that."

"Maybe you overheard something?"

"Nope."

"Did you see anybody at all who sticks in your mind? Maybe some foreigners?"

He frowned and shook his head. "I was busy most of the time. Truth is, I didn't pay much attention to visitors."

We talked a while longer, then I strolled back to the house, feeling again the emptiness of the place. What could I do? I wasn't a professional investigator. But Charlie wanted me to help, and I could try for an old friend. I could sure as hell ask questions and pry around and use some common sense doing it. When I came in, Charlie asked if I would stick by the phone while he made a short trip to town.

He'd hardly pulled away from the house in the pickup when the phone rang. I picked it up and said — "Valley View Ranch." — and a syrupy feminine voice said: "I'm calling from Santa Fé, New Mexico. May I speak to Mister Charles B. Vann?"

"Mister Vann isn't in. Could I take a message?"

"May I ask who is speaking, please?"

18

Boy, did she have a pleasant voice, so intimate she could have been beside me in the room. "A family friend," I said.

"Very good. Then you can pass on this communication I have about the stolen stallion . . . It came to me in a dream last night. I am Madame Alpha, well-known in Santa Fé for perceiving things beyond the natural range of human senses. It is quite likely that you've heard of me."

"Sorry, ma'am, but can't say that I have."

I thought that might discourage her, but she went on. "Please tell Mister Vann that I know where his horse is. But I'll have to come to Oklahoma to pinpoint the exact location. Once there, some travel will be necessary. My fee is five hundred dollars a day, three days' cash in advance, plus first-class airfare and car rental."

Naturally, I didn't believe her. Just another nut with her hand out. Yet . . . "That's interesting," I said. "But you'll have to be more specific to convince Mister Vann."

There was a long pause, and then her voice reached me like a dreamy whisper. "In my dream . . . and dreams are the inner voice of oneself speaking, you know . . . the extrasensory perceptions from far out that are in all of us mortals, but which surface into reality only in those of us responsively gifted to psychic forces . . . In my dream, which is before me now on the screen of my mind as I speak, I see a large bay horse with a star on his forehead . . . He is standing outside a red barn with a white fence around it . . . There is a noble cast to his head . . . Nearby is a Spanish-style house . . . In the distance, I see lofty trees and a winding river, low

19

this time of year . . . yes, it is low, I see . . . However, I cannot quite pin-point the horse's location from here . . . There is an obscuring haze over everything . . . though I know it is somewhere in central Oklahoma, and I know I can locate it precisely when I arrive there at Mister Vann's bidding. I also sense . . ."

"No need for you to make the trip at all," I broke in. "I can tell you exactly what you see. You're describing Mister Vann's Valley View Ranch, which you've seen on the television news. Good day, Madame Alpha." I hung up.

Soon after that the phone rang again. A man's voice this time. The guy wanted to talk to Charlie about The Never-Fail Watch Dog Security System, which he would install at a special ten percent discount. A little late, I told him, like locking the barn door after the horse was stolen. Call back after Jim Ned was recovered.

More calls came in. Friends offering their help. I took down their names. Another nut call — this time a man claiming he'd seen a horse answering Jim Ned's description in a trailer going through Kansas City. For a "reasonable fee," he'd be glad to check it out. Just wire the money. Forget it, I said. Then a Dallas detective agency spokesman said he would send his top man immediately with contract in hand. The FBI would do for a while, I said, and he made a sniffing sound. One man wanted Jim Ned's picture. Another said he was going to check some barns west of town. I told him to go ahead, but be careful. A man could get shot that way.

By the time Charlie came back my ear was bent down and I was fed up with vultures. "I've had more phone calls than a bootlegger on Saturday night in a Baptist town," I said, and told him the score.

He was discouraged. "I was hoping we'd get a call from the thieves."

"There's still plenty of time," I assured him, not that I felt that certain. I heard a car drive up fast and stop and, through the picture window in the living room I saw a portly man in a brown business suit and gray Western hat get out and stride up to the house same as if he owned it.

"F. Jerome Tucker," Charlie groaned. "*The* F. Jerome Tucker. Corporate raider and candidate for governor. Also a syndicate member. The last man I want to see today."

Tucker knocked at the unlocked glass door, and Charlie waved him in. Tucker didn't just walk in, he strode in. "Hello, Charlie," he said, hand quickly out, election-day style. Charlie shook and introduced us.

"Buck Clegg," the man said, tossing off the name, and seated himself. He had a high forehead and an aggressive set to his broad mouth, a big man with heavy shoulders and a mane of thick gray hair. Impatience marked him. He reminded me of some oil-country folks I'd known who could never understand when their horses ran out of the money.

"Have a drink?" Charlie offered.

"No time for that." Tucker's eyes put me at a distance, and I guess he saw a man of medium height with a battered face, gray eyes, thinning hair, and a lean frame imposed by making weight. Turning to Charlie, he said: "Can we talk in private? This is important."

21

"No need to. Buck rode Jim Ned in all the Triple Crown races. Came up from Ruidoso to help. What is it, Jerome?"

"I heard on the news that you've put up a ten-thousand-dollar reward and may even raise the figure."

"That's correct."

"Well, I want you to know that I oppose that. So do a majority of the stockholders."

Charlie looked amused. "Mean you've called that many?"

"I've talked to a number, and others have called me."

"You went to a heap of trouble, Jerome."

"If the reward goes any higher than ten thousand, you are in the area of ransom, which we shareholders oppose on moral grounds."

"All I want is my horse back . . . call it ransom if you like."

Tucker straightened himself, a gesture of self-importance he made no attempt to hide. "The racehorse industry could never bow to that. If you pay ransom, then no racehorse would be safe, quarter horse or Thoroughbred. It would be like paying for the return of hostages."

Again, Charlie looked amused. "I think you're a little far out in the pasture on that one, Jerome."

"Not at all. I think you fail to see the widespread effect of all this."

"An even higher reward would be better than allowing the horse to be maimed, then put down when found, or even killed by the kidnappers."

A sort of patronizing expression moved into Tucker's face. "I don't like to bring this up, but some shareholders are talking about suing over the lack of security here, over negligence the way Jim Ned was handled."

I thought Charlie would rise to that; instead, he fed Tucker a little half smile. "You know, I could almost agree with 'em."

"However, I would never go along with that," Tucker said, backing off. "You know me better than that, old friend."

Charlie's smile grew even thinner. "Might hurt the honorable F. Jerome Tucker's campaign, eh? I can see the headlines now . . . 'Candidate Sues Old Friend, Charges Negligence Over Stolen Racehorse.' Wouldn't look good, would it, kickin' a man in the butt when he's already down?"

Tucker flushed.

"Furthermore," Charlie said, "I'll buy back your share anytime you like. Furthermore, you can tell any shareholder who asks you that I intend to raise the reward to fifty thousand. Maybe I'll go to a hundred thousand. If that sounds like ransom, so be it."

Tucker snapped to his feet, glanced once at Charlie, and strode from the house.

"Now," said Charlie, in the same tone he might use saying pass the salt, "help me write this new reward notice. Let's put some punch into it."

CHAPTER
TWO

Next day I drove what Charlie called the family car, a Chevy long past retirement age, to Remington Park outside Oklahoma City. Along shed row, I visited with trainers and jocks I'd known at other tracks over the years. Since I was aboard in all Jim Ned's big races, they wanted to know if there was any good news. Had I come to Oklahoma to help Charlie Vann? No and yes, I said, and told them about the increased reward money, hoping maybe they knew something I didn't. Nobody did. Sorry. Mighty sorry. But one thing for sure — they'd know Jim Ned if somebody tried to race him under another name, which we all agreed was pretty remote, with the serial number tattooed inside every running quarter horse's lip for identification.

Everybody wanted to help, everybody had notions why the horse was taken. Reckon some rich Arabs wanted Jim Ned's speed to breed to their European racing stock? Colombian and Mexican drug kingpins liked fast horses. Maybe one of them had done it? Or maybe international terrorists planned to trade the horse for big bucks to carry on their feud with the Western world? But the wildest theory of all was that Jim Ned's sperm was being sold to create a new breed of super speed horses. So the well-meaning guesses ran, most of them gleaned from stories by over-imaginative sports writers.

I left them before post time, feeling more unqualified than ever for the task at hand, and mingled with the crowd in the grandstand. I watched quarter horses fly by in two races, my mind wandering. I bought a program and, looking it over, placed six dollars across the board in the fifth race on the favorite, a nice-looking quarter filly named Miss Go-Go. She broke well, she ran straight, and won by daylight. She'd been bet into the ground, only paid $2.40 to win. I delayed going to a pay window, enjoying once again the expectant mood of the crowd, the hum of many voices like a steady pulse of people having a good time. The feature of the afternoon was coming up, the Oklahoma 550 Championship, a stakes handicap for three-year-olds and older. A nice purse of $20,000.

I was content just to watch the horses as they came out for the post parade. On the tote board the crowd was going for Rambling Reb, Prairie Boy, and Our Sal. As the horses filed by the grandstand, I could see why. The two chestnut colts looked smooth and powerful, little to choose between them based on conformation. The bay filly, fine-boned and balanced, looked quick. I went to a window, collected my winnings, and bet a ten-dollar show ticket on her.

At the break, Rambling Reb shot into the lead from the two hole, with Prairie Boy, the four horse, up close. My filly, sprinting out of five, wasn't far back. It was a fairly solid front all across until about the first furlong.

There a big gray stud, carrying number eight, came charging down the outside and tore into the lead. The two horse rallied and moved ahead. Then Prairie Boy, responding to the whip, made his run. Around me everybody was jumping up and down and hollering and all I could see was the bunched leaders as they crossed the finish line. Maybe, just maybe, Our Sal was in the money.

A pause. Then the tote board blinked. There was a big roar, and I saw that Prairie Boy had won. Rambling Reb was second. Our Sal third. The gray stud had faded to fourth.

I started making my way through the milling crowd for the pay windows. A man stood aside, still watching the tote board, a stricken look in his eyes. It was Tom Shelby. Suddenly he threw down a ticket and slumped away. He didn't see me. He didn't seem to see anyone.

Some instinct beyond invasion of his privacy caused me to pick up the ticket and glance at it. I had to shake my head in sympathy. It was a thousand-dollar win ticket on the two horse, which had run second in a blanket finish. Shelby, who knew horses, had picked the probable winner, only probable winners don't always win.

Later, easing the old car through snarls of traffic, I found myself thinking about Shelby's wager. That was a big bet and a big loss for the manager of a horse ranch.

"All I've had are calls from TV and newspaper reporters wanting to know more about the reward," a

26

disappointed Charlie told me at the house. "I thought the notice was plain enough."

"Main thing, we made the morning news," I said. "Did you get the money?"

"I did. Do you think we made the provisions of the reward too strong?"

I ran the wording through my mind again: **A reward of $50,000 will be paid for the recovery of speed horse champion Jim Ned, alive and in good condition, and another $50,000 will be paid for information leading to the arrest and conviction of the person or persons responsible for the theft**.

"No," I said, "but you may have to settle for just the horse for a while."

"I want both . . . I want these bastards to go to jail. We used to hang horse thieves in Oklahoma . . . still should."

"I couldn't agree more. But try to look at it this way, Charlie. Let's get the horse back first, if that's the way it shapes up. That done, we can go after the crooks."

While we sat around and talked, waiting for a call that might never come, I saw Tom Shelby drive by the house, and I thought of the big bet he'd lost. I said nothing to Charlie about it, because I wasn't about to play the rôle of informer on a friend.

The afternoon was nearly gone by now. We had a couple of bourbons, ate supper, and watched the evening news and weather. The sports announcer repeated the new reward offer, but said, as yet, there was no break in the case. Next, we watched a half-hour game show without interest.

Charlie turned off the TV, and we sat in glum silence. When the phone rang, we both jerked. "You answer it," Charlie said. "If it's anything, I'll get on the phone in my bedroom."

I picked up the receiver, said — "Valley View Ranch." — and a mocking voice asked — "Would this happen to be Mister Buck Clegg, the famous jockey?"

"I don't know about the famous part," I said, a little startled and not flattered, "but this is Buck Clegg. What can I do for you?"

"Understand from the papers you're here to help in the investigation about the stolen stud?"

"I'll help any way I can, you bet."

"Well, I've got news you can't afford to pass up."

I waved Charlie to the other phone and said: "Who is this?"

The guy laughed. "Think I'm fool enough to tell you? I'm also calling from a pay phone, so you can't trace it."

"You can give me your name if you're on the up and up."

"I'm on the up and up, all right, but my name's not important. What I know is."

"Just what is that?"

"I know where the big stud is."

I didn't trust the caller. He was sounding more cocksure the longer he talked, yet we couldn't ignore him, we couldn't afford to ignore anybody who might have a lead. "That's great news," I said. "Where is Jim Ned?"

I got back a sarcastic snort. "Hey, Clegg, you've had one too many falls off last-place platers. Must've landed on your head. Think I'd tell you over the phone? You'll know when you and your banker friend bring the fifty thousand reward."

He was fast losing any credibility with me. Just some spook on the look-out for easy money. Still . . . "Well, partner," I hung on, "that's mighty interesting. How do we go about this?"

"You bring the money across the river tonight, and I'll lead you to the horse."

"Instead, why don't you bring the horse over here and collect your money? That's all you need do. Cash on delivery." I couldn't hold back throwing in some sarcasm of my own. "Stove up as I am, after all them falls you said I had, I don't like to get out and drive after dark."

His voice exploded in my ear. "Hey, pony boy, you puttin' me on?"

"Not one bit. But I don't believe a word you've said. You bring the horse, you get the money. No horse, no money."

"And have you waitin' there with the law? No way!"

"Hold on!" Charlie broke in. "Now, whoever you are, this is Charles B. Vann, the owner of Jim Ned. If you'll get down to taw and cut out the smart-alecky talk, maybe we can come to some sort of agreement. Otherwise, get off the line. Maybe the *real* person who has the horse will call."

The voice calmed down at once. "All right, Mister Vann. I have the horse, and here's the deal. At exactly eighty-thirty tonight, traveling at thirty miles an hour, you cross the South Canadian River bridge and blink your lights three times and drive on. A car will swing in behind you. Better be sure nobody's tailin' you . . . From there you proceed west on the Blanchard road. At the first section-line road turn right and go exactly half a mile on your speedometer. At that point you stop. When you see a flashlight blink twice, throw the money in the bar ditch, drive on ten yards, and stop." He seemed to pause for wind. "I want to see the color of the money when I pick it up, Mister Vann. I'm funny that way. Wrap it with string or rubber bands. No sacks . . . no bags like you bankers use with the red dye that explodes, you understand? Try that, you'll get shot, the horse, too. You wait there till I check the money. If it's all there, you'll be allowed to proceed. A hundred yards down the road, you'll find your horse tied to a fence post."

"You're all wrong on the most important thing," Charlie said. "You show me the horse first, then you get the money. Not until."

"That's the way it has to be, Charlie, my boy." More sarcasm.

"Not if you want the money."

"Is, if you want the horse."

Charlie said no more, letting it hang. Then the guy, sounding nervous for the first time, said: "To please you, forget the hundred yards. The horse will be nearby when you drop the money. You'll see him in your lights. Fair enough, huh? But you have to come alone."

30

"That won't do, either," Charlie said. "Buck Clegg comes with me."

"No!"

"Yes!"

Like a cagey horse trader, Charlie waited him out with silence.

"All right," the guy said suddenly, "it's a deal. But stay in your car, till I say so. You'll be covered from both sides of the road . . . I'll be lookin' for you." The line went dead.

Charlie came into the living room, looking grim. "What do you think? This bird on the level?"

"He seems mighty eager to make a quick deal. Maybe too quick."

"No quicker than I do."

"You want to clue in the sheriff?"

"Might scramble the whole thing. Get the horse hurt. Besides, there's not much time, which obviously is the way they've planned it." He disappeared back into the bedroom. Coming out, he held a pack of greenbacks tied with broad rubber bands. "All thousand dollar bills," he said, and glanced at his watch. "Let's go."

I held up a hand. "Is there a gun in the house, Charlie?"

"I've got a Thirty Eight. Why?" Charles B. Vann, wise in the world of finance, otherwise like a babe in the woods!

"Hell, Charlie, many a man's been murdered for far less than fifty thousand dollars. Down along the border

. . . maybe for as little as thirty-five cents. Let me have the handgun."

It was right on eight-thirty when, groaning along in the senile pickup, we reached the bridge. A sickle moon dripped sallow light through drifting clouds. My slow thirty miles an hour brought an indignant honk from a driver speeding up from behind. He swept around us with a tire-burning screech, riding the horn.

"A true Okie gentleman-motorist," Charlie muttered.

Across the bridge, I blinked the lights three times and watched the rear-view mirror for a car to pull in behind us. Nothing changed. I slowed down some more. Maybe the guy had lost his nerve. But as we turned off the interstate on the road to Blanchard, suddenly lights flashed back there.

"There he is," I said. "He wanted to make certain nobody followed us."

Before long I saw a section-line road and turned in on it. The trailing car dogged us closer. I checked the speedometer, slowed to twenty miles an hour, and switched the lights on bright. Charlie hunched forward, clutching the money. My hands on the wheel began to feel a little slick with sweat. The .38, on safety, stuck inside my belt felt cold and puny. I wondered how many thugs we'd be up against if things reached a stand-off. At least two so far — the trailer, no telling how many siding him.

Just as the speedometer registered half a mile from the highway, our headlights picked up a bay horse tied to a fence post.

"There's Jim Ned!" Charlie called out, and started rolling down the window.

I slowed down, my eyes trailing over the horse, then glanced around for the horse thieves, primed for trouble. As I braked to a stop, I eyed the horse again. Something about his conformation bothered me and kept nagging at my senses.

A flashlight blinking twice from the bar ditch on my side broke my concentration, and a man stepped out onto the road. He wore a gorilla mask.

As Charlie started to pitch the money out the window, the wrongness about the horse hit me full on, and I jerked Charlie back with one hand and yelled: "Hell, that's not Jim Ned! That short-coupled bay won't stand fifteen hands. It's a ripoff. Hold on . . . we're gettin' outta here!"

I gunned the pickup. The worn motor protested, caught, and after a moment we took off with a roar. The masked man, planted in the middle of the road, waved a handgun at us to stop. I couldn't go around him, so I drove right at him. He tried to leap out of the way, but he was too late. I felt the jar and heard the crunch of metal on bone mingled with his scream. The impact threw him up and flopping across the hood. He was still screaming when he rolled off.

I wasn't about to stop. We tore past the horse. Charlie yelled: "You sure that wasn't Jim Ned?"

"Positive," I yelled back. "Furthermore, when did Jim Ned acquire two white rear fetlocks? I saw 'em as we went by."

I glanced back. The driver was charging hell-bent after us in one of them fast, slope-nosed jobs. Although the pickup was still on the lead, he roared up on our tail after a few yards. In a flash, he swung around on my side to cut us off. On instinct, I shut him off before he could draw even. It was crash or pull back. He pulled back, then came at us again. This time we scraped metal. He dropped behind us, and I figured he'd quit.

Just as I thought that, the pickup's rear window shattered and glass flew.

"Get down, Charlie! He's shootin' at us! And here he comes again!" Charlie had to rear up and look back, of course. "Now stay down!" I yelled, and that time he did. As I ducked down, a second shot knocked out more glass.

Ahead of us the road narrowed. I had the pickup floorboarded, but the speedster sailed up to us like a hawk after a dove. I couldn't let him come even with that gun. So I eased up a notch to draw him on, and, when he tore around, I headed the pickup into him, ready to cut back the moment after we crashed. We did, with a crunch. The car faded away. The pickup bounced and swayed as I jerked the wheel to straighten us out. For a tick, I thought we'd go over. But the heavy old clunker righted itself, and we raced on. When I glanced back, Slope Nose was in the bar ditch, with one eye out.

When we came to a west-running road, I took it and circled around to the Blanchard highway. No word was spoken until Charlie let out a big breath and said: "What'd I tell you, Buck? There's still plenty miles left in this ol' baby."

34

CHAPTER
THREE

After breakfast next morning, we sat around the table reading the paper and watching the news on TV, in case Jim Ned had been found. We agreed that was a long shot; if there was any news, it would most likely originate from the ranch.

Charlie, shaking his head, said: "I still get the jitters whenever I think of how close I was came to tossing fifty-thousand, hard-earned dollars into a bar ditch."

"But you didn't," I said. "If you'd had time to take another look at that horse, you'd've come to the same road I did. Looking back at it, I think that horse was even a little sway-backed. Probably an old workhorse they'd sneaked off some farm. It was a pretty slick scam at that." He started to turn off the TV, but I stopped him. "They're comin' on with a bulletin."

The announcer said: "The Highway Patrol reports a three-car pileup on Interstate Thirty Five south of Guthrie. Two fatalities . . . three injured are being rushed to hospitals."

As the news went off, I realized once again that we were still in the position of reacting to what others did, instead of taking the initiative ourselves, because we had nothing to go on. I was pouring myself more coffee, when the thought took hold. I glanced at Charlie and saw an expression break across his face that was a mirror of mine.

"Hospital," he said, his eyes lighting up, and I said: "Yes, hospital . . . that gorilla-masked *hombre* with the gun had to be taken to a hospital, or maybe to a morgue."

"Norman Municipal Hospital is the nearest. Let's give it a shot."

I grabbed the phone book, found the number, called the hospital, and got a quick connection. I said: "Was a man injured in a car wreck brought into emergency last night or early this morning?"

"Do you know his name?"

"I'm trying to locate my brother . . . uh, Ed Turner. He didn't come in last night, and I heard there was an accident off the Blanchard road."

"Let me check." After a bit, she said: "There was a wreck victim brought in before midnight . . . a Mister Earl Smith . . . Broken leg and arm . . . multiple contusions."

"What room is he in, please?"

"Number ninety-two. But he isn't seeing visitors or taking calls, and, obviously, he isn't your brother."

"No, ma'am, but he might know whether my brother was in the wreck. If not, so much the better." I thanked her and hung up and turned to Charlie. "A guy was brought to the hospital last night . . . broken arm and leg. This could be a break for us."

I saw him overrule his urge to go with me. "Somebody had better stay here."

In less than an hour I was walking down the hallway to Room 92. A nurse hurried by. An attendant pushed a

36

cart. I moseyed down a way and back, and, when no one was looking, I gently pushed open the door to Room 92.

He lay asleep on his back with his right leg and right arm in casts, the arm in a sling. I stopped . . . *Earl Smith*. Although there were a lot of Earl Smiths in the world, somehow the name struck me as phony. His clothes hung in an open closet to my right. In the hip pocket of a pair of torn and bloodied trousers, I found his billfold and started going through it. A gasoline credit card carried the name of C. D. Cole. So did his driver's license. I put the billfold back and crossed over to the bed.

I saw a sandy-haired man about my age. His hard-featured face was long and thin, offset by a strong underslung jaw. He groaned, blinked, and bold yellow eyes, startled wide, seemed to jump out at me. "What the god-damned hell you doin' in here? Who are you?" Of a sudden he reached with his left hand to press the call button on the bed panel. I caught his hand. He jerked back. "I say, who the hell are you?"

"Why, I'm Buck Clegg, the famous jockey. Also known as 'pony boy.' Remember? However, I don't recognize you without your gorilla mask, which is a damned sight better-lookin' than you are. You tried to hijack me and my friend for fifty thousand last night off the Blanchard road."

He sneered. "You're outta your head. I got busted up east of town on the way to Tecumseh when my pickup blew a tire."

"You're in here as Earl Smith, but your name is C. D. Cole on your driver's license. You'd better have some answers!"

"What's it to you . . . and what the hell'd you mean goin' through my pockets?" His outraged voice, high and sharp, didn't exactly jibe with the low, mocking persuasion I'd heard over the phone. Yet there was a certain likeness in tone.

"I want to know where Jim Ned is," I said, grabbing his call-button hand by the wrist.

He tried to laugh it off with a snicker. "Jim Ned? Who's that?"

"The world's fastest quarter horse . . . as if you didn't know. I'll break your other arm, if you don't come clean. Where is he?"

He struggled to reach the call button. When I pinned his arm, he yelled — "Nurse . . . nurse! Help . . . help!" — and kept yelling.

In seconds, the door flew open, and two nurses rushed in.

"This man's hurtin' me! He's accusin' me of something I didn't do!" Boy, how he could whine.

They had me cold. I still had hold of his arm. I let it go and faced them, feeling my face flush.

A pretty little black-haired nurse, blue eyes blazing, confronted me. "What do you mean, sir? This man is seriously injured. Get out!"

"He's wanted in connection with a stolen racehorse. That's why I'm here. I'm a private investigator for Charles B. Vann, the Norman banker and horseman."

Charlie's pride would've taken a nose-dive if he'd seen how his name didn't even register on her. She folded her arms and planted herself firmly between the bed and me. "That can wait. He'll be here for several days, at least. But you'd better bring a court order. Now get out . . . else I'll call security."

"Ma'am," I said, "I haven't hurt this man. I'm just tryin' to find out where he's hid the horse. He's our number one suspect. Surely, you've heard of Jim Ned, the great quarter horse stallion that's worth millions?"

Just as I said that he raised a great big ol' put-on moan and moved his head back and forth, like he was about to pass out. Blue Eyes'd had enough. She told the other nurse: "Get security!"

I was still trying to explain, and Smith, alias Cole, was still carrying on like an actor on amateur night, when two uniformed young men, both the size of college football tackles, charged in.

Although it was obvious who the culprit was, the second nurse had to point an extra nasty finger at me. "There he is . . . that's him!"

"Out!" one of the guards ordered, jerking a thumb, and out I went with what little dignity I could muster. Behind me, I could still hear the great Oscar-winning performance. The guards not only bodily escorted me downstairs to the entrance, but told me not to come back, despite my explanations.

Going out to the pickup, I played everything over in my mind. A gut instinct told me What's-His-Name? was the right hold-up man. Whether he had Jim Ned or not, or knew who did was something else. But now was no time to pull up in a race that had just left the gates. We needed to follow through on the first and only lead in the case. We needed help now. That was when I remembered Bill "Smiley" Evans. I'd met him at the ranch last year. Not only a runnin' horse man, but the long-time sheriff of Cleveland County.

I found him in his office at the courthouse.

"Hey, Buck!" he hollered when the deputy showed me in, "you're just the man I need to talk to. Come in!" He started shaking hands twenty feet away, a heavy-set, florid-faced man with a smile that never quit. Charlie had said Smiley never forgot a name or a face, or anybody who'd done him a favor, which explained why he was in his fourth consecutive term.

He seized my hand, and, before I could get in a word, he said: "I've got to tell you about this little filly. I've nominated her for all three futurities at Ruidoso. These fees are killin' me. To get through next winter, I may have to sell my pickup and pass the hat at country pie suppers. But I think I've got me a once-in-a-lifetime runner. She's by the mighty Dash for Cash, out of Sail on Sue, who's by Shoot Yeah. You remember how fast he was? And Sail on Sue won five straight before she bowed a tendon. I'm callin' this little girl Quick Cash. When she moves, she just ripples." He stopped himself short. "Kinda got carried away, didn't I? What's on your mind, though I've got an idea it's about Jim Ned?"

I told him in detail, beginning with the phone call at the house, to the attempted hold-up on the road, to the scene at the hospital. "I want a court order so I can get

40

back in there and question him . . . you with me . . . and I want him arrested as a suspect."

"Whoa, now. Didn't you say the hold-up man wore a gorilla mask?"

"That's right."

"Then you can't identify him."

"But I know he's the guy, the way he's busted up."

Smiley turned a weary smile on me. "I know plenty of crooks I can't arrest, and I've been sued for false arrest a time or two. None held water, but . . ."

"But you can help me question him."

"Oh, I'll do that. But we'd better go the court order route. I know the high priestess at the hospital. We've met before. Miss Harriet Sawyer. A real corker. Guards her patients like a mother hen. Court's in session right now. Be early afternoon before I can come down with the court order . . . You go on to lunch. Be back here around one-thirty or so. Meantime, we'll check around on this Smith-Cole gent. Something tells me he's got more aliases than an old-time outlaw on a fast horse."

I drove back to the ranch to report to Charlie. He slapped me on the back. "This is the break we've been looking for. This'll lead us straight to Jim Ned."

"Don't count on it, Charlie. Could be he's just a two-bit crook who read about the reward in the paper."

When I walked into Smiley's office at one-fifteen, he was waiting for me. "I've got the court order," he said, smiling big, "and your man's got a record from here to the county line. Not only goes by C. D. Cole, but by C. D. Reese and C. D. Blaine . . . likes that C. D. The Earl Smith is a new moniker. Served time in Texas for burglary and car theft . . . has a weakness for Lincoln Town Cars . . . Got off a cocaine distribution charge in Oklahoma City last year when the witness didn't show up. Wonder why?" Smiley studied a long sheet of paper. "Was a suspect in a warehouse arson case in Tulsa two years ago. That was as far as it got. Always hires good lawyers. Beat a rap for assault when the victim dropped charges. Again, wonder why? The list goes on and on. A lot of petty stuff in his younger days, gradually building up to more serious offenses. Fits the profile of a habitual offender who's now moved into big money drugs and greater violence. Like the other night, when he and his accomplice tried to kill you and Charlie for that fifty thousand."

"Nothing in his sheet about stealing valuable racehorses?"

"Nothing, but no reason why he wouldn't. To him, a horse would be just another commodity to sell, like drugs."

"But there had to be a horseman involved in this . . . somebody who knows how to handle a horse, particularly a powerful racing stud. Somebody who knows how to inject a tranquilizer, if needed. I don't see how this guy fits the part."

"Easy enough to find a jackleg vet or some hanger-on around race tracks . . . Well, are we ready to go?"

Miss Sawyer's dark head snapped up at the sound of us clomping down the hallway in our cowboy boots to her desk.

Smiley swept off his hat with a flourish. "How'do, Miss Harriet. You're lookin' mighty fetching as usual. If there was a cowboy dance Saturday night, I'd ask you to go. It would be an honor."

She raised her firm little chin and leveled him a straight, blue-eyed glance. "Flattery will get you nowhere, Sheriff. Besides, you're on safe ground. They don't have cowboy dances around here any more, and, besides that, you're married."

"A man can fantasize a little, can't he?"

"What is it this time, Sheriff?"

"Well, Miss Harriet, what I have here is a court order to interrogate one of your patients, a Mister Earl Smith, alias C. D. Cole ... wanted for questioning in connection with the theft of a very valuable racehorse ... one Jim Ned ... and also in connection with attempting to rob and murder Mister Charles B. Vann, of Norman, owner of said Jim Ned, and his friend, Mister Buck Clegg, here." He held out the court order to her.

She started to take it, then did not. Her mouth fell open. Her eyes widened and she grew rigid as alarm spread over her face. "Sheriff," she said, stumbling over the word, "Mister Smith left the hospital during the noon hour without checking out. Two men came for him. They carried him downstairs. Didn't go to the business office. Left us with another unsettled bill."

"Why, Miss Harriet," Smiley said, as though shocked. "How could that happen?"

"I was at lunch. Of course, it was against doctor's orders. It happened so fast, before anyone could stop them. They were brazen about it, too. Marched right out the front door. I mean carried him."

"Did anybody notice the kind of car they drove off in?"

"Yes. I believe it was a Lincoln Town Car."

Smiley looked at me. "Fits."

"Did they happen to take down the license number?" he asked Harriet.

"No. But if I'd been on duty, I would've tried to stop them."

"Good thing you weren't," Smiley said. "They might have killed you."

"I'm sorry he got away, Sheriff."

He favored her a forgiving smile. "Not your fault, or the hospital's. It just happened. I'm glad nobody here got hurt. Now, I need to use your phone to get out an all-points bulletin for three thugs in a blue Lincoln Town Car."

Going to the parking lot, he said: "We had one hooked, but he got away. If he wasn't involved, why did he break and run? By now, they've switched cars. I doubt we'll catch 'em."

I called Charlie from the sheriff's office, and hung around till late afternoon, waiting for something to happen. Nothing did, as Smiley had predicted; discouraged, I drove back to the ranch. Charlie had to know the whole story all over again, down to the last detail. I obliged him while we lowered the level a notch on his Maker's Mark.

"At least," I said, "we saved your fifty thousand and smartened up considerably. We found out the hard way that this bunch plays for keeps. Even if they don't have the horse, they may pretend they do to make another try for the fifty thousand."

"And we'd have to take the bait, in case they do have Jim Ned."

We settled into our evening routine of an early country supper and TV news and weather. In no mood for a game show, we reminisced about Jim Ned. How his conformation and balance as a youngster soon caught the eye and raised our hopes as he matured that he would get a chance to prove his evident promise on the track. No matter how fast and sound and intelligent a racehorse is, or how smart his trainer and owner are, bad luck always seems to lurk around the corner: colic surgery, a wrong step wrecking a knee, thousand-pound bodies tangling at the break. After years of good luck, Charlie's bad luck had struck late. He got out some photos of Jim Ned crossing the finish line, and we looked at them and re-hashed the races.

The evening was on the verge of turning into a wake when we heard the gunshot. A boom, like a shotgun's blast, from the direction of the barns.

We stared at each other for a second, then Charlie muttered — "What the hell?" — and we ran to the front door and stepped outside. I could see a light in the bunkhouse and a low glow in the tack room.

A figure dashed out of the darkness. It was Rick Hinton.

"Mister Vann," he panted. "It's Tom . . . Mister Shelby . . . in the tack room. It's awful!" He started crying.

We ran there. I looked in and jerked back. Charlie froze. Shelby lay on his side. He had stuck the barrel of a shotgun in his mouth and pulled the trigger. His face was hardly recognizable.

In a choking voice, Charlie said to me: "Go call an ambulance, but I don't think it will do any good."

As I made for the house, I could hear a woman screaming without let-up.

CHAPTER
FOUR

The rest of the night passed like a nightmare. All the ambulance crew could do was take poor Tom Shelby's body away, while we tried to comfort his widow, Wilma. Charlie put in painful calls to the children, a son in northern Oklahoma, a daughter in Texas. After that, he called a neighbor woman friend of Wilma's so she wouldn't be left alone later in the night. There would be more ladies from the church tomorrow.

"Tom blamed himself too much for Jim Ned," Charlie said. "You saw that. He was always such a conscientious man. I should've seen this coming."

I didn't say anything. Now wasn't the time. But I couldn't put that thousand-dollar betting loss out of my mind.

Next day was almost as bad. Smiley Evans drove out early with the coroner, shortly before the news media got wind of the story. By ten o'clock the phone was ringing, and soon reporters and cameramen appeared at the house. It was the Jim Ned thing all over again, Charlie said. More questions that he couldn't answer, particularly inferences that Shelby's suicide might be linked to the theft.

"All I can tell you is that Mister Shelby took Jim Ned's theft mighty hard," I heard Charlie tell them. "He practically hand-raised that horse. He helped me start this horse ranch. It will be impossible to replace him. This is a terrible shock. One of the saddest days of my life."

The day after the funeral Charlie and I went to the Shelby house for our morning call on the family. When the children left to take care of some details in town, Wilma asked us to stay. The way she said it made me look at her. A ranch woman to the core, she was small but not frail. She clasped work-reddened hands. I remember Tom saying once that, from habit during the lean early years of their marriage, she still raised a few chickens and put up fruit and vegetables every spring and summer and baked bread every week. Her round, pleasant face, now gray with grief, her large, brown eyes, puffy from weeping, regarded us with a sad concern.

"I need to talk to you, Charlie," she said, rubbing her hands.

"What is it, Wilma? You know I'll help in any way I can. You don't have to leave here. You have a home here as long as you like."

"Thank you very much," she said, managing a sweet smile. "Right now, I think it best that I stay with one of the children for a while." She glanced away and back. "I keep thinking about what happened . . . and why. I can think of only one reason. Tom gambled a lot at Remington. He'd go there on week-ends. He knew horses, and sometimes he won. But he bet too much, so, when he lost, it hurt. It was like an obsession with

48

him. He left us heavily in debt, though lately he seemed to have done better."

Charlie went over and, sitting down beside her, took her hand. "Now, Wilma, everything will be taken care of . . . everything. Don't start rushing off. Let things settle down. It's far too soon to make big decisions. I know from experience." Now he had a smile for her. "I believe you're the one who told me that when I lost Elizabeth, when I wanted to sell the ranch. You told me to wait and see. In a short time, I realized what a mistake that would've been. I needed the ranch, I needed my horses, and I needed old friends to help see me through. You were absolutely right."

"I just wanted to clear this up in my mind, and with you, as to why it happened. What led up to it."

He patted her hand. "I know, too, that Tom blamed himself for Jim Ned. Time and time again I'd told him it wasn't his fault, but mine, if anybody's, when it really wasn't anybody's."

She thanked him with her eyes. "I feel better now that I've told you."

"I'm glad you did. I feel better, too."

Going back to the house, Charlie said: "I didn't know Tom gambled that much. I'd been to Remington with him, but he never gambled big."

"He lost a thousand dollars the afternoon I was there. I know, because I picked up the ticket. I did, because he had a dazed look on his face. I was standing near him, but he didn't even see me."

Charlie stopped. "And you didn't tell me?"

"It was none of my business. Why tell on a friend?"

49

"I'm still surprised Tom got in too deep. He was always a very sensible man about the ranch. Had good judgment. That's what I'll miss now, his judgment about things. He earned every penny of the good salary I paid him. Was conservative. Yet he took what he thought was the only way out. I'd have helped him, if he'd told me. But he was a proud man, as you know. It wasn't in him to ask for help. Too much pride has been the downfall of many a good man, Buck."

"And messed up others," I said, thinking of Lori Beth.

Time crawled while I helped young Rick around the ranch and at night sat around with Charlie, hoping something would break. Two days slipped by. Should I go back to Ruidoso? My boys would be ready to ride soon. Why not get out of this? I considered that, then scrapped it. A special brand of stubbornness kept me here. A mixture of hope and concern and downright anger that somehow we'd get Jim Ned back and bring the thieves to justice. So I said nothing to Charlie, though I could see that he was discouraged.

Charlie was at the bank, when the phone rang and a voice said: "Is Mister Vann in?"

"No. This is Buck Clegg. Can I take a message?"

"Yes. Tell him that we have his horse."

Feeling charged through me as I tried to hold my voice steady. "That's been said before. The last time it was a hoax. Mister Vann and I got shot at. You a part of that bunch?"

"Disregard that."

"That means you are, then?"

"Think whatever you like, Mister Clegg."

This voice didn't fit Smith-Cole's mockery. It was all business. It was deeper, very distinctive, very courteous. I guess you'd call it vibrant, a rich baritone, not that I'm a music critic. I couldn't even make the eighth grade glee club. It was an educated voice. A voice that belonged to a big-time actor. A voice you'd remember.

"Let's get down to business," I said, feeling my way.

"Before we do, I want to know if we're being recorded?"

"We are not."

"Would you tell me if we were?" he said, chuckling. So the guy had a sense of humor.

"No, I wouldn't. But you're in the clear."

"I'm calling from a pay phone, anyway."

"First, I want to know how Jim Ned is. Are you taking good care of him?"

"He's all right."

"Just what do you mean by *all right?*"

"I mean he's standing on all four feet . . . that's what!" So the guy could get edgy.

"Any rope burns?"

"A few rope burns won't hurt, Mister Clegg."

"Shows you don't know how to handle a horse. He has to be delivered in good shape or no fifty thousand. I want that to be understood. Mister Vann would tell you the same."

"I've read about the reward and the conditions set forth by Mister Vann," he replied, a superior tone in the stagy voice.

"Good. Now, pardner, I'm gonna tell you something about feeding a runnin' horse, any horse, for that matter." I realized my voice was on a rise with my temper, so I pulled myself in. "Stalled horses, particularly, need to be kept on a regular feeding schedule, twice a day, morning and evening ... otherwise, they might colic. Feed hay and oats for fiber ... no corn ... Eighty percent of what a horse eats should be fiber ... no corn ... Corn is a high energy feed, for horses bein' worked hard. Give plenty of water, preferably lukewarm ... Mix bran with the oats. Bran helps keep a horse open. Mineral oil in the food is helpful when you transport horses. That way you'll keep things open so there'll be no impaction."

"I didn't know I was gonna get a lecture." Mocking me now.

"Well, I've fed a lot of horses and listened to vets. Now, about the horse!"

"It will be necessary for either you or Mister Vann ... alone ... to make a trip to western Oklahoma."

"Why so far?"

"So we can talk away from the ranch."

"I hope you mean face to face."

"I didn't say that. It will be to your advantage to do so. We'll talk, all right. Bring the money with you."

"I've heard that before. Will the horse be there?"

"I'll tell you where he is when you get there. I repeat ... it has to be you or Mister Vann ... alone."

"Where?"

"Elk City."

"When?"

"Be there at high noon tomorrow. Go to the restaurant at the Flamingo Hotel, which is on the west side of town on the main drag. You'll be contacted there."

"Mean you'll page me on the phone?"

"I'll decide later. However, I know what you look like, since you've been in the newspapers lately and on TV. If I may say so, Mister Clegg, you have a rather unforgettable face. Have you ever been in the ring?"

"Just in some barroom brawls, and I've had a number of racehorses go down with me. You get the same general effect, minus the cauliflower ears. I was a lot better-lookin' when I was eighteen."

"Ah, I like a man who can see beyond the boredom of everyday life and find the lighter side. I do believe you are a true gentleman of the turf, Mister Clegg."

"Don't brand me with that. I've been called everything but a gentleman." It was my turn to mock him a little. Rub it in. "By the way, have you ever been on the stage, or on television? You have a great voice." I might as well soft soap the thievin' bastard. He might let something slip.

"As a matter of fact, I have." He sounded surprised and genuinely delighted. "I've been on the stage, here and there. I also sing. Solo or in small groups. I've been in several movies, and I was in a long-running TV series."

"I'm not surprised. Was it a soap opera?"

"It was."

"Hey! I'm a big soap opera fan." Which was a big lie; actually, I can't stand soaps. I go for James Garner. The real stuff. And stomp-and-go country music. "What was the name of the series?" I slipped in.

The line went silent. I could almost sense him drawing back. When he came on, his voice had changed, a kind of hurt in it. That told me he was a vain so-and-so. "You're sly like a fox, Mister Clegg. You very nearly got it out of me. I know now to be on guard. As for tomorrow, I warn you that, if you bring officers, the horse will be shot."

"No need to get riled. Why, I may be a big fan of yours. Too, I thought you boys wanted your horsenap money? Won't if you shoot the horse. What kind of logic is that?"

The baritone voice hit a dramatic high. "It's simply a pre-caution, Mister Clegg, with the additional warning that, try any funny stuff, and you as well as the horse could be shot. I advise you to keep that firmly in mind. Do you get it?"

"Couldn't miss, hearin' that great voice of yours." Before I could get in another word, he hung up.

I took off the next morning. Elk City would be more than a three-hour drive in the family car, even taking the interstate west of Oklahoma City. I had the fifty thousand in a money belt, and I carried the .38 in an old shoulder holster of Charlie's, a relic from his young buck days when he worked a stint for Wells Fargo and kept a sharp look-out for hijackers.

"I still don't like this Lone Ranger stuff one little bit," he'd argued again at breakfast. "I think I ought to go along."

"I don't, not this time," I had said, trying not to hurt his feelings. "We've got to follow the kidnappers' instructions up to a certain point. After that, once we locate Jim Ned, we'll call in everybody, and go for broke."

He had been stubborn. "I could follow you in another car. Smiley Evans would love to go along."

"No, Charlie. Let's try it this way. One thing will be in our favor . . . it'll be daylight. They sure can't pull that staked-out-horse act on us again."

"Well, damn it, be careful!"

As I drove out on the river highway and turned north for Oklahoma City, a green Nissan pickup went by me fast, headed south. I got a brief glimpse of two men. By now I was suspicious of anything that moved. So I watched the pickup in my rear-view mirror, watched until it faded from sight, apparently going into Norman.

Once traveling west on the interstate, I settled down to the old car's plodding but steady gait. I figured I'd make Elk City well before high noon. Everybody passed me. I virtually had the road to myself. Observing the landscape, I noted that the shortgrass pastures looked green and lush. Good horse country.

Long stretches of interstate can be monotonous. I relaxed, content to enjoy the rolling reddish land. Now and then I checked the rear-view mirror. After a time, I began to notice a green pickup. It had crept into view, then slowed and seemed to keep the same careful distance of half a mile or more. Why the slow down?

A feeling took root in me: it became a cold knowing. I was being followed, and I told myself I should've expected that.

My next instinct was to drive faster. But soon I realized I couldn't outrun anybody in the vintage sedan, so I dropped back to my usual forty-five miles an hour, a speed that had drawn curious stares from Highway Patrolmen passing me. Much slower and they'd have pulled me over for obstructing traffic.

As more time passed and the distance between us did not change, it came to me that maybe I was wrong. Maybe that was just a farmer easing along in an old pickup. To find out, I decided to play a game. I stepped the sedan up to sixty, hearing it clatter at my lack of respect for its declining years.

When I did, the pickup moved faster, yet maintaining the same margin as before. I dropped back again, this time to a bare forty miles an hour. Whereupon, the pickup did like-wise.

For certain, I was being followed.

We continued like that for about half an hour. When a roadside filling station and café took shape, I turned off, parked, and entered the cafe. A radio was airing country music. Buying coffee, I chose a table where I could watch the parking lot and highway.

Cars and trucks roared by. A station wagon loaded with adults and kids wheeled into the parking lot, and everybody piled out, hurrying for the restrooms.

Sipping coffee, I waited until more than enough time had elapsed for the pickup to cover the half mile. It wasn't coming — not yet. Whatever that meant, I had to go, if I was to reach Elk City by high noon.

I was at the door, when the radio changed to another song. It tore at me all at once, checked me in my tracks. *Hell*, I thought, *that's "Let Love Linger," Lori Beth's top hit!* I bent my head, drawn to every sweet note, but didn't want to hear any more and went out and started the sedan.

Waiting for a gasoline transport to pass, while the song stayed with me and I fumed about the pickup, I saw the cross-over road from the eastbound lane. An impulse seized me, and I drove across and turned east, aware that I was looking for trouble, a trouble I was likely to find.

A van, two cars, and a truck gunned by me, the truck's wake shaking the sedan. After them, came a string of cars. All this blocked my view of the westbound lane. When the highway ahead of me cleared, I saw that I was past the pickup, parked on the shoulder. There was no crossover this soon, but the median strip looked fairly level. We bucked across and headed west.

The Nissan pickup looked brand new. I could see two heads, instead of only the driver I had expected. Two men, like in the Nissan pickup that had passed me when I left the ranch.

I slowed down, easing off the paving, and drew alongside. As I did and the two faced me, I felt a jolt that wasn't far from pure shock. They wore gorilla masks that grinned at me in a hideous way as they nodded.

I know I'm not a coward, but over the years I've learned to let well enough alone when the odds are against me. I pulled the sedan back on the highway and put the accelerator to the floor. Looking back, I saw the pickup come on, following at a leisurely speed.

From there on to Elk City, it was the same scenario, as they say on television. Me holding to my forty-five miles an hour, the pickup pair keeping the half-mile gap. In town, I drove down Main Street to the west end. When I saw the Flamingo sign, high on my left, I turned and parked and stood by the car, ready for the pair to show up. When they hadn't after fifteen minutes, I went inside the crowded café and ordered lunch from a booth where I could eye the parking lot. It was seven minutes till high noon.

Looking over the luncheon crowd, I found mostly businessman types, several heavy-set guys in baseball caps, jeans, and colorful shirts I took for truckers, some ranchers in big hats, chatty office girls, and quiet old couples. I wondered if the actor could be among them. In the swell of voices, I couldn't find one that sounded remotely like that distinct voice on the phone, or any man that fit the picture I'd built in my mind: tall, bearded, well-dressed, puffed up with self-importance, and sneaky eyes.

The phone on the wall behind the cash register rang. The cashier answered, flung an inquiring look around, said a few words, and hung up. When it rang again, after about five minutes, she glanced about and said even fewer words, and hung up. In the next half hour, it must have rung three times, but she didn't page anybody, just glanced over the room, and snapped a reply into the receiver.

Finally, I went over there. "Ma'am, have you had a call for Buck Clegg?"

"Buck Clegg? Naw, just some fool girl who's tryin' to locate her boyfriend. He stood her up. I know 'em both. Take my word, she'll rue the day, if she marries that deadbeat."

I bought a cigar, idled back to my table, and had more coffee.

The crowd started thinning out before one o'clock, and by one-thirty I had the place to myself except for a lingering old couple and a vanful of tourists. The phone had stopped ringing.

Two o'clock passed. Not only had I been stood up, like the girl, but I was out of humor. There was no reason for this, unless they didn't have the horse, and, while they pretended to, they couldn't work out how to get the money, or they had the horse and got cold feet at the last minute about the swap for the money. I kept thinking about the pair in the pickup. The gorilla masks, meant for intimidation purposes, definitely linked them to Smith-Cole, who could have had the money if he'd had the horse. So, did they really have Jim Ned? I doubted it, but what else did we have to go on?

I walked out to the parking lot, stood around, came back, and wasted almost an hour.

I jerked when the phone rang and was at the cash register before the lady hung up. She turned to me with the I-told-you-so expression of an older woman who's been around the track more than once. "Her boyfriend finally showed up at the house," she said, and made a puckery little face. "Ever'thing's just fine. He had a flat on his old pickup. Boy, have I heard that one before!"

"But it still works," I said, and went to the pay phone and called Charlie.

He was so excited he spluttered: "What happened?"

"That's it . . . nothing. I wasn't contacted. Nobody showed up. But two guys in gorilla masks trailed me on the interstate into town."

"The bastards."

"They drove a green Nissan pickup, but I didn't see it again. Wish I'd thought to get the license number, though it's probably stolen, or they switched plates. I'm heading back in a few minutes while there's plenty of daylight."

"Just hold on now, speed hoss. I'm gonna ask the Highway Patrol to keep an eye on you. They've been great about helping. Give me fifteen minutes to work this out with Oklahoma City headquarters before you hit the road."

I had to rib him. "Guess they won't have any trouble spottin' me in a museum piece. What model is it, Charlie?"

"A Nineteen-Sixty-Seven Chevrolet Bel Air, de luxe, no less, and don't you run it down."

"I know. There's still plenty miles left in the ol' baby . . . if you don't drive over forty-five. I think it needs a valve job."

"When that's necessary, I'll have it done. Meanwhile, you sit tight for fifteen minutes, you hear? And check the oil. It may be down a shade. There's a quart of forty-weight in the back end."

The "shade" turned out to be a quart low. With a final look around, I left the Flamingo and drove east to the interstate. Nobody followed when I came on. Everybody snorted by me. About five miles out of town, a black-and-white patrol car barreled up beside me. The patrolman waved and smiled as he eyeballed the sedan. Waving me on, he dropped back like a rear guard. I held to my steady forty-five miles an hour or so. I hadn't been on the road more than ten minutes, when here he came again and signaled me to roll down the window. Then he hollered: "Won't that thing run any faster?"

"If I do, you may have to tow me in."

He grinned and dropped back, shaking his head.

I had patrol escort all the way back to the ranch, the black-and-whites changing about every fifty miles.

Charlie was both relieved and angry. We'd come to another dead-end, left without a single follow-up clue, and, again, all we could do was wait and react, instead of initiating something.

Two Maker's Marks later the phone rang. Charlie answered it. His face hardened as he said: "He wants to talk to you."

"Hello, Mister Clegg, I hope you enjoyed your lunch?" the actor's voice came on, as courteous and pleasant as if nothing had gone wrong.

I'd had enough of his slick talk. "What the hell happened to you?" I said. "You stood me up."

"The situation changed at the last minute."

"How?"

"I can't go into that."

"It was all in your hands. You even had two of your thugs in gorilla masks follow me in a pickup. What's the big idea? It ain't Halloween, and it ain't funny. That two-bit hoaxer wore the same face the night I ran over 'im. You got a zoo or somethin'?"

"Disregard that, Mister Clegg."

"I can disregard just so much. I don't think you planned to contact me at the Flamingo at noon, at all. I think the idea was to get me to hang around long enough till I had to start back here after dark, so the funny face boys could hijack me on the highway."

"I was at the Flamingo, but I didn't contact you because the situation changed, as I just said."

"How do you mean it changed?"

"That, I cannot divulge."

"I don't believe you ever entered the place."

"You will when I tell you exactly how you were dressed."

"Tell me, *compadre*."

"For a start, you wore a light-gray Western hat."

I'll be damned if he wasn't right.

He went on in that superior theatrical tone of voice that was beginning to rub my temper. "You also wore brown lizard boots, probably made by Tony Lama or Larry Mahan. A blue shirt and tan jacket and gray trousers, with a green turquoise belt buckle."

He was right about everything except the bootmaker. I wear Luccheses. I like the feel of that soft goatskin. So I'd been closely eyeballed all the time, except for when

I smoked the cigar. He'd have mentioned that. He'd left by then. It all gave me an uncanny start. I swept my memory back over the crowd for a person that answered the description I had been putting together, but nobody came to mind that was tall, bearded, well-dressed, puffed up with self-importance, and had sneaky eyes. I was far off. Maybe the guy looked like an ordinary businessman.

"You're right," I said. "Now where does that leave us?"

"At another beginning, Mister Clegg. I am quite willing to set up another meeting, and I apologize for the last snafu. I do, indeed." Golden Voice was pouring on the persuasion again.

Before I could speak, Charlie was on the other phone. "This is Mister Vann. There will not be another meeting until you show us proof that Jim Ned is still alive. I want photographs of the horse. A front-on photo of his face and a side view. We get those or the deal is off."

"That is an unusual request, Mister Vann."

"Not at all. They still make Polaroids, don't they? You send the photos to me, here at the ranch, Route One, Norman. After we get 'em, I'll talk again. Not until."

Then Charlie hung up.

CHAPTER
FIVE

I've always believed in instinct as a true sense that guides a man many times when nothing else works. Therefore, next morning, I decided to call on an old horseman friend who lived on the out-skirts of the little town of Blanchard, the home of two All-American Futurity winners. Not that Doc Young had won The Big One. Something always happened in the trials. Rearing in the gate. Bumped at the break. Breaking stride on a slick spot when on the lead. Running into a strong head wind, which can be fatal in a quarter horse race when the time is broken into one-hundredths of a second. Once he'd missed making the final field by that little pinch. I know first-hand, because I was aboard his Red Dobber, a colt with speed to spare. Doc'd had the necessary go in several horses, but not the luck to get him there. You need both.

I found Doc cleaning out a stall at the horse barn across the street from his home. That close proximity, I remembered, was a joke to everybody but Doc, who used to say: "This way I can keep a keen eye on my horses. If I catch anybody sneakin' around the barn or corrals, day or night, don't bother to call a doctor . . .

just call the undertaker. And I'm a dead shot." He kept a loaded 12-gauge shotgun right by the front door.

Doc was eighty if he was a day: stooped, thin, wrinkled, gray. But there was still spring in his movements and alertness in his eyes as he leaned the pitchfork against the wall and turned to greet me.

"It's about time you showed up over here after all that's happened." His grip made me flinch a little. "Now bring me up to date."

After I had, briefly, he pointed to a big cottonwood in a grassy pasture below the barn where a few horses grazed. "When I was a boy, I saw a horse thief hangin' there. He hung there for days, till the smell got so bad it was a public problem, so they had to cut him down. He'd stole a fine buggy horse from my uncle, and the sheriff had caught him with the horse." Doc snorted upright disgust. "We don't hang 'em any more. Oh, no. It ain't proper. Might violate a thief's civil rights." He slapped his leg. "But, by God, it was justice!"

"Did he have a trial?"

"You bet he did. Right under the cottonwood."

"How long did it take?"

"About five minutes."

"Kinda sudden, wasn't it?" I was guying him.

"Was . . . but it sure thinned out the horse thieves around here. Don't recall there was another instance of that till about the time we whipped Kaiser Bill. And, if my memory's right, Jim Ned's theft is the first in about thirty years." He took my arm. "We've just commenced to talk about this. But, first, I want to show you my yearling stud colt."

We walked down to the pasture, and my eyes caught on a colt romping near the fence. He was midnight black and moved with easy balance, already showing exceptional muscle. I liked the way he held his head. I liked everything about him. A corner, if all went well.

"By none other than Mister Master Bug," Doc intoned in my ear. "You know what he did? Rolled up close to two million. Speed index one hundred and ten."

"Looks just like his daddy," I said, remembering.

"Out of my Pie in the Sky mare, Early April. I wanted to take her to Jim Ned's court, but I couldn't see that twenty thousand dollars, even on the credit that Charlie would have given me. Not at my age, this late in the game. I don't blame Charlie for the size of the fee. I'd do the same if I had the horse. If you're smart, you take advantage of what you have and what the market will bear. Makes up for the bad luck you had before."

"This colt couldn't look any better."

Doc gave me a 'possum grin. "That's why his name is Masterpiece. He's my last shot. I aim to be very careful with him. Just a few races as a two-year-old. I've seen too many young horses run too often and too far. I want him to reach his peak when he's matured, when he can take the wear and tear."

"I wish you luck," I said.

"What if he made me rich at two and had to be put down?" Doc went on. "I wouldn't enjoy the money. An old man can eat just so much and drink so much . . . not much of either." He laid a hand on my shoulder. "Which reminds me. It's time to go to the barn."

There, after a glance around, he reached inside the oat bin and lifted out a brown jug with a cob stopper. He pulled the cob, wiped the mouth of the jug with his shirt sleeve, and handed it to me. "Try this," he said. "Made by an old friend who farms a little on the Washita River. It'll put snap in your walk and brighten your eye. However, it does have a little whang to it."

I took a pull, swallowed, shuddered, and said: "Believe it does have a little whang to it, Doc."

He smiled like a man complimented for his choice of whiskey, which is always appreciated. "Just right. The next one will go down a lot easier."

He took the jug, and we went to the east side of the barn and sat with our backs to the wall in the late morning sun. "This is the best-lookin' colt I've had since Red Dobber," he said. "Red won his share. At that he was unlucky, when you think of the close ones he lost and the speed he had and the heart he showed. I got hard up and sold him to a man in New Mexico. Been sorry ever since. That's been my trouble, Buck. I get too fond of my horses. Hate to give 'em up, and sometimes, if you don't, you don't eat, and a man's got a family to feed. Take Masterpiece. I've already got one regret."

That surprised me. "What's that?"

He passed the jug. I had a pull and handed it back, and he had a pull before he spoke. "I wish you could be on board when he steps in the gate for his first out. A young horse needs an old hand in the saddle."

"I'd like that. But they tell me I'd be a fool to ride again."

"I know. I heard what the docs said. Well, here's to the olden days." — and he passed the jug again. After a bit, he said: "I was eighty-four last March. Now the wife wants me to sell all my horses an' just sit on the front porch an' watch folks go by. Says I'm too old to be handlin' runnin' horses . . . might get hurt. But I say . . . 'Why, Annie, I'd be dead in six months. I'd just mold away.'"

I put on a half smile. "And what does Annie say to that?"

"Still says I ought to quit. What do you think, Buck?"

I knew how he felt. I also had to be honest. "Keep your horses," I said, "as long as you enjoy it and can take care of 'em."

"I was hopin' you'd say that, Buck. But I know the day will come when I have to hang 'em up. Meantime, my hopes ride with that black colt there. He's the main reason that brings me here every day."

"That's reason enough." I knew all this had been preliminary to the subject of Jim Ned. I had come here because I felt, in some vague way, that Doc Young might help. If nothing more, he would be a good listener. So, after a pause, I said: "I feel Jim Ned is in this area. That my trip to Elk City was just a move to throw us off balance. However, I know I was eyeballed in the Flamingo restaurant then, because he told me over the phone how I was dressed."

"You sure there's only one bunch involved in this? City crooks would need a barn somewhere and somebody to feed the horse."

"So far only one outfit has contacted us."

"Jim Ned would be worth considerably more than fifty thousand in places other than Oklahoma."

"You mean foreign countries? Now don't make me feel any worse."

"I mean foreign countries, a batch of 'em. Horse thieves come in all colors and nationalities."

"Charlie told the guy on the phone that we had to have proof Jim Ned's still alive before we'd talk again. So we're waiting for some photos as proof."

"That's good. Charlie was cagey to demand that."

Our talk trailed off. We just sat there, enjoying the morning and the sight of the promising black colt running and playing and tossing that proud head now and then. As Doc started to pass the jug again and I shook him off, I was reminded again why I'd come, and I said: "Doc, I want you to help us find Jim Ned. I believe you can."

"Me?" he said, taken by surprise. "An old codger my age? What could I do?"

"You know every major horseman from here to Texas and up to the Kansas border. Keep your ear to the ground. You may hear something."

Now Doc fed me a half smile. "Don't tell me one of my old acquaintances might have taken Jim Ned?"

"You just said horse thieves come in all colors," I said back at him. He passed the jug on that, and this time I took it. "You know what I mean?"

"True. I know most of the old breed of horsemen, but I don't know many of these Johnny-come-lately boys, in the runnin' horse game just for tax purposes and quick payoffs. I avoid 'em, if I can. They come here, askin' for advice. Maybe they want to get around vet fees. Maybe their horse is coughin'. 'What do you do, Mister Young? How do you get a horse over sore shins?' Most of 'em want to know how to develop a quick winner, not how to bring a horse along at a rate fair to the horse. They don't realize, or don't care, that two-year-old racing is hard on a horse and there's a price to pay in leg problems over the long run, simply because a young horse's bone structure is not developed . . . Well, I've lectured enough . . . you of all people."

"You will lend us a hand, won't you, Doc?"

"Sure. But I don't know what I can do."

"Maybe just circulate around, listen."

"I'm just a short horse any more. My range is about from here to the old hangin' tree, yonder. I sure as hell ain't no detective."

"Neither am I, but here I am, and I've already been shot at. But I don't want you shot at."

He laughed, we shook hands, I gave him Charlie's phone number, and left for the ranch.

On the way back, I came to the section-line road down which Charlie and I had been all but ambushed and Charlie had come within a hair of pitching fifty thousand good dollars out the window. Curious, I turned in and drove the measured half mile, recalling step by step what had happened. About there, the bay horse was tied. About here, I had run over the hijacker.

I stopped my car, got out, and started a slow walk down the road. About here, I figured, Slope Nose had made his run at us, crashed, and ended up in the ditch, one headlight busted. Searching along the edge of the road and in the grass of the bar ditch, I found broken pieces of chrome. I picked it up and examined it, playing over in my mind the bullets smashing the rear window, Slope Nose racing up for the kill, then the crash and the lucky way the old pickup had kept its wheels on the ground, like a balanced horse that didn't go down when bumped at the break.

Suddenly I dropped the chrome and hurried back to the car. Why hadn't I thought of this before? Buck Clegg, the great detective! I hung my head.

I tore into Norman. Stopping at a motel, I went to the pay phone and scanned the directory for body shops. I found three listed and took down the addresses. At the first place, Bill's Body Shop, a long-haired boy in jeans and a sweatshirt was in the last stages of installing a windshield in an '88 Olds. I waited.

When he was free, I introduced myself and asked him: "Have you boys repaired the right front fender and put in a headlight on a slope-nosed car the last few days? The chrome was also missing on the right side."

He looked me up and down, from my boots to my hat. He seemed amused. "You a detective?"

"You could say that."

"Well, mister, there's all kinds of slope-nosed cars. There's the Daytona, the Pontiac Grand Prix, the Mazda R X-Seven, the Chevy Camaro, the Ford Probe, the . . ."

I stopped him. "Partner, I'm impressed with your savvy about cars. I can see you're smart as a bunkhouse rat in that department. Question is . . . did you make repairs like I described? I don't know the make or model."

"I just started working here today. The boss is out, rushed up to Oklahoma City for some parts."

"I'd sure be obliged to you if you'll ask him, when he comes in, then give me a call at this number if he repaired such a car." I wrote down the ranch phone number in my little memorandum book and tore out the page.

"Guess I could."

With the page, I stuck a twenty dollar bill in his shirt pocket. "Would this help you to remember?"

He looked at the bill. "You bet!"

"One more thing. On repairs here, do you take down the license numbers?"

"Most times, I'd say. What's this all about?"

"It's about a great racehorse that's been stolen around here. His name is Jim Ned. You've heard of him, haven't you?"

"Oh, yeah! And I heard about that."

"Then you just might be the one that helps us trace the thieves. Ask for me, Buck Clegg, or Mister Charles B. Vann. He's the owner."

He stuck out his hand, now as interested as a bug-eyed country boy at his first county fair. Who wouldn't like to help solve a mystery? "My name's Don. I'll sure check on this for you."

I thanked him and, after some searching, located the Sooner Body Works on a wide street off Main, led there by a wrecked sedan, probably totaled. Inside, the building had the dark and greasy look of what likely once had been a garage. There a heavy-set man crouched, beating out a fender on a Ford pickup.

I watched him as he expertly shaped out the crushed fender. Before long, he saw me and hollered: "Be with you in a minute!"

"No hurry," I said.

He banged a while more, then put down the hammer and came out to me, sweating and puffing, his expression genial. After I told him what I wanted, he studied a bit before he spoke. "A few days ago . . . in fact, it was four . . . a bird came in here with a Camaro banged up about like you said. He didn't have any insurance. Wanted to work out a credit deal. I said no way. Go to the bank. He left in a huff."

"The right front headlight was broken?"

"As I recollect, it was smashed."

"Was chrome missing on the right side?"

He studied some more. "Uh . . . I believe it was. What I noticed mainly was the fender and headlight. Yes, the chrome was gone."

"Can you tell me what he looked like?"

"A rat-faced little white guy. Say, thirty-five. Brush mustache. Talked fast, in a rush. In fact, he was tryin' to rush me into fixin' his car. I remember what he looked like because he was so nasty. Hope this will help a little?"

"It does. Don't suppose you got his license number?"

"It was an Oklahoma tag. I remember that. But I didn't get the number. No reason to."

"You've helped a lot. I'm much obliged to you."

I left him the ranch phone number in case the guy returned, which sure wasn't likely, and drove to the Southwest Paint & Body Shop, the last on my list. If the Camaro had been repaired there and the license number jotted down, I was in business. Smiley Evans could trace ownership in a few minutes with the State Motor Vehicle Registration office in Oklahoma City.

The shop owner was obliging when I made my spiel, but no slope-nosed vehicle of that description had been repaired in some weeks. Yes, they did put license numbers on all work orders, just like a garage. I'd learned that much. Disappointed with my attempts at birddoggin', though not surprised, I left him the ranch number, and he promised to call immediately if the Camaro came in.

Charlie showed more interest than I did over the day's results. "This proves again the gang is in the area," he said, bitter and frustrated. "That was plain dumb for the rat-faced bird to bring his car to Norman. Imagine that!"

"Which reminds me I'm no smarter," I said lamely. "I'm gonna call every body shop in Oklahoma City, if it takes that to get that tag number."

"Only I don't have an Oklahoma City directory here," Charlie said. "I'll call the bank and have one sent out right now."

He made the call, and, while we sat around waiting, the phone rang. Charlie grabbed it, spoke, then passed it to me.

When I answered, a young man's voice fairly crackled in my ear. "This is Don at Bill's Body Shop. The boss says he fixed up an 'Eighty-Seven Camaro two days ago, just like the one you described. It had an Oklahoma tag, C L Four Four Zero Eight."

The C L stood for Cleveland County, and with Norman the county seat tied the thieves even tighter to the vicinity of the ranch. For the first time today, I felt my pulse leap. "Great work, Don. We can trace that to the owner. What did the guy look like?"

"Let's see. I'd better ask the boss." In a few seconds, he said: "He was a squinchy-faced little cuss with a short mustache. Talked fast. Real cocky."

"What name did he give?"

"He didn't give one till the boss asked him. He kinda hesitated, then said it was John Brown. The boss smiled a little, but he didn't care what the guy called himself, since he paid cash. If you ask me, Mister Clegg, that name's as phony as a three-dollar bill."

"You're sounding like a real detective, Don. But you have to remember there are many good people named Brown."

"Yeah. But I'll bet he's the one that stole Jim Ned."

"We'll see. Meantime, pardner, you keep a sharp lookout. Hear?"

"You bet I will, Mister Clegg. Anytime."

I hung up, smiling, more than a little proud of the boy. After I told Charlie, I called the sheriff's office and got the undersheriff. Smiley Evans was out, but would be back shortly. Meanwhile, the undersheriff would check the Camaro's ownership for me.

I sat back, feeling on a high. At last, we were getting close to something to work on. Something we had done ourselves.

Within minutes, the phone rang. It was Smiley.

"What've you got, Sheriff?" I was feeling confident.

"Buck, that was a cagey thing you did, checking on the body shops. Should've thought of that myself. But . . . afraid we're right back where we started. That Camaro checks to none other than our old nemesis, one C. D. Cole, alias Earl Smith. Address, General Delivery, Norman."

CHAPTER
SIX

Smiley's report was about like bein' nosed out at the wire on the last jump in a big stakes race. I'd pictured all of us on the bulge, driving up to this Smith-Cole *hombre*'s address and taking him in for questioning and breaking the case wide open and, later, finding Jim Ned alive and sound. Smiley did leave me one crumb of hope, though. He would put out an all-points for the Camaro's number, with the warning to approach the driver with extreme caution. This John Brown I described to Smiley, after he'd let the air out of my sleuthing, not only had to be the driver who had tried to knock off Charlie and me, we agreed, but Smiley said he also seemed to fit the general description of a tough Dallas hood known as Dapper Thompson, wanted in three states for strong-arm robberies and car theft.

So . . .

I was moping around the house next morning, wondering what to do next, when Charlie came in on the run from a trip to the mailbox on the road.

"Got 'em!" he shouted. "Photos of Jim Ned!" Fumbling in his eagerness, he drew two from a brown envelope.

I saw a Polaroid of Jim Ned's face and a side view. Like Charlie had requested of Golden Voice.

"How do you think he looks?" Charlie asked hopefully.

I didn't answer for a moment. I hated to tell him I thought the horse looked dull in the eyes, which are a mirror of any animal's condition. The other photo showed weight loss.

"He's lost flesh," Charlie said, worried.

"You would expect that, but he's not down much. Hell, Charlie, this horse's been under stress. At least he's alive. How many days has it been now?"

"Eight, ten? I've lost count. Seems like a month." Suddenly he pointed. "Look! There's no postmark on the envelope. Just now noticed it. They drove by last night and put it in the box. All they had to do. Proves, once again, the bastards aren't far away." In frustration, he laid the photos on the coffee table and punched the air again and again.

"If I have this figured right," I said, "we'll be getting a call before long from Golden Voice."

"Golden Voice?"

"That's what I call him to myself, that and The Actor. He is one, you know. He let that slip first time he called, when I buttered him up, told him what a great voice he has. A vain son-of-a-bitch. Did he go for that! Told me he sings, or has. Been on the stage. Was in a TV series, but he was smart enough not to reveal the title. I guess you'd say he's a fine example of misused talent."

★　★　★

78

Promptly at seven o'clock the phone rang. Charlie, who was seated by the phone, grabbed it. "This is Charles Vann," he said, motioning for me to go to the bedroom phone.

As I picked up the receiver, I heard Golden Voice say: "I hope you found the photos, Mister Vann?"

"I did."

"Don't you think he looks good?"

"I can't say that. The horse has lost weight. Obviously you aren't feeding him right."

"We are doing our best under the trying circumstances, Mister Vann. Even trying to follow the regimen that Mister Clegg suggested. Plenty of hay and oats and water."

"That part is good. Do you have him stabled, or is he cooped up in somebody's one-car garage in Oklahoma City?" Charlie said, his bitterness spilling out.

"He is in a well-ventilated barn, Mister Vann. However, it would not be judicious of me to say that he is or isn't in Oklahoma City."

"But he is in Oklahoma?"

"Yes, you may say that with assurance."

Golden Voice couldn't be any more respectable; in fact, he was so unctuous it was sickening. My disgust and anger grew. In my mind's eye, I could see him waving a cigarette as he talked, making gestures like an actor on stage, playing a rôle.

"All right," Charlie snapped. "We've beat around the bush long enough. Let's get down to taw." From Charlie's tone, I was afraid he'd lose control and cuss the man out, but he left it hanging there.

"A rather bucolic way to put it, Mister Vann, but clear enough and one in which I wholeheartedly agree. It is my desire to make this as convenient for you as possible. I realize this has been a most trying experience. We left you the photos for two reasons . . . proof of possession and to allay any fears you might have that we were not sincere." The way this dude talked, I knew that he loved to hear the sound of his own voice and to show off his command of the language.

"Then make it clear," Charlie barked. "Cut out the bullshit. You've got the horse, we've got the money. It's that simple. Where can we make the exchange?"

"I am coming to that."

"All you've got to do is bring the horse here and collect your money."

"I fear that is somewhat too simple. You'd have an army of officers waiting."

"I wouldn't. And my word is a damned sight better than yours, after that empty gunny sack deal you pulled on us at Elk City."

"As I explained to Mister Clegg, the situation changed."

"You changed it. Buck drove out there alone, waited, and you never contacted him. He followed your instructions exactly."

"I know he did, and I apologized for the snafu."

"Whatever that was. Maybe you boys couldn't agree on how to divvy up the money. Too many sticky fingers. Now what the hell do you suggest?"

"This. Simply this. Bring the money in a paper sack to the abandoned filling station across the river tonight at nine o'clock."

"Abandoned filling station across the river?"

"Yes, it's still standing. A momento of Oklahoma's glorious past." Some stagy sarcasm there.

Charlie broke into instant laughter. "They used to sell whiskey there before Oklahoma went wet. They could get by with it in McClain County. You drove under the overhang. A guy raised the little window, asked what you wanted. You told him, and he said he had only one kind of bourbon . . . take it or leave it. You took it."

"That's it."

"If you know, you must be a local Okie of the early days. Maybe you got past the eighth grade somehow and managed to slip in at OU and enrolled in drama? With that smooth voice of yours, I can just see you on the stage at Holmberg Hall, in short pants and long socks, struttin' back and forth, declaiming . . . 'To be or not to be. That is the question.' Or, more to the moment at hand . . . 'A horse! A horse! My kingdom for a horse.' "

I was impressed, not far from being spellbound. Had the circumstances been peaceful, I would've been entertained. Where had Charlie picked up all that Shakespeare? Not that I am a student of the bard of Avon, as they say. But Lori Beth is college-educated. Taught high school English before she followed her heart and instincts into country music and met me at Ruidoso. Some of that had rubbed off on me as she

81

tried to smooth my rough edges with scant success, particularly my horse barn grammar. Charlie had never been to college. Just read a lot, I reckon. Anyway, he was pouring it on the guy, bulling him, airing his pent-up frustration and bitter anger.

I thought Golden Voice would lose his temper, but he was as oily as before, when he said: "Mister Vann, I'm just trying to reach an agreement with you as to time and place."

Charlie calmed down. "All you said was bring the money. You said nothing about the horse."

"You didn't give me time. The horse will be there, waiting to be picked up."

"Tied to a fence post, of course, just like before? And as we drive up, we won't know whether it's Jim Ned or another bay nag you stole off some poor farmer . . . not till it's too late . . . just like before? And you boys will have the drop on us this time for certain, because there's no way out but to turn around. You'd have us dead, like you almost had us the first time. No. No more of these nighttime meetings. I want a daylight deal."

"The first meeting was bungled, Mister Vann. I know that. But I wasn't there."

"But you probably planned it."

Golden Voice said nothing.

"Tell you what," Charlie said. "You tie the horse at the filling station tomorrow morning, say ten o'clock, or you name the time, and I will leave the money there for you to pick up."

"And when I go to pick up the money, you'll have me trapped. Officers coming in from all directions. No way, Mister Vann."

"And no way am I going to walk into another set-up like this."

The bland voice changed. "We could kill the horse, you know."

"How would you profit from that?"

"There would be no profit, which would be most regrettable. Circumstances could force us to that extreme. Your inflexibility, for one. Fear of apprehension, for another."

"I don't believe you'd do that."

"You may see, Mister Vann. You may." He hung up.

Charlie was sitting there like a man turned to stone, when I came in. "I've just come to a terrible conclusion, Buck. They want the money, but they don't want to give up the horse. Figure that out. What does that mean? There's no sense to it. Why would they take the horse, except for the money?"

We finished out the evening mostly in glum silence, each man alone with his thoughts.

Next morning Charlie called Sheriff Evans and reported the details of The Actor's call and threat. Smiley said he would put out deputies to check more ranches, especially barns that appeared abandoned. Smiley said his men and city police and the Highway Patrol were looking for the Camaro and one Dapper Thompson. Texas authorities had obliged with a description of the gun-toting hood, believed to have murdered a storekeeper in Vernon, Texas, two years ago, and a car salesman in Ardmore, Oklahoma, as recently as last April. With the second killing, he now had the dubious honor of making the FBI's Most Wanted List.

"It's a good thing you boys didn't go out there last night," Smiley told Charlie, "or you might not be talking to me now. That Thompson is a cold-blooded killer. From now on, count us in on anything that comes up."

Charlie promised. He was wearing down and showed it. He'd lost weight. His sad eyes were more doleful than usual. Discouraged, he sat around, saying little. Twice he called the bank, brief calls. He mentioned Tom Shelby, what his loss meant to the ranch. His judgment would be missed with the young horses. I stayed with him all that day, figuring he needed me. When evening came, we expected a call, but nothing happened. For the first time, I thought he had given up hope. I think we both felt that it was likely we had lost the great horse for good. There was no way we could safely meet the thieves' conditions. The money was waiting. Why did they hold back on an easier exchange? It was beyond us. We couldn't fathom it.

After the news and weather on TV, Charlie said he'd turn in. I followed a little while later, taking one of his boys' rooms. The wind was up, a threat of weather, about like the night Charlie had said Jim Ned was kidnapped. Oklahoma weather can change in seconds, from bright springtime to the dark havoc of a snake-like funnel, from a fooling January thaw to a blowing blizzard. As the wind increased, I heard the first

84

drumming of the rain, but soon the wind seemed to ease, and before long all I could hear was the rain sweeping in softly. At that, I slept.

I'm a light sleeper, which goes back to years of rising to be at the track by five a.m. to exercise horses. Some sound had unsettled my sleep. I sat up. A car passed on the river road, traveling fast, the roar of the motor sounding like a pickup. I could hear Charlie snoring down the hall. No, it wasn't that. It was something else, inside or near the house, something foreign to the night, something that had jarred across the gentle drumming of the rain. Something that didn't fit. Like a heavy *plop*. I listened for several minutes, but the sound didn't repeat. Still puzzled, I dropped off to a restless sleep.

Tension makes a man an early riser. We both were up soon after first daylight. Usually, Charlie didn't walk out to the mailbox for the newspaper until after the housekeeper had fixed breakfast at seven. This morning he first went for the paper.

I heard him open the front door, then his horrible scream. "Oh . . . my God! Buck, come here!"

I ran to the door and, jerking it open, stopped short, horror-struck at the grisly sight.

A horse's bloody head lay on the steps. The head of a bay horse.

"It's Jim Ned," Charlie croaked. "They did it. They've murdered him . . . like they said they would . . . the bastards!" He was raging and crying at the same time, while he knotted his hands and beat the air.

I glanced away and back, forcing myself to stare at the head. A late connection struck as I did. At once I understood about the *plop* I'd heard, and the pickup roaring off.

The mess had to be taken away.

"I'll get a feed sack," I told Charlie, and, as I started to go to the barns, glancing again at the ghastly thing, I noticed something I hadn't before. "Charlie," I said, "this horse has a star and a white stripe. Jim Ned has a small star, no stripe."

He stopped moaning and waving his arms and suddenly bent down to peer closer. When he looked up at me, the most wonderful relief spread across his ruddy face, like the face of a kid suddenly reprieved from disaster. "That's right. I hadn't even looked at the forehead. Jim Ned is still alive!"

Charlie immediately called Smiley Evans, who hurried out and looked for clues but didn't find any. What else could there be besides the head? But Smiley said, if he didn't look around, people might think he wasn't doing his duty. He said the theft was the first nationwide case of his experience as sheriff. He used words like "bizarre" and "baffling," which Charlie said later Smiley fancied to impress the voters.

"Let's keep this out of the papers," Charlie said.

"But if some farmer reports a stolen bay horse, what'll I tell him?"

"Just tell him the truth and describe the head."

The evening paper reported more wild tales as to Jim Ned's whereabouts. These stories seemed to bob up every few days. This time the big horse had been seen in a trailer pulled by a diesel truck speeding toward the vastness of the Navajo reservation. The witness: a guy reeling out of a roadside bar in Farmington, New Mexico. Another person reported a bay horse offered for sale at a stock sale in Fort Worth, then suspiciously withdrew it at the last moment. Purported owner and horse then vanished. In the wildest rumor of all, a Japanese horseman had purchased a bay race-horse at a small track in California for export to Japan. The tale bearer even called the ranch. He'd bird-dog the horse and buyer plumb to Japan if Charlie would pay air fare there and back, plus *per diem* expenses. No thanks, Charlie said, and hung up.

When the phone rang a little after six-thirty, I answered it and The Actor could've had a mouthful of molasses, he was so chummy. "By now, you've found the regrettable spectacle," he apologized.

"How could we miss it?" I said, and heard Charlie come on the line. "I hope you paid the farmer for his bay horse!"

Ignoring that, he said: "You and Mister Vann forced us to make that drastic demonstration of what we could do to your horse."

"There are two sides to this," I said. "You don't want officers brought in, which we've agreed to, and we want the horse delivered under conditions safe to us."

"I understand that, Mister Clegg." Boy, was he courteous tonight! "Are you listening, too, Mister Vann?"

"I am," Charlie growled. "Keep talking."

"The same arrangement holds as before. We'll meet you at eight o'clock tonight at the old filling station across the river. The horse will be tied behind the station."

"I told you I had to have a daylight exchange," Charlie said.

"We can't do that. It's too dangerous."

I sensed that Charlie was weakening as he said: "And nighttime is dangerous for us, after what happened off the Blanchard road."

"That will not happen again, sir, I assure you. That man is . . . uh, no longer with us."

"He tried to kill us!" Charlie said.

"I'm told those were merely warning shots."

"Warning shots, hell!"

"Now, Mister Vann, I want to make this as convenient as possible for you as a horseman. I must say you've played square with me, including the wasted Elk City trip. As for my part, I've tried in turn, but sometimes . . . 'the best-laid schemes o' mice and men gang aft agley,' as the poet said."

"'An' leave us naught but grief and pain,'" Charlie added without pause, to my surprise and The Actor's, who exclaimed: "Praise be, Mister Vann. You are a scholar. Indeed, you are, sir." He was spreading it on heavier than ever now with the sickening *sirs*, and damned if Charlie didn't seem to like it.

"Hardly that," Charlie said modestly. "Happens Bobby Burns is a favorite of mine."

"Much more of this and we'll be forgetting the matter at hand. Mister Clegg may come with you tonight, since one man alone couldn't drive the car and lead the horse back. How does that strike you?"

"Better."

"Just don't forget the money."

"Don't you forget the horse."

Golden Voice even chuckled.

Disgusting! Charlie had agreed without saying so, and I didn't go along with it one bit. Hell, they might as well be discussing a well-secured bank loan over lunch.

And then Golden Voice said: "Shall I look for you gentlemen at eight o'clock tonight, with the money?" Another chuckle.

"You may."

"One last caution, Mister Vann. Bring officers with you and this great horse of yours will be shot on the spot. I know you don't wish to risk such an irreplaceable loss." The rich voice changed, took on an edge. "Furthermore, this is the last chance you'll have to get your horse back. I do not intend to call again. We have other plans if you mess up."

That threat and he hung up.

Catching my disagreeing look, when he rushed into the room, Charlie said: "That smooth-talkin' bastard's not about to shoot my horse, and he knows it. It's his ace in the hole. No horse, no money." Then he frowned. "I'd like to know what he meant by other plans."

"But, Charlie, this is the same situation as before. We bring the money, they claim they'll have the horse there. I think we'd better call Smiley Evans. There's not much time, same as before. They planned it that way, I'm sure."

Charlie smiled like a 'possum. "This has gone on far too long. I decided to call his bluff, win or lose. Smiley can be here in a few minutes. He and his deputies can cross the river . . . it's low . . . and work down to the filling station on foot in twenty or thirty minutes. If they're slow gettin' here, we can time our arrival a little late."

The phone rang on the heels of his words. Charlie answered and winked at me as he listened and said: "Just checking, you say? You thought I might be calling the law? Don't you trust me? I want my horse back more than you want to keep him. See you around eight, with the money."

Grimly, Charlie put down the phone. "I had a hunch he'd check up on us. Why I didn't call Smiley immediately. Best way was to call me quick. If the line was busy, I was calling for reinforcements. Smart s.o.b . . . Better play it safe, in case he checks again. Of course, he can't wait much longer to get out to the filling station. So slip down to the bunkhouse and call Smiley. Tell him what's cookin', for him to tear ass out here with a deputy or two and be prepared to cross the river on foot. Tell him not to come in a sheriff's car. He don't need to put on a show for the voters. Siren wailing and lights flashing. Some bird might be watching the main road west out of town for a while."

I could see a determined change in Charlie. He'd taken his fill of the kidnappers. Tonight was showdown time, hell or high water. I caught Smiley at home and explained what was planned. He'd be out *pronto* in his personal car with his boys.

At the house, Charlie was loading a double-barreled, .12-gauge shotgun. I went to my room and got the .38. After that, we just waited and looked at each other.

In a way, that made me think of a kid wishing for something he wanted more than anything in the world. He said: "Do you reckon Jim Ned will really be there? Will we really get him back?"

"It's a long shot," I said, "but the only chance we have. So we have to take it."

Smiley Evans wasn't long rolling up to the house. He introduced us around. Undersheriff Will Quinn, deputies Hap Bagby and Orville Moon. Everybody loaded for bear. Two six-shooters wobblin' on everybody's hips. Shotguns in the car. Quinn and Bagby, I took for old hands. Both in their late thirties or early forties. Quiet, cool men, steady of eye and manner. Moon a stocky, brown-haired, eager young man who smiled a lot, obviously new on the job. He kept fidgeting and touching his guns and rubbing his chin. I wondered how he would perform in a pinch.

"We're ready," Smiley said. "Now, let's work out the details. Tell you boys something. I got more respect for bank robbers than I have for horse thieves."

"I don't respect either," Charlie said.

There wasn't much to decide. Timing was vital. Smiley and young Moon would cross the river at dark and move down the riverbank to the old filling station, keeping in mind the eight o'clock meeting with the kidnappers. But they wouldn't close in until they saw us drive up. Quinn and Bagby, in Smiley's unmarked car, would follow Charlie and me at a distance. After we crossed the river bridge and turned off the highway onto the dirt road to the station, they would shut off their lights and stop on the road, blocking any getaway to the highway, shotguns at the ready.

It was too early to leave yet, so we sat and talked.

"Wasn't sure you remembered the location of the old filling station," Charlie said to Smiley, something more behind his words.

"Finally came to me," Smiley said, rolling his eyes. "Let's see. The old station is about a hundred yards off the highway. Maybe fifty yards from the river."

"That's right."

"I was a young buck then. Went to a country dance every Saturday night. We'd swing those gals till they got dust in their pockets. Seems I do recollect that sometimes we'd drive across the bridge and turn off real fast to the station, hopin' nobody we knew saw us. Four of us would go together and buy a pint." He leaned back and stared at the ceiling. "It looked like a real filling station. Even had two pumps out in front. If somebody drove up that wanted gas, the guy would just say he was out. Was waitin' for a delivery. But I can't remember the brand of whiskey we got most times . . . generally they had only one. Whatever they could haul in at night from Wichita Falls or Arkansas or Missouri."

"Old Belmont, wasn't it?"

"Believe it was, now that you jibe my memory."

"Just didn't want you to get lost tonight," Charlie said.

"No problem. A dog never forgets where he's been fed or who fed him, and an Okie never forgets where he could buy a bottle back then. Why, Charlie, I even remember what the little man at the window looked like. He was freckle-faced, had a tooth missing in front, and wore an eye patch. Once I got up the nerve to ask him what his name was. To this day, I remember his exact words. He said . . . 'I don't have no name.' They even had a sign stuck up out front, not a big sign, mind you, and it said 'Good Gas.' I failed to realize it at the time, but such keen observations laid the groundwork for my future as an officer of the law. I've been keen on details ever since in my investigations. Just ask the boys."

They nodded like grinning puppets.

"Are you sure that Old Belmont didn't add to your power of observation back then?" Charlie asked.

"Not one little nip," Smiley said, and we all smiled with him.

After Smiley and young Orville left, we sat in tense silence until it was time to hit the grit. I drove the pickup, whose back window was still shot out. Charlie came aboard with the shotgun, a pocketful of shells, and the fifty thousand in a paper sack, just like Golden Voice had ordered. I didn't see why a paper sack was better than bare folding money. So much for the whims of kidnappers. As for the extra shells, I hoped the showdown didn't come to a pitched battle. If so, all the shells I had were in the .38. I'm not much of a hand with guns. It was all horses when I grew up.

Reaching the river road, I looked back and saw Quinn and Bagby leave the house. Farther on, I saw their lights at a distance of about two hundred yards. Good. Well, here we go again, I thought. It sure wasn't *déjà vu*, which Lori Beth had explained to me one time. It wasn't an illusion of having experienced something actually being experienced for the first time. Hell, no. This was a true repeat with some added features: officers backing us up, the thugs cut off front and rear. Something had to give.

We crossed the bridge and slowed down. Charlie had to help me find the road to the filling station, it was so dim, two pale tracks angling off through the grass and weeds, bent from the passage of the kidnappers' car, and trailer, I hoped. I took it at ten miles an hour. We had gone about fifty yards when our lights picked up a square-looking little building with an overhang in front and two sagging gasoline pumps. That — but no horse. No trailer, no car. Nobody in sight.

"Goddammit, where are they?" Charlie said.

I drove on a short way and stopped. Still nothing showed. "Charlie," I said, "we're not gonna drive up there and have them take us from the side. Two sittin' ducks in a car."

"You mean leave the pickup here and go on?"

"Seems best." I wasn't too certain what to do.

"I think we'd better take the money."

"Yeah."

We advanced down the road in the pickup's lights, side by side, guns in hand, Charlie holding the money sack under his left arm. Still no movement around the

94

station. Somewhere off to my left in the brush I thought I heard a car's motor running. I wondered whether Smiley and the deputy had come up yet. They should be close by now.

We'd come within ten yards of the station when suddenly two figures appeared. Both wore gorilla masks that looked yellow in the light. Both carried handguns.

We froze. So did they.

"Where's the money?" one said. It was Golden Voice! I could tell that rich baritone anywhere, I'd heard it so often. Charmed, I'm sure. All I could make out about him was that he looked about five ten, was slender, had a haughty way of holding himself, even here, and gestured with his left hand when he spoke. Very dramatic. Just like I'd imagined. The other guy, short and lean-looking, with an aggressive stance, could be Dapper Thompson, the two-time killer. I turned cold at the thought.

"In this sack," Charlie said. "Where's the horse?"

"Behind the building."

"Bring him out."

"We want to see the color of the money first." His tone was demanding, and his head rose higher. I could just see the bastard on stage in a dramatic scene.

"You'll see it when you lead out the horse."

"Mister Vann, you are being most uncompromising. I believe there's another word for it . . . intransigent." Showing off again, even now!

"Just plain English," Charlie said, raising the shotgun. "No horse, no money. Nothing fairer than that."

Golden Voice seemed to hesitate and shot a quick glance at the other man.

"If you make one wrong move," Charlie said distinctly, "I'll blow you both to kingdom come with this double-barreled shotgun. I'm fed up with you! Now, one of you lead out the horse. You go with him, Buck."

I was proud of Charlie at that moment. He'd taken control of the situation. His shotgun made the difference at this short range, something maybe they hadn't expected.

"Go on," Charlie ordered. "Get the horse!"

Golden Voice still hesitated. We'd reached a stalemate for certain. They weren't going to give up the horse, and they wouldn't get the money, if they didn't. Yet, if not, why bring the horse here? Strange. If they chose to shoot it out for the money, we still had the advantage. I knew now that the second man was more dangerous than The Actor, so I eyed him hard. I'd go for him first. He held the gun in his right hand, but he didn't point it at either of us. Just held it ready. I knew he could get off a shot almost as fast as Charlie could fire the shotgun. In a shoot-out, we'd all go down.

It happened then, jerking at the four of us. A sort of brushing sound that came from behind the station. Not the stamp of a restless horse, but lighter. Now a shot from back there. And a shout. And pounding boots.

Golden Voice broke first, shouting: "Come on! They've set us up!"

The other guy didn't hesitate. They sprinted for the brush where I'd heard the car.

Things changed so fast it didn't occur to me to shoot. I was thinking of the horse. So was Charlie, who ran ahead of me toward the rear of the building. Rounding it, we almost bumped into Smiley and the deputy. No horse was tied there.

Smiley was short of wind. "We's comin' on the run. Orville . . . he stumbled . . . dropped his gun and it went off. Where'd they go?"

The roar of a car, tearing away, took us back on the run to the front of the station.

"They can't get away," Smiley said confidently. "Quinn and Bagby have got the road blocked."

So we started running down the road. Coming to the pickup, we stopped together, startled by the wrongness of bouncing car lights heading not for the river road, but to our right, toward the Blanchard highway. In moments, the lights turned west along the highway, the car going full blast. Even as we watched, it raced out of sight.

"I'll be damned," Charlie said, let down. "Never knew there was a back road to this place. Guess I never stayed long enough to see."

"Must've been used in the old days as a way out when they got raided by officers comin' down the river road," Smiley said.

We hurried on to where Quinn and Bagby waited. Smiley explained to them, adding: "We could give chase, though I doubt we could catch 'em, but we don't even know what make of car they're in. Charlie, did you and Buck get a good look at 'em in the car lights?"

"Both wore gorilla masks, like before. So how could we identify anybody?"

"You couldn't in court."

"Just like before," Charlie said again. "Just like before."

"We'd've been there sooner," Smiley said in a regretful voice, "but we had to detour around a deep wash. Fact is, we fell into the damn' thing . . . couldn't see it. Took us a while to get out. Otherwise, we might have caught 'em from behind."

"And I'm sorry about dropping my gun and it goin' off," Orville Moon said, his tone sheepish. "I'm mighty awkward at times."

"Another fact is, your shot probably prevented a shoot-out, and Buck and I might've been killed," Charlie said forgivingly. "The situation was about ready to pop. Because they ran when they heard the shot. If there's any fault, it's mine. I should've shot 'em when they took off. But my only thought was my horse. I thank you boys for all your help. I guess now it's time to go home."

Charlie and I trudged back to the pickup and sat there in silence, like spent athletes after a long race. Finally, to cheer him up, I said: "Well, you've still got your fifty thousand, and we didn't get killed. That's something. It was building up to a sure 'nough corpse-and-cartridge occasion, as they used to say. That little bird was just itchin' to burn powder. I think that was Dapper Thompson by the way Golden Voice seemed to look at him to open the ball."

"Yes," Charlie said. "We are very lucky in some respects. But they still have Jim Ned."

CHAPTER
SEVEN

Let down, we stayed close to the ranch next day, doing chores to pass the time. But by afternoon, word must have leaked out in town about the aborted exchange — probably from one of the deputies — because the housekeeper rushed to the barns and said Charlie was wanted on the phone. It was the Norman *Transcript*. Not long after that, the *Oklahoman* called, then the Associated Press.

Charlie, keeping in mind that he didn't want to rile the thieves any more than we had, gave them all about the same general account. Not many specifics. "Yes, there was an attempt to pay the kidnappers for the horse, but it didn't work out. Where? Across the South Canadian River. Yes, we talked with the kidnappers last night, but no agreement was reached. They wore masks, so we couldn't identify them. We think the horse is still alive, because the kidnappers sent us its picture. We still have hopes something will be worked out. That's all I can tell you at this time. Thanks for calling."

That evening as we sat around after the late TV news and weather, Charlie looked up from a magazine he was aimlessly thumbing through. "I see here that Shergar, the brilliant Epsom Derby winner, hasn't been found yet. Been six years since he was taken from Ballymany Stud in Ireland. No trace whatever. If the horse wasn't kidnapped for ransom, was it revenge? Somebody who had a grudge against the owner, the Aga Khan? Seems there was a mix-up. No proper reward was offered.

"The Aga Khan is the spiritual leader of some twelve million Muslims. Colonel Gaddafi of Libya is an enemy. Another writer thinks the kidnapping was the work of an international gang, helped by the Irish Republican Army. Whatever, the horse is either dead or standing under another name."

"Wouldn't that be caught by blood tests?"

"Would, I guess, if they followed through on every new registration. But think of the thousands of Thoroughbreds foaled every year, some forty thousand in this country alone. There are always ways to get around rules, if people are slick enough." He put a hand to his forehead and closed his eyes. "We've offered a big reward, which we might as well call a ransom, but we've had nothing but evasion and frustration. I know they planned to murder us for the money at the station."

"Only we got the drop on 'em with your shotgun. They figured we'd just pull up there, and they'd take over."

"I'm very discouraged, Buck. It's plain as a mule's kick they won't give up the horse. Never intended to. I'll be damned if I understand it. They say money talks. Well, it's dead silent in Jim Ned's case. After reading about Shergar, makes me wonder if there might be an international angle to this case."

"The nearest logical conclusion would be Mexico," I said, thinking of the Town Policy case.

"If so, they've had plenty of time to fly the horse there. Yet, the photos were recent."

"They could've been taken soon after they took the horse."

"But why then? They didn't send the Polaroids till I asked for proof that he was alive."

Once again, all we could do was wait. After what had happened, I didn't think the kidnappers would call again, an opinion I kept to myself. Charlie was low enough, ready to grasp at anything. Why would they call? Any credibility they had before was shot after two attempted hijackings and the dry run to Elk City. Next time we might not be so lucky.

Around midnight, the phone ringing jolted me out of uneasy sleep. I heard Charlie answer in his bedroom and call: "It's for you, Buck."

On the living room phone, I recognized a familiar, but somewhat blurred, voice say: "*Señor* Buck. This is Chip. I'm back in Ruidoso."

"That's good," I said. "Means you're able to ride again."

"I am, man. But when you comin' out here?"

"I'm still tied up, trying to help Charlie Vann find Jim Ned. Do you know about that?"

"Yeah. It's been in all the papers. That's bad, stealin' racehorses." His outraged voice sounded more blurred. "I need you, man. I do better when you're here."

I could understand why. I'd tried to protect him, and had to some extent. Chip was only nineteen years old, not long out of Chihuahua. A poor, honest, good-looking Mexican kid, as vulnerable as a baby. But not poor long, because he was a natural rider. Knew when to wait on a horse, when to ask a horse for more run. And he had courage. He wasn't afraid to take a horse through a narrow opening on the rail. With his money had come the usual problems: salesmen with "hot deals" on everything from condos to fast cars, and pretty women and parties and booze and drugs. Busted once for drugs, but only once.

"Chip," I said, "you'll have to free-lance till I get back out there. You can do it. And tomorrow morning I'll call some trainers for you. Tell 'em Chip Romero's back in town."

"*Bueno*. I like that."

"Meantime, I don't mind if you have a few beers with the boys, Chip. But no heavy booze, no drugs. You know what I mean?"

"I know. I remember what happened before."

"You OK tonight?" I could hear loud music and voices in the background. He was in a club somewhere.

"I am, man. On the lead."

"That's good. Now, Chip. You know I want you to take care of yourself. You have to. If you don't, you'll be back in Chihuahua behind a mule in a bean and chili patch."

He laughed his quick, boyish, catching laugh, which made me laugh. "*Señor* Buck, you always make this Chihuahua *hombre* feel good. I am OK. I be looking for you *muy* soon, after you have hang them coyote horse thieves for the buzzards. *Hasta la vista*."

But I wasn't so certain he was OK. It's very difficult for a talented young jockey, likable with matching good looks, generous and easily influenced by swarms of fair-weather friends, suddenly gleaming in the public eye and plenty of folding money and credit cards in his jeans, to ride a straight course through the early years. Difficult to keep all the glitter in perspective, after going from virtually nothing to much. I hadn't done so well myself, when I was riding high, which helped me to understand Chip Romero better.

My thoughts trailing back, I sat by the phone and searched my mind for where my main obligations lay. It would be easy to fly back to Ruidoso, claiming my duties as an agent. Charlie would understand. Then what? My conscience would be back at the ranch. This was far from finished, hardly more than started. In only the opening stages of what was now the biggest quarter horse theft in history. It had taken this long to learn, for certain, that the kidnappers wouldn't surrender Jim Ned for good money — figure that out, if you will? — nor had they asked for more money — figure that, too. Also established that we were up against cold-blooded killers. There was no telling what direction the case would take from here. Bizarre, as Sheriff Evans would say, and sure as hell baffling. If kidnappers would turn down fifty thousand, they must have bigger money in mind elsewhere. No way, in view of all the nationwide publicity, they could run the horse for big money and get away with it. I had to rule out revenge as a motive. I couldn't see anybody hating Charlie that much; besides, this was the work of a gang, not one individual.

At least three men involved: Smith-Cole, Golden Voice, and Dapper Thompson. Maybe four. Two characters had rushed Smith-Cole out of the hospital that day. I couldn't place Golden Voice as one of them — he wasn't physical enough. Maybe he was the mastermind behind the whole thing. We faced a long haul, and it was all uphill. I was ashamed I'd even thought of ducking out on my old friend, Charlie, not forgetting Jim Ned. If the kidnappers killed Jim Ned, which they might do if pressed, the racing industry would lose its fastest blood. Another Shergar case.

So much for the deductions of "Detective" Buck Clegg, ex-bull rider, ex-jockey, ex-husband.

I called several trainers in Ruidoso next morning and told them that Chip Romero was available again, after suffering minor injuries in California. That he usually stayed at the Inn at Pine Springs Cañon, across the highway from the track. I laid it on thick about the races he'd won on the West Coast. Sure, two said, they needed a first-call rider and would get in touch with Chip. I felt better after that. The only problem was whether my boy, with me not there, would fall off the water wagon again, or, worse, do drugs again? New Mexico had always tried to run a clean racing program, and the stewards at Ruidoso were cracking down hard on alcohol and drugs around the track, particularly among the riders, with no exception.

Charlie said we needed horse feed. Would I go into town for the order? You bet. We both needed to keep busy till something broke, if it ever did. He had Rick Hinton working on fences.

I was unloading feed sacks back at the barns, when Charlie said Doc Young had called while I was gone and left his number for me to call back immediately.

"He sounded like it was urgent," Charlie said. "Rick's coming in now. He can finish unloading."

Doc must have been next to the phone, because he answered at once. "Buck," he said, "reason I called, I've run into a little something that may or may not be important. Thought you ought to come over, and we'll have a look into it. I won't tell you over the phone. Would take too long." His voice, an old gent's scratchy voice, sounded a mite higher than usual.

"I'm on my way," I said.

"What is it?" Charlie asked.

"Doc's picked up something. Said it would take too long to tell me over the phone. May be important, may not. Wants me to come over."

"Call me, if you need me," Charlie said.

I took the pickup. Doc was standing on the front porch, waiting for me. Instead of taking me inside the house, he led me across the street to his barn. "I didn't want to say much around the house. Annie might get upset. She's already of the opinion, as I told you, that I ought to rock on the front porch and mold away, instead of makin' myself useful." He eyed me straight. "I read and heard about what happened across the river. Didn't tell me much. What really happened, Buck?"

I told him, leaving out nothing.

"So it was that close," he said, nodding. "They was gonna kill you. The old filling station brings back some memories. I used to know the two fellers that ran it. Got tired of hard times, farmin', decided to perform a public service, you might say. Something the public needed. Anything respectable out of a bottle tasted pretty good then. Beat cañon run." He seemed to find pleasure at the thought and to dwell on the memory.

"What was it you called me about, Doc?"

"I was comin' to that. After you left the other day, it occurred to me, as a matter of common sense . . . that, when a man steals a horse, he has to feed it . . . if he aims to make use of the horse later. So . . . I've been checking feed stores in this vicinity and as far southwest of here as Chickasha. I didn't come into Norman. Didn't figure a horse thief would be fool enough to buy feed nearby where he had taken the horse."

"You must have found something suspicious?"

"You could say so. Also unusual. A citified feller buyin' oats and hay. You might think he was one of these get-rich-quick city horsemen I was tellin' you about, also in it for tax write-offs. But this fellow never bragged about his horse or horses. Like most of 'em do. Chickasha was where it was. I think we ought to run down there. The feller who runs the feed store is an old friend of mine."

"Let's go."

We set off southwest at a laboring gait, with Doc curiously examining the interior of the bullet-marked pickup. Little bits of glass still crunched on the floor.

"Looks like somebody got plumb personal," he said.

"We think a guy known as Dapper Thompson shot at us," I said. "He's wanted for a murder in Vernon, Texas and one in Ardmore. Now's on the FBI's Most Wanted List. His specialty is strong-armed robberies. He had a gun in his hand at the filling station, but, when he looked into the mouth of Charlie's double-barreled shotgun, I guess he decided he'd better not open the ball."

"I didn't know Charlie could be that gun-wise in a pinch, him bein' a banker used to a desk job. Lucky he was."

"It was a tough lay. But when it comes to Jim Ned, Charlie can be whatever it takes. He's learned a good deal about himself lately, and so have I, about myself included."

Chickasha wasn't far, and, before long, Doc directed me to the Washita Feed & Seed. There he introduced me to Ben Watts, a stout, jovial-faced man whose lively blue eyes told us he knew why we had come. After we shook hands, he invited us into his cubbyhole office and poured us coffee.

"I don't know any more than I did," Watts said. "The man hasn't been in here since."

"What did he look like?" I asked, thinking of Dapper Thompson.

"Just an average-looking man. In his thirties, I guess. Nothing stood out about him that I remember. He did have a brown beard, though."

The beard eliminated Thompson, I thought.

"What did the guy say?" I asked.

"Not much. All he said was that he wanted hay and oats for a horse."

"Just one horse?"

"He just said *a horse*. Seemed in a hurry. I figured what he'd need for a week or so. He didn't argue. Paid cash, and that was it."

"Do you remember how his voice sounded? What was it like? Anything special, that sounded different?"

"Not a thing. Just an ordinary voice."

So it wasn't Golden Voice.

"Didn't say where he kept the horse?"

"He didn't say, and I didn't ask him. I supposed it was a saddle horse. But he didn't say."

"He came in only once for feed?"

"That's right. Three days ago."

"Did you see what he was driving?"

"I didn't take out his order. One of the boys did. Want me to ask?"

"Might as well."

Watts stepped to the doorway, and hollered: "Hank, can you come here a minute?"

A muscular young man appeared. "Yes, sir."

"Remember the city-lookin' feller who bought hay and oats three days ago? One that seemed in a big hurry?"

Hank didn't have to think long. "Do I? He tipped me a quarter. Just that! Not that I'm used to big tippers. I started to say keep it, he might need it. Too, he griped, said I was slow."

"You say he was a city-lookin' feller," I said. "Just how do you mean?"

"Well," Hank said, "he had on a suit . . . gray suit, though I can't say it looked brand new. Wore one o' them little-batty hats with the little-bitty brims. Farmers and horsemen around here wear Western hats or caps with bills . . . Sorta baseball caps, like we give away here at the store with our name on 'em for advertising. It was how he acted. Even asked me how much you're supposed to feed a horse a day. When I told him, he just nodded. Like he knew, but it had slipped his mind. He was a city feller, all right, not used to bein' around stock. I could tell." The young man smiled to himself. "And when I was loadin', he kept lookin' around, real careful, like he was in a cow lot and he might step into something."

I could see that Hank liked to talk and enjoyed being the center of attention. This could go on and on. For all that, however, he had a keen eye for details.

"I don't suppose," I asked, "he gave any hint where he was taking the feed?"

"He just drove off. Even spun the tires a little."

"What was he driving?"

"A Nissan pickup. A green one. Looked pretty new."

I jerked upright. Now, finally, maybe all this conversation was leading somewhere. I glanced at Doc and saw that he'd caught it, too, connecting what I had told him earlier about the Elk City trip and the two men following me in the green pickup. Not that there's only one green Nissan pickup in the country.

I said then: "Which way did he go, Hank?"

Hank mulled that over. He seemed to be calling up all the pertinent particulars, every little-bitty one, and then some, and I got ready for another long, roundabout spiel. He waited so long I was about to break in, when he said: "Normally, I don't pay attention to where a customer goes when he drives off, but this time I did. Guess it was how he'd acted like a dude wrangler, and was so obnoxious, and the way he squealed the tires when he took off. So I watched him go." Hank stopped and put a hand to his chin, like a man in deep thought, though I figured he was just playing to his three-man audience, waiting for somebody to ask him to continue.

I was willing to oblige him, when he said: "That feller he headed straight east. I watched till he went over the river bridge."

A great excitement grabbed me. Finally, we had a location, even though it was only a general one — the east side of the Washita River. I glanced at Doc, and he nodded. We both stood up, ready to go. But there was one more point.

"Did you happen to see his tag number?" I asked.

Hank gave the old country sign of disgust, a snap of his fingers and a toothy grimace. "Sure didn't. Didn't see any need to."

"There wasn't," I said.

Once again, we seemed to have a special problem with tag numbers.

"You fellers maybe workin' on something that has to do with the law?" Hank asked.

"Depends," I said. "Maybe so, maybe not. Thanks for your help, Hank. You have a good memory."

He grinned like a schoolboy complimented by his teacher. "Mister Watts tells us to be nice to folks. If they ain't nice in turn, we're still nice."

110

No need to bring Ben Watts up to date on the case. Doc had done that. We thanked him and struck out east, over the Washita River bridge, traveling at a steady trot for the pickup, thinking what lay ahead of us.

"Now," I said, wondering, "all we have to do is cover this side of the river, up and down for miles, maybe on east. What we need is another clue, Doc. Got any ideas?"

After a short run, Doc said: "A man goes where he's appreciated and there's know-how. Let's go see Wildhorse Johnson."

"Wildhorse Johnson? No wild horses any more."

"He used to catch 'em out in west Texas and eastern New Mexico for the big cow outfits. Was a first-rate bronc' stomper. Rode in all the big Texas rodeos and around . . . Fort Worth, Midland, Amarillo. You name it. One of the best. Could ride anything with hair on it. But the inevitable caught up with 'im. Got all stove up. Never married. Never had time to get into double-harness. Always had another place to get to down the road . . . When the fun wore out, himself with it, came back to the Chickasaw country, where he growed up, and took up farmin', which he never was any good at. Like a fish out of water. When that wore out, he took up a talent he'd picked up from an Arkansawyer that had taken a likin' to him . . . learned how to make good whiskey with a whang to it. Same as you had at my barn. To this day, it has kept him goin', besides contributing to the general public good at prices the public can afford . . . Let's go see Wildhorse Johnson, whose first name is Luke."

CHAPTER
EIGHT

At Doc's direction, I turned south onto a rutted country road. We began winding and bouncing through oak timber and patches of prairie and around grain fields. Good country through here for horses and farming. Now and then, off to our right through the trees, I caught the bright gleam of the river. We passed a farmhouse where a bony, gray horse stood head down in a corral that needed some fixing up. Paint on the sagging red barn had peeled off long ago. The one-story frame house, likewise neglected, showed a sad face of better days. Except for the horse, I saw no sign of life. Not even the essentials of a hound dog running out to bark at us as we drove by, or the usual farm pickup. There was a run-down, hard-time air about the place, an abandoned look. I wondered about the horse, which looked old and poorly fed. However, judging by the tire tracks leading up to the house and inside the corral, somebody must live here at least part time and feed the horse.

We rattled across a bridge over a clear-running creek. On a way, we passed a farm where somebody had been at work recently. A new board was nailed into the gate of the corral at the barn. In the house I could hear voices. Nice place. But the house and the barn both needed painting. Maybe a family had just moved in. Something for Buck Clegg to consider someday, a settling down. I'd like a place like this, with the pleasure of building it back. First thing, I'd paint the barn a pretty red. You can't beat red for barns. Horses would come first. Lori Beth had accused me of that when we broke up. In a way, she was right; in a way, she wasn't. I never made that clear enough. Maybe because I didn't know how to say it.

For a few moments, I'd allowed myself to dream a little and look back. As the twisting road led us closer to the river, the going suddenly toughened. Sand pulled at us, and the pickup strained and growled and balked. I shifted to low gear, the motor roaring now. We crawled along at five miles an hour for about fifty yards, and then, as suddenly, we pulled out of the sand onto solid ground.

"When a car starts to bog down in the sand, and the motor roars, it's a warning signal to Luke that somebody's comin'," Doc explained. "I've even accused him of bringin' in sand from the river when the road gets packed down. This way he always has time to put things away around the house. He needs that time, if it's a nosy deputy."

"What's to keep a deputy from leaving his car and walking up to Luke's house?"

"Did you ever hear of a deputy that likes to walk? It's a good half mile to Luke's place."

I drove on, expecting to find only more rutted road to Luke's house. But before we'd gone another hundred yards, I had to slow down for a steep-banked wash, the pickup's motor complaining all the way as we made the climb out.

"Warning signal number two," Doc explained.

"Is there a number three?"

"That's the last one."

"Do you call him Luke or Wildhorse?"

"Either one, but he dotes on Wildhorse. Reminds him of when he was a top rider. I forgot to tell you he also rode at Pendleton and Cheyenne. Won first money many times."

Our twisting and squirming continued as the ruts grew deeper. Signs of travel on the road, some car tracks straddling the ruts, indicated Wildhorse Johnson had no lack of visitors. Finally, we drove through a screen of trees and found a little farmhouse set back in a clearing. A smooth-looking dog, showing Collie blood, charged out barking.

"Easy now, Bud," Doc said, getting out, and the dog trotted back to the house.

A man came out on the porch. From a distance he looked runty. As we approached, I saw, instead, a well-knit, wiry individual, with bowed legs and a hawk-like face. A mane of snow-white hair hung to his shoulders. His eyes, quick and gray under thick brows, met us with a warm greeting. Although he limped, he moved like an athlete, balanced and sure, when Doc introduced me and he shook hands. An older man, probably near Doc's age, but not old.

He smiled with easy assurance. His voice had a warm twang. "About time you brought me some decent company, Doc. You boys come in."

The room, that served as both a dining room and kitchen, was as neat and clean as any woman's. I smelled the pleasant mingling of fresh bread, woodsmoke, and tobacco. He swept us to seats on cane-bottomed chairs, with — "Believe this calls for a little drink. I'll be right back." — and limped out.

"He heard us coming, so he hid what he calls his house jug out back," Doc explained. "He's never told me where, but I believe it's somewhere around the corral."

"Has he ever been raided?"

"More than once, but they've never found anything. He always heard 'em comin'. He's too proud to put his mash in a bottle bought at a liquor store in town, which would make it look legal. Says he won't downgrade his product under a foreign label with no whang in it. He never keeps much around the house. Just a jug for personal use and, like now, for company. He never sells to women or kids or Indians. Just old friends, of which he has a number, and he don't deliver. Most folks comin' here would never suspect that he's in the business. He's close-mouthed, even to me. Has never told me where his still is, but I think it's where a little spring runs down to the river. Since he's always home in daytime, I figure he does his work at night."

"How do you go about getting a jug?"

"Seldom by direct approach. When I tell Luke I'm almost out of my mornin' phlegm-cutter for medicinal purposes, he'll say . . . 'I'll see what I can do. When you drive out, look behind that stump on the right side of the road just after you leave the clearing.' Then he'll be gone from the house a few minutes. When he comes back, I pay 'im ten dollars a gallon, and that's all that's said."

"How does he get around? I didn't see a pickup."

"It's parked behind the house in a shed. The deputies even went over that. Checked for a false bottom. Luke, he just laughed. Invited 'em in for coffee. One time his friends complained to the sheriff that his deputies were harassin' Luke, him just an ol' retired stove-up bronc' stomper. The raids quit after that, but the deputies still pop in now and then. They get plenty of coffee."

With a backward glance, Luke slipped through the back doorway with a brown jug, saying: "You boys help yourselves now." He set out glasses from a cupboard.

Doc poured himself half a glassful. I took about a third. Luke had half a glass, and we all sat down.

"Well, boys, here's to the olden days," Luke said, lifting his glass, "when a top bronc' stomper was known as the rider of the rough string, and everybody knew his name, and the sun came up bright every mornin', and even bad whiskey tasted good on Saturday night." Luke and Doc downed their drinks without a blink.

I took a tentative sip, shuddered as I had at Doc's barn, and headed for the cedar water bucket on the bench washstand.

"It does have just a little whang to it," Luke admitted. "But remember, it's as pure as a country girl's first kiss, made with untreated spring water, and cooked in the shade."

Unable to speak, I could only nod and put my glass down.

"Now, what brings you boys here on this auspicious occasion?" Luke asked.

I motioned for Doc to go ahead, since he'd gone to the trouble to search around on his own and found the feed store lead, if it was a lead, and he began to lay out the story from the beginning, when Jim Ned was taken. Now and again, he would look at me to fill in a gap. The facts told, down to the green Nissan pickup, Doc added: "Buck was in the irons when Jim Ned won all his Triple Crown races . . . in fact, in all his big stakes races."

Luke nodded. "I remember, and I was mighty proud it was an Oklahoma horse. As for these late doin's, all I know is the little bit I've heard on the radio and what little more I get in my daily paper. I know just about everybody on this side of the river for some distance above and below here." A sly smile trickled across his face. "Most of 'em are acquaintances of long standing. Nobody's let drop that anything of a suspicious nature has happened. Not that it couldn't have. I don't see my neighbors every day." The sly smile surfaced again. "Only when they drop in for medicinal needs and want to visit. Or when I go into town. Or pass 'em on the way in. Then we just wave."

"Has anybody moved in around here lately?" I asked.

"Not that I know of."

"Comin' in, I noticed we passed two farms. The first place looked deserted . . . just an old gray horse in the corral, and he looked done for. At the second farmhouse, we heard voices. Both places looked run-down."

"The first place," Luke said, "is what we call the Old Homer place. Old man J. A. Homer passed away about two years ago. Raised great watermelons. It's been in litigation ever since. Two kids can't agree on the time of day . . . Fight like cats and dogs, they say. One wants to sell. Take the money and run, move to Dallas, they say. Other one wants to rent it out or maybe live on it . . . keep it in the family. Fix it up. I don't know about the gray horse. But I haven't been to town for two weeks or more." Rising, he took Doc's empty glass and filled it halfway, like a man who remembered from practice. I passed, when he looked at me, though to humor him, I sipped again and found some of the fire had gone with the water I'd added at the bucket. Fixing his drink, Luke had settled himself for more talk.

"You said the second farmhouse looked occupied. Glad to hear that. That's the Old Binger place. Been rented out just lately, I guess, after standin' empty for six months. Makes me wonder who the renters are, and what they aim to do with it." He took a long sip. "Let these places not far from the highway stand idle long enough, hippies will move in and hole up like rats in a woodpile." He trailed off, lost in thought. "The gray horse must mean that one of the kids has moved in. That would be the oldest boy, J. A., Junior. Maybe he put the old horse out there to make the place look occupied."

Our talk wandered while Luke reminisced about catching wild mustangs in Texas and, later, his free-roving days as a star on the rodeo circuit, "when a stomper threw money around like chicken feed, and the purty girls bunched up around him like bees to a hive, him thinkin' his luck would go on forever, till that day

118

his foot hung in a stirrup at Cheyenne and a man-killer rolled over on him and the game was over."

While I listened, and Luke touched up Doc's glass and mine again and again, the afternoon had slipped away. The sun was a vanishing red eye, as bleary as my own, ready to drop behind the wall of trees along the river.

I looked at Doc. "Think we'd better go?"

"You boys are going to stay for supper, then spend the night," Luke said, emphatic about it. "First horsefolk company me and Bud's had in a long time."

"I told Nellie we might stay over," Doc said, which he hadn't told me.

Luke treated us to sourdough biscuits made cowboy-style and gravy, fried potatoes, and steak. As we sat around after supper, talking horses, I asked him: "Did you know Tom Shelby?"

"I did, and can't believe what happened."

"It was a shock to all of us, still is."

"It don't make sense, a man as level-headed as he was about horses, I've wondered what might be behind it."

"We don't know," I said. Why bring up the gambling losses and smear a man's good name? Gambling could be addictive, like some other human failings. I could vouch for that. Only I was lucky. I'd broken away from mine. It had been the amphetamines more than the whiskey, the combination of the two. Now I could handle drinks with friends and be in control of myself and not have to have a drink next day. Believe me, I'd got down on my knees and prayed for help many times alone in motel rooms. It didn't come to me till after I'd lost Lori Beth. Guess I didn't deserve it till then, maybe

119

not even then. It happened right before the West Texas Futurity at Sunland. Something seemed to come over me all at once one evening while I prayed. Like somebody had placed a hand around my shoulder. I found myself actually crying like some kid. Like a great burden had been lifted from me and I was my true self again. Well, pardner, the next afternoon, aboard a game little bay filly called Get Along Babe who liked to go to the front, we took that stakes money by daylight. You could have driven a hay wagon between us and the second horse. I never rode a better race. I think a man has to hit rock bottom before he can start back up, because by then he can't drop any lower. If there was another factor than gambling involved in Tom Shelby's sad case, I guessed it would never be known.

"Maybe Tom was bad sick and didn't want to tell anybody or didn't want to end up that-a-way?" Luke said, shaking his head.

"Maybe so. There is another thing. Charlie said Tom blamed himself for Jim Ned, but there was no way it was Tom's fault. Charlie made that clear, never blamed Tom, only himself for not taking more precautions at night when he stalled the horse."

"But not many people are gonna steal a stud horse. Not many are gonna know how to handle one. It would take a horseman or a vet."

"It would," I said, thinking how Jim Ned didn't like trailers . . . Jim Ned. Would any of us ever see the big bay horse again?

The night seemed without end. I kept waking up, my mind fixed on the green Nissan pickup. In my

120

off-and-on dreams, I'd always see two gorilla-masked men in the pickup, and I'd always see us chasing it and about to catch up. But something always happened at the last second. The green pickup would run off and vanish from sight, or, just as Doc and I roared up even, Charlie's old pickup would blow a tire or start steaming. We never caught the green Nissan. Dreams of frustration, no less true when daylight filled the room and I was still awake.

After a bountiful cowboy breakfast, during which Luke promised not once, but twice, to keep his eyes peeled, as he put it, we took off in an uncertain state of mind. What could we do? Discussing it as we drove along, we decided to check the country roads north of the highway, where there would be a scattering of small farms, maybe a horse ranch or two.

We crossed the deep wash, rattled on to the sand pit, and, as we struggled through it, the motor groaning, Charlie said: "Now Luke can tell we're leaving." We neared what Luke called the Old Binger place, where I'd noticed signs of life. Now a blue sedan with a trailer hitch was parked in front of the house. Lazy smoke curled up from the rock chimney. A horse trailer stood backed up to the barn's open breezeway.

As we chugged by, gawking, I spotted movement inside a stall in the barn. A flash of bay hide. "Did you see that, Doc?" I said. "A bay horse is in there!"

"I missed it, but my eyesight ain't what it used to be."

"Let's go see. Looks like they've just unloaded a horse."

121

I backed up, wheeled into the road that led to the house, squealed to a stop by the gate to the barn's corral. Getting out, I saw heads suddenly appear at the front window of the house. I didn't even wave or slow down. I slid free the bar on the gate and strode up to the open barn. Doc was puffing right behind me. In the middle stall I could see a tall bay moving around. It was too dark to catch his markings.

I ran over there, peered inside the stall, and froze, hoping. The horse was munching hay. As he raised his head, I saw the white stripe down his face.

Well . . . I slumped a little. Wrong horse. Jim Ned had only a small white star.

"What the god-damned hell you two doin' in here?"

An agitated young man stood in the barn's entrance, pointing a shotgun at Doc and me.

I raised my hands. "Easy," I said. "I can explain everything. We're not horse thieves. We're looking for a stallion stolen near Norman a short time ago. I saw this bay horse from the road. Thought he might be it."

"Well, you won't find him here." Still suspicious, he continued to point the shotgun, that was shaking in his hands.

Talking faster, I said: "My name's Buck Clegg. This is Mister Doc Young of Blanchard. We're looking for the champion quarter stallion, Jim Ned. You must've heard of Jim Ned?"

"I have. But I don't believe anything you say, mister."

"Under the circumstances, I can see why. But just point that shotgun the other way. Meantime, for identification, you can call Sheriff Smiley Evans in

122

Norman. Or Mister Charles B. Vann, the Norman banker. I can give you the number, if you'll allow me a few seconds to remember it. Doc, who could he call in Blanchard?"

The shotgun wavered for the first time. "Wait a minute," the young man said. "Did you say this is Doc Young?"

"I did. He's well-known there. Has had quarter horses for years?"

He was staring hard at Doc, his expression hopeful yet still suspicious. "Do you remember a filly I took over to you a couple of year ago named Little Lela that had shinbucked bad?"

Doc looked down and up, scowling. "A bright chestnut filly?"

"Yeah, that's her." The shotgun was cradled in his arms now.

"And," Doc said, still scowling, "she was by Shawnee Bug, out of . . . Her dam escapes me. Little Lela also toed out in front. Sure, I remember her." Doc looked straight at him. "And you, although I can't call your first name, are George Flint's boy."

"Right, Mister Young!"

"And how is Little Lela these days?"

"She lit up the board every time she was out. Now in foal to Kitaman. I like that Go Man Go blood. She's over at Dad's place now. I've just leased here. Moved in a few days ago. I'm David Flint."

"Well, David," Doc said as they shook hands, "you'll have to excuse the way we've busted in here on you. Jim Ned's a bay, and, when we saw your bay, we just rushed in. A dangerous gang of criminals took Jim Ned, and we're on the lookout. We stayed last night with Wildhorse Johnson. Sorry we caused all the commotion. I don't blame you for runnin' out with a shotgun."

"Oh, that's all right. I understand."

"We'll get along, then. By the way, David, has anybody new moved in around here lately, besides you?"

David Flint shook his head.

"Wildhorse Johnson said the Old Homer place has been standing idle since J. A. Homer passed away, but we saw a gray horse in the corral yesterday. Somebody's moved in."

"I've seen the horse, but nobody around the place. Guess they aim to move in later."

"Well, if you hear of anything, call me collect at Blanchard."

"Will do, Mister Young. I may be bringin' a horse over to you before long."

"Be glad to help, if I can."

"You did last time."

Driving off, I was reminded that Buck Clegg, "the great equine detective," had missed again. I said: "That wasn't smart of me to barge in there without a gun."

"If you'd had a gun and as nervous as that boy was, we both might've been shot."

"And if that had been Jim Ned in the stall, and that had been one of the kidnappers . . . maybe Dapper Thompson . . . we'd have been shot for certain. From now on, Doc, we call for help if we spot something. No more rushing in bare-handed."

Approaching the Old Homer place, I slowed down to look. The back side of the sagging barn was closed. I could see day-light through the weathered siding where the hayloft was. Nobody in sight back there. Driving on, I saw the bony, gray horse in the corral as before. Poor old critter!

But, to my surprise, a four-door sedan was parked in front of the house. Beside it a one-horse trailer. As we drove by slowly, a man I'd not seen before left the house, headed for the corral. But seeing us, he seemed to hesitate and strolled over to the sedan, opened the front door, glanced in, and went back into the house. Why the sudden change of direction when he saw us? But couldn't a man change his mind?

I drove on down the road about a hundred yards. There, in the timber, I gave in to my suspicion, or maybe it was more curiosity, turned around, and started back. As I sighted the gray horse again, I noticed that the barn door was closed. Was it open when we went by the first time? I didn't remember. Hell, I hadn't looked. The front of the barn was back and off to my right. I was too busy watching the man. Now two men stood talking on the porch, the first man I'd seen, a chunky-looking individual dressed in a dark suit and small hat. City or just a small-town guy. The second man was rangy. He wore a Western hat and a dark leather jacket. So what?

I took my time driving past the farmhouse and turned around. When we poked by again, the two men were still on the porch. A woman came to the door, and they went inside. My last glimpse was of the old gray horse, standing like a wooden horse. Old horses get that way in their last days. They just stand and stand, seldom seem to move, unless it's feed time, then they sleepwalk to the barn. I felt sorry for the old fellow. He deserved better, no matter what he'd been. Probably a small workhorse.

The farmhouse was lost from sight when Doc, giving me a look, said: "For a while, back there, I thought you were fixin' to go up to the house and ask what was in the barn."

"It did come to me. But when I saw the woman, I changed my mind. So far as we know, there's no woman in the gang."

"You're forgettin' Bonnie and Clyde. You saw that woman and figured everything was on the up and up."

"Guess I did."

"I felt the same way. We could both be wrong. Looking back to the olden days, as Wildhorse Johnson said, I believe the toughest person I ever met was a woman. Her name was Kate Hill. Least, that was the name she used. Smoked black cigars, could cuss like a muleskinner, drank her whiskey straight, and never staggered a step."

"Tough and ugly, eh?"

"No, she was the best-lookin' woman I ever saw outside of my Annie. Snappy black eyes and long black hair. Perfect teeth. When she smiled, you wanted to please her. Great figure. A man could circle her waist with both hands."

"How'd you know that?"

"I found out when I took her to a cowboy dance. Every cowpoke there sidled up to her. How she could dance! And flirt! But that was as far as it went. She'd kinda drifted into this part of the country, you see. Came alone, driving a nice sorrel team hitched to a light wagon with a canvas top. A camp wagon, you'd say."

"How'd you get acquainted with her?"

"She needed help handlin' one of her horses. I happened to be ridin' by, so I helped."

"What happened after that?"

"Like I said, I took her to a dance. Then another dance. I was stuck on her. But she wasn't as stuck on me as I was on her. I always felt like her stay was temporary, that she was just markin' time. She never let on where she was from or anything about her background. One day, as I rode toward her camp, I heard shots. I spurred my horse into a run. Lucky me. Kate was in trouble, and I'd be the one to rescue her. That would impress her! I always packed a gun then. I could just see her fallin' into my arms and me strokin' that black hair, tellin' her not to be afraid. But as I rode up, I saw it was the opposite. She was out behind the wagon, firin' a six-shooter. At each shot, she'd knock the head off a thistle at thirty feet. I tell you, my eyes bugged.

"She smiled up at me and said . . . 'Just having a little target practice. A girl has to protect herself, you know.'

"I told Miss Kate I thought she was well-protected and need not worry. As I rode on, my thoughts turned

127

serious. Where had Kate learned to shoot like that? Mmm . . . Well, a few days later a stranger on a fast horse loped up to her camp. I know because I happened to see him. Next morning, when I rode that way, Kate and wagon and team and stranger were gone.

"Wasn't long after that when word got back what happened down at Bonham, Texas. Kate and a man rode into town to rob the bank. Kate shot the banker right between the eyes when he went for a gun. The man grabbed the money, and they ran outside. What they didn't know was that a hardware merchant across the street had a Henry repeating rifle. He shot Kate dead before she could get to her horse. Then he shot the man out of his saddle.

"Who was the man?"

"Turned out he was known by more than one name. His latest was Blue Lucas. Seems they'd robbed a string of banks up in Kansas. Kate would dress up like a man . . . To this day, I think of Kate and the way she could smile at a man. But she shouldn't have shot that banker, and no tellin' how many more she had put down. The point is a woman could be involved in this, too. Kate taught me that."

"I get your point, Doc. There was also another point back there. Even if we had decided to go in, we didn't have a gun. From now on, I'd rather the sheriff or the Highway Patrol did my gunfightin'."

"A good point. Trouble is, the sheriff and Highway Patrol can't be wherever we happen to be."

"Which right quick will be north of the highway. Let's go scout out the country."

CHAPTER
NINE

Coming to the highway, I turned east. Not long after, Doc pointed, and we turned north into a dirt road not much better than the way to Wildhorse Johnson's. So far, without the sand.

"For a man who lives miles away," I said, "you seem to know this area unusually well."

"A mighty nice-lookin', red-headed girl named Hannah used to live up this road," he said. "Her daddy raised some good horses."

"And you took her to some cowboy dances?"

"I did . . . only she up and married a fast-talkin' cowman from Texas. Was he flashy? Rode a leggy Thoroughbred. Sported a new saddle, new Stetson, new boots. Wore a scarf around his neck. Used a lot of bay rum and slicked down his hair. But about that time I met Annie, who saved me from a life of regret."

"You've been lucky, Doc."

"You don't have to remind me. I found out later that Hannah had a terrible temper. Him and her broke up a few years later, and she ended up in double harness with a drummer out of Kansas City. A man can sure get foolish when he listens to fiddle music, an' his feet feel light, an' his head's made lighter by a jug in the wagon.

An' every girl looks like a rodeo queen in the moonlight."

Before long, Doc recognized a man plowing a field behind a team of mules. Doc waved; the man stopped. Doc eased through the barbed wire fence, and they must've talked for a good twenty minutes. That was the way it started and stayed. Every little while, Doc would spot an old friend, and even the ones he didn't know seemed up to date about their neighbors. No strangers had moved in. Nobody had brought in a big bay stallion. Even so, we didn't take everybody's word for what they said. While Doc yarned, I'd wander around and eyeball the barns and sheds. Sometimes, just to be social, we'd have to size up a man's quarter colt or filly and discuss their breeding back to early day foundation blood, and then listen to the owner's high hopes. At times, when Doc got to reminiscing too long, I'd have to suggest that we needed to move on. One old-timer even remembered the red-headed Hannah. He smiled at Doc when he brought it up, and Doc didn't expand on the subject, which saved us some time.

As we went along, my mind would swing back now and then to the old gray horse at the Old Homer place and the two men we'd seen standing on the porch. Something about the man nagged at my memory, but I couldn't place it. When you're up against a problem like that, it'll work out most times if you'll let it simmer a while in your head, then it'll come to you in a flash — most times, that is, if it's really back there in your memory.

130

We kept working north, with the only results the renewal of old friendships and no bay horse and no green Nissan pickup, not that all green Nissan pickups are driven by horse thieves. In the meantime, we turned down three invitations to dinner, which is still the noontime meal in the country.

Close to two hours had gone by when we realized we'd run out our string on this expedition. The green pickup must have gone much farther east and turned off, which left us with the impossible job of a big chunk of McClain County to investigate. Instead of retracing our way south to the highway, Doc said he knew a road that would take us straight east to where the highway bent to the northeast, a few miles from Blanchard. Along the way we could scout out more farms.

The farms turned out to be farther apart this way, so we moved faster. Doc's old-time acquaintances, therefore fewer, had no news for us, but they promised to keep a look-out. As we bumped along, the notion occurred to me that, instead of going on to Blanchard and giving up our plan, we could angle back to the southwest on the highway and check farms, off to our right. It would be like throwing a loop around that section. The idea appealed to me, and Doc agreed. We couldn't quit yet. I marveled at Doc, who seemed as fresh as when we'd started, rejuvenated by visiting old friends.

It was near noon, when we pulled in on the highway and found a filling station and a little eating place. We stopped and ordered lunch.

131

"This way," Doc agreed, as we rehearsed the plan, "after what we've covered this morning, we'll work out everything between here and the river north of the highway. Since that bird bought his horse feed in Chickasha, he can't be far away."

"If he is the real party," I said, feeling my first doubts. "He could be south of here. There's a world of country to hide a horse in."

"I saw more old friends today than I have in years," Doc said, over a second cup of coffee. Still in a reminiscent mood, he added: "When I saw all those good horses today, it made me think maybe I'd be a lot better off today if I'd gone to vet school and stuck with it and got me a diploma."

"Vet school?" I said, my mind circling back to the gray horse and the two men at the farmhouse.

"Yeah, vet school. Up at Oklahoma A and M, or up in Kansas. Been a country vet on the side, and got paid for it. As it is, unless it's a Johnny-Come-Lately, I doctor mostly for free. But all I wanted to do was raise fast horses and race 'em. Even if I do say so, I'm a fair-to-middlin' vet. Learned it the hard way, hit or miss. Read horse-doctor books and stock magazines."

I looked at him, my mind seeming too come full circle. "Vet . . . vet? That's it, Doc!"

"What d'you mean? That I should've gone to vet school?"

"I mean I used to know one of the men on the porch back there at the Old Homer place. I mean I know who he is. The rangy one. The one in the Western hat and leather jacket." I rubbed my head hard. "His name . . .

132

his name is Grubb . . . Grubb . . . Doctor Grubb. Hell, yes! He's a vet! Suspended a few years back . . . for illegally dispensing drugs at Ruidoso Downs and Santa Fé. Oxymorphone and Mazindol."

Doc stiffened, his eyes getting bigger and bigger.

Everything came in a rush to me now. "The beard . . . the spade beard. It's Emil Grubb. Doctor Emil Grubb. That's it! I heard some of the horses won big . . . Never heard whether he was reinstated or not by the Racing Commission . . . What's a shady New Mexico vet doing at an unoccupied farmhouse in Oklahoma? This is the break we've been lookin for, Doc! But we need help. Where's a phone?"

I found it behind the counter and put in a collect call to Charlie at the ranch. The phone rang and rang. Where was he? If he wasn't there, he was at the back or *en route* between the two. Charlie, you said you'd stick close. Of all the times! The operator came on. Did I want her to place the call again later? "Keep trying now," I told her. She did.

I was about to give up and call the bank, when Charlie answered in a winded voice, like he'd been outside when the phone rang.

"Charlie, this is Buck. I think we've got something."

"I wondered why the hell you didn't come back yesterday, and why you didn't call later. What is it, another long shot go-'round?" He not only sounded hurt because I hadn't called, but tired and skeptical, which I couldn't blame him for after all the stress over what had happened.

"It could be, but this is too odd a connection to ignore." Then I told him about recognizing the suspended New Mexico vet at the farmhouse. How the farmhouse had been unoccupied till just lately. How I didn't think it was safe for Doc and me to barge in, and could Charlie bring in the Highway Patrol, and have Smiley Evans call the McClain County sheriff for help? Smiley would need it, being out of his jurisdiction. We'd wait on the main highway just east of Chickasha, where the first country road turned south. The farmhouse wasn't far. They couldn't miss us.

Charlie was still kind of skeptical. "Did you see Jim Ned?"

"No. The barn door was closed. They wouldn't let him run out in the corral, would they? They'd keep him inside."

"They would, of course, if he's there."

"The whole thing hinges on this Doctor Grubb. What would a suspended New Mexico vet be doing at such an Oklahoma farmhouse? Not to lease the place. They had to have a vet along when they took Jim Ned. They had to have somebody to sedate a horse that acts up in trailers, didn't they?"

"No argument there. I'm a little slow on the uptake today, but I'll be there as fast as I can. You bet I will!" The old Charlie was talking now.

"Bring your shotgun and the handgun."

"Will do."

"Charlie's gonna round up some help and meet us at the turn off to the farmhouse," I told Doc.

134

Knowing there'd be a wait, I didn't race the pickup to the rendezvous. While we chugged along, I reviewed what little I remembered about Dr. Grubb's troubles. You could hear all sorts of bits and pieces of hearsay around a track, some no more than idle rumors, some pure exaggerations of what had really happened. But there'd been several indictments for "knowingly and intentionally" dispensing illegal substances to quarter horses. I was certain about that. Grubb had been the vet for more than one leading trainer at Ruidoso Downs. One of the charges specified a positive on a horse after winning one of the Triple Crown futurities, which meant hundreds of thousands of dollars at stake, with ten percent to the trainer. A hearing before the New Mexico Racing Commission was scheduled. That was the last I recalled, which was about the time my own world was breaking up.

When we reached the turn-off road, I pulled over and parked where we couldn't be missed, and we could wave down anybody rushing by.

Time dragged till it seemed locked. I'd sit a while and stare up and down the pickup, then get out and walk around it, and stare up and down the highway. Traffic was light. Doc had an older man's patience. He sat and waited. What, I thought, could we do if the green Nissan came barreling out of the timber pulling a one-horse trailer? I could give chase, but Doc would have to stay here to direct the pursuit. So much for what I hoped didn't happen.

It seemed longer, but in no more than thirty minutes, I know, I saw lights flashing east on the highway, coming fast. A Highway Patrol car in front, a sheriff's vehicle close behind.

I went out and waved, and they slowed down and drew off and parked. Charlie got out of the patrol car, gripping the shotgun and handgun, one trooper in step with him. Smiley Evans and Undersheriff Will Quinn left the other car. I was relieved in a way that Smiley hadn't brought Orville Moon, the green deputy. A good boy, but, as he himself had admitted, awkward with a gun. Might shoot himself in the foot, if he was along today. We all gathered for a parley. Charlie introduced the trooper as Joe Harper.

"The McClain County boys are tied up on a two-car smash-up with fatalities, but will be here directly," Smiley said. "Now, what's the lay-out, Buck?"

I described how the house and barn lay back from the road, and said I'd seen two men and a woman at the house, and parked at the house a sedan and horse trailer.

"I think it'd be better if we approach the house on foot," Smiley said, "instead of roaring in there. Quinn, you make a little circle to come in on the back side of the barn, in case they try to sneak the horse outta there."

I said: "The other man I saw on the porch, besides the vet, didn't fit the description we have of Dapper Thompson, the Dallas killer. But if Thompson's in the house, there'll probably be shooting."

Harper spoke up next. "It might be wise if I park the patrol car where it will block the road from the house."

136

All details agreed on, Doc and I got in the patrol car with Charlie, and we started down the rutted road. Soon after, when the farmhouse and barn became visible beyond the timber, the trooper turned off and parked the car so it blocked the road from the house. Smiley and Quinn arrived now. With a look all around, we spread out like stalkers, while Quinn continued along the rutted road on his assignment to watch the rear of the barn.

As we moved through the woods, I kept thinking about Jim Ned. My hunch grew stronger with every step. The vet and the horse connected. This was it, finally!

But when we came out of the timber and I looked across the clearing toward the house and barn, I halted in sudden and sick shock. The horse trailer was gone, the four-door sedan was gone. Only the old gray horse was left.

I glanced at Charlie. "Looks like they've pulled out!"

"Maybe somebody's still at the house," Smiley said. "Maybe the horse is still in the barn. Come on!"

At that, we all started running, Doc at a fast walk.

To prove I was wrong, I wanted to see signs of alarm at the house, startled faces at the windows or somebody running out. But nothing stirred anywhere.

Charlie and I legged it for the barn, Smiley and the trooper for the house. When we reached the corral gate, I wanted to see movement around the barn that would tell me we'd come in time, even if it meant a shoot-out. But nothing happened. The whole place was absolutely still.

I slid free the gate's bar and ran past the gray horse to the barn. Together, Charlie and I yanked open the heavy, barn door, then just stood there, guns ready, hoping, staring into the gloom for bay horse flesh. Splinters of light leaking around the weathered siding told me enough, told me what I'd feared — the barn was empty.

We stepped in and looked about. Fresh horse droppings, all right, but maybe the gray horse had been stabled and fed here. Heads down, we went back to the barn's entrance. Neither of us had said a word. Quinn walked up from behind the barn and shrugged. We shook out heads, meaning likewise. Smiley and Doc and Harper joined us.

"The house is empty," Smiley said, disgusted.

"Like the barn," Charlie said, almost choking, as down-hearted as some kid. "Makes me wonder if Jim Ned was even stabled here. But, hell, yes, he was. Buck and Doc picked up the trail when they spotted that vet. What would a down-on-his-luck, out-of-state vet do here at an old farm that a share-cropper would think twice about before he'd live on the place? You boys tell me, will you? Had to be dirty work. I want to take another look."

He moped inside, head down, refusing to give up. We all followed. Quinn went back and opened the rear door of the barn. The added light made a big difference.

I looked at the recently used stall again. The walls not only showed the normal scars of an active horse, the boards were shattered in places, the sign of a big, powerful horse, dented in others. Some horse, or horses, had raised hell in here, and not long ago.

"Look, Charlie," I said. "There's been a ruckus in here."

He looked and said — "I see." — and, hurt more, started to turn away.

I guess we both saw it about the same time: the shoe prints on the floor of the stall. Charlie seemed to throw off his gloom. "Hoof prints with a bar running across the shoe," he said. "Remember?"

"Ever since the start of his three-year-old racing season," I said, "when he developed a sore foot. The shoe worked fine."

"Jim Ned was really here," Charlie said, looking down. "We came this close, Buck. This close!"

The rest of our bunch crowded around to look.

"Sure the prints of a bar shoe," Smiley agreed, "and they sure don't belong to a workhorse."

I was looking at Charlie in apology as I said: "What must've spooked 'em was when we drove by the place three times. First time, we noticed one man who seemed a little nervous by the way he acted when he saw us. When we turned around and came back, another man was standing on the porch with him. The second man was the vet, it came to me later . . . too late. Third time we drove by, we saw a woman at the door. She seemed to say something, and the men went inside. I guess seeing the woman cooled any suspicion I had at the time. So we drove on. Proves a man should follow his hunches. I should've gone to the first phone and called you, Charlie."

"Now, Buck, I won't listen to any blame. Not one bit! We're lucky to find where they kept Jim Ned. Furthermore, we know now that Jim Ned is still alive. I'm mighty grateful about that."

My old friend Charlie. But I knew something then of how Tom Shelby must have felt when Jim Ned was taken.

"We can put out an APB for the horse in a trailer," Smiley said. "Trooper Harper and I can do that. How much time has passed since you and Doc drove by here, Buck?"

"Well over two hours, I'm afraid."

"What was the color of the trailer?"

"White."

"What was the color of the sedan?"

"Blue, I think. A dirty blue."

"It's not too late to get something out statewide." Smiley kept roving his gaze over the floor of the barn. "They must have unloaded and loaded the horse in here. Look at the tire tracks."

Seeing the tracks, I thought of the green pickup. Maybe it was a false lead after all, maybe not. Maybe the pickup was parked in the barn when we had passed. Whatever, it had led us down this road to the hide-out.

The old gray horse caught Doc's attention and mine when we left the barn. We stood there feeling sorry for him. "The poor old fellow was just a front," I said. "Left here to die when they pulled out. Guess they threw a little hay to him once in a while. I see a water bucket over there. He's not even shod. Never got a square meal here. The bastards!"

Doc crossed his arms and pulled at his chin, in an attitude of deep, if not impish, thought. "I believe Wildhorse Johnson is just about to get himself another horse around the place. Might make them deputies think he really farms a little, since Old Timber here is a workhorse and needs a home. What do you think, Buck?"

"I think that's a super idea, Doc. We can lead him behind the pickup."

We moved on to the house. Curiously, everybody went in. There wasn't a stick of furniture in the living room, in the kitchen a wood-burning stove, a cigarette-burned table, and four worn chairs, a box for stove wood, a few dirty glasses by the sink, and a litter of cigarette butts, vodka bottles, paper cups, napkins, and paper plates from fast-food places. A half-eaten hamburger of recent making and some scattered french fries.

"Looks like somebody left all of a sudden," Smiley said, going through the litter. "Didn't quite finish his lunch."

It was a two-bedroom little farmhouse. The one off the kitchen was bare. The second one held a broken-down bed-stead and springs, on the floor a brand-new bedroll.

"Now, why would they leave a new bedroll?" Smiley said, sniffing. "Even smells new. Forgot it. Left in such a hurry. Got scared. I tell you, it didn't take this tinhorn bunch long to clear out. Didn't have much to take. If you ask me, they've been movin' this horse around from place to place." He opened the bedroll, examined it inside, even shook it out, then turned it over on its backside. Something caught his attention. "Now, this is interesting," he said. "Charlie, you and Buck look at this."

It was s square-shaped blue label sewed into a corner of the bedroll. It read: **Jim's Outdoor Outfitters. Ruidoso, New Mexico. We Know Your Needs.**

Charlie and I swapped looks. "Well, I'll be damned," he said.

Smiley placed the bedroll by the front door to take along, then we all trooped through the back door, onto the porch, and into the back yard. Between the house and the outhouse near a rick of stove wood lay a low mound of scattered trash, much like what we'd found in the house, except for tin cans.

"Maybe been here longer than I figured," Smiley said, sizing up the trash. He picked up a piece of stove wood and started digging into the litter while we all stood by. "Why, they can even read," he said, snatching up a torn piece of wind-blown newspaper. He scanned it fast. "Something about an airport, but one not around here." He held it out for Charlie and me.

It was just a few paragraphs of weather-stained newspaper, one column, circled with a pen, no room for the name of the paper. No date. Something about the airport near Fort Stanton, New Mexico, being completed.

"Fort Stanton?" Charlie said. "I don't remember any airport at Fort Stanton."

"It's on the Fort Stanton road, not at the old fort. They shut down the Ruidoso airport. Too dangerous.

142

Built the new airport on a mesa, where it can handle bigger planes. A lot safer. They call it the Sierra Blanca regional airport."

We dropped the matter there, and afterward scouted around the farmhouse and barn and corral and back to the cars, and found nothing more of importance. Before now, Trooper Harper and Smiley had put out the APB. It was time to go, time to get in the pickup, and lead the old gray horse down to Wildhorse Johnson's and head back empty-handed again for the ranch.

At the highway, Charlie thanked Smiley and Trooper Harper again and again before they drove off.

But there was something still unfinished today, something that bound Charlie and me closer together, so far unspoken, but felt, I sensed, by both of us.

"I feel this thing leads straight back to Ruidoso," I said. "It's a gut hunch after seeing the vet and the few scraps we found at the house. Yet, why would they take the horse to Ruidoso? They can't run him there. I ignored my first hunch, but I don't want to let this one go by . . . that is, if you agree?"

"It's a long shot."

"But a long shot is still in the race."

"It's all we have," Charlie said, as low as I'd ever seen him. "I won't rest till we get the horse back, or find out what happened to him. The theft has never made sense to me, as valuable as the horse is, and it makes less now, with this possible link back to Ruidoso, which is even more strange. Why? Why? Could it be revenge, after all? Somebody out there getting back at me for all

143

the good luck I've had? Plain old jealousy tied to revenge? There is jealousy among horsemen. We've both seen it more than once. Maybe that was behind Jet Deck's murder?"

"If so, somebody went to a helluva lot of trouble to get back at you. No. We've been through that before."

"Somebody went to a helluva lot of trouble to murder Jet Deck."

"They did. But I can't see the same motive here. The people in it don't match up for plain jealousy and revenge. This is a gang of scums. That bird in the hospital, that self-styled Earl Smith. And Golden Voice and Dapper Thompson, now the vet, and probably some fringe dead-beats. No. Money . . . big money . . . has to figure in this somewhere, far bigger than the reward money, Charlie, though they sure wanted that, too . . . What say, we lead the old gray horse down to Wildhorse Johnson's? I've got another hunch he'll offer us a drink, and we could all use one."

CHAPTER
TEN

Two days later I checked into the Amigo Hotel in Ruidoso. Charlie would follow as soon as he could find somebody to look after the ranch. Once again, reliable Tom Shelby was missed. In a few days, Smiley Evans would trailer in his fast filly, Quick Cash, for the trials of the Kansas Futurity, a 350-yard sprint for a $500,000 purse. The situation hadn't changed back in Oklahoma. However, the statewide APB put out after the too-late raid on the farmhouse did pick up one report of interest: a green Nissan pickup seen pulling a one-horse trailer through Chickasha about noon, headed south. Which figured that the kidnappers had vacated the farm soon after seeing us drive by. Which placed us a good two hours behind the thieves. Headed south? Headed where? Another hide-out in Oklahoma? Or down into Texas? New Mexico, I hoped. And that damned green pickup! As elusive as a bedbug in a bunkhouse mattress. We hadn't seen it at the farm, which meant it was either parked inside the barn or the driver came in after we scouted north of the highway.

The more I thought about the case, the less confident I felt about returning to my old haunts and selling Charlie on the idea. But what else was there to go on? We were back to instincts, plus one dirty bedroll, a scrap of newsprint, and a shady vet out of the past.

In spring and summer, Ruidoso is like a magnet drawing horsemen off the hot Oklahoma and Texas plains to the cool pines of the Sacramento Mountains. On stakes-race weekends, it swells from a small village to a frenzy of thousands, mainly free-spending Okies and Texans mixed with just plain tourists, swarming in to bet and enjoy the scented air, and stroll the shops along the main pathway called Sudderth Drive, and pack the eating places. They drive Cadillacs, Lincolns, customized vans, motor homes, and fast pickups. The horsemen wear big hats and big buckles over big paunches, and the women still go for turquoise jewelry. All come to watch and bet the world's fastest quarter horses run for the world's biggest purses.

I still felt uneasy about Chip Romero, so my first concern next morning was to locate him. Going out to the track a little after daybreak, I hoped to find him exercising horses. He wasn't in sight on the track, and he didn't show up after some time. A rider I knew said he hadn't seen Chip in days. By that, I knew my boy was in trouble. I soon found Mike Peterson, Jim Ned's old trainer, around the barns.

"I heard you went back to Oklahoma," Peterson said. A stocky, unhurried man, pushing fifty, his broad face and genial eyes reflected a rare patience with horses and people. He used to say the key thing in training is to get to know your horse. He did with Jim Ned, kept the big horse tuned to a peak for the stakes races. "Anything new on Jim Ned?"

146

"Still looking. Charlie's coming out before long. Thought we might pick up something around here."

His eyebrows shot up in surprise. "Here? It's a long way from here to Oklahoma."

"For this reason." And I gave him a rundown about seeing Dr. Emil Grubb at the farmhouse, and what we'd found, including the telltale bar shoe, and how close we'd come.

"That bar shoe!" He fisted a hand. "Yes!"

"Tell me about Grubb."

"I haven't seen him in Ruidoso this season. Not since last spring, I guess. He was the vet for a filly that won the Rainbow Futurity two years ago and tested positive for Oxymorphone. They held up the purse. About the time you were in California. Grubb said he was innocent, hired a big-time lawyer out of Albuquerque, but the Racing Commission suspended him. That was some months later. You know how these things take time. There was another stink up in Santa Fé." He broke off. "I'm hazy about most of the details. A federal grand jury returned a number of counts . . . Grubb pleaded innocent all along . . . The case has dragged on and on. He hasn't come to trial yet. Last I recall he was out on bond, with the provision he can't practice till after his trial next fall. I've heard he's been around, but I don't know a trainer that would risk usin' him. I wouldn't now, though he was in the clear till the filly showed up wrong at the test barn. I'd say, he's been hard-up since the suspension, with his attorney's fee and other things . . . Buck, it gets me that you'd recognize him after all this time."

"Well, I knew him when he was the vet for other trainers. Not that we were buddies. What told me was that spade beard. He always wore one. Only guy I know. He always took pride in it. That, and the way he talks with his hands. Like windmills. Different, too. And the rest of him fit . . . a long, tall guy I used to see around the barns."

"What a mess."

"I came out here to find Chip Romero. When he called me back in Oklahoma, I felt he was headed for trouble again."

"He was, and still is. Bad test for cocaine. Suspended for sixty days. I wanted him to ride for me, but . . ."

I had to take a step back. I'd sensed this coming, but it still shocked and it hurt and I felt a stab of guilt. Maybe I failed Chip along the way. "Is he still at the Inn at Pine Springs Cañon?"

"Last time I talked to him, just before he got set down, he'd taken a little apartment in the complex across from the Y, on the right when you come into town."

I didn't remember the name of the apartments, but I remembered the location. The office manager threw me an odd look when I asked Chip's number.

"Is he doing OK?" I asked. He only shrugged, and I said: "I'm Chip's agent." He shrugged again. As if to say, so what? Great guy.

A stretch of silence followed after I knocked on the door. I knocked again, louder, and called — "Chip, it's Buck Clegg!" — and that time a slim Mexican girl in a red blouse and stone-washed jeans opened the door and greeted me. "Come in, *Señor* Buck. Chip is here. I'm Rosa."

She held out her hand and gave me a firm shake. I liked her instantly: great, warm, black eyes, no deviousness there whatever, no hint of drugs, and a nice, open smile that made me feel welcome and smile in turn. High cheekbones set off a smooth-skinned face. Straight black hair down to her shoulders. Some Indian blood in those high-boned features. I guessed her about Chip's age, maybe a year or so older, but she had a maturity that Chip didn't have and needed. A product of hard times along the border, I figured, like so many young Mexicans, except the recent good times, if any, hadn't changed her. For sure, Chip had upgraded the quality of his company compared to what I'd seen previously among the fair-weather crowd.

The apartment, a one-bedroom affair, showed a woman's neat hand, a far cry from Chip's usual disordered den at the Inn after a wild binge: bottles and beer cans, the clutter from fast-food orders, and loaded ashtrays. I missed another familiar item — the sweetish stink of the weed. This place was clean. Rosa clean!

I was standing there, wondering what to say next, and how to approach the subject of Chip Romero, suspended race rider, when a shouted — "*Señor* Buck!" — startled me.

He stood in the doorway of the bedroom, and he looked like hell. Long, black hair like vines across his face. Eyes puffy from sleep, or the lack of it. Slumped. Mouth agape. In pajamas that hung like green drapes on his skinny frame.

I said — "Chip." — and crossed over to him and wrapped my arms around his shoulders in the damnedest *abrazo* I could muster. He hugged me hard. I could hear him choke a little. My throat was tight, too. When we drew back, both of us got embarrassed and looked away for a moment. "Glad to see you, Chip."

All he could do was nod the same. Then he seemed to remember something and, looking at Rosa, said: "Meet Rosa, my wife."

I looked at her and got the big smile again. "Fine," I said. "I'm glad to hear that. Chip's a lucky man."

"We are both lucky," she said, turning those eyes on Chip.

"Rosa's from Chihuahua, too," Chip said. "Been working in El Paso. But no more will she work like burro there. This *hombre* rescued her. She is my burro now." He forced a semblance of his quick, boyish laugh. The guy was really hurting, and I was thinking what could I do?

"I will get your robe so you will be decent talking to *Señor* Buck, your good friend," Rosa told Chip.

"See, man," Chip teased, "how this Chihuahua woman jumps when I speak."

The light moment passed. He was not really fighting his sickness, he was trying to hide it from me, a fact that had to come out sooner or later. I decided to let him tell me. When Rosa brought him a robe, he settled down on the divan. He asked me about Jim Ned, and I set forth what we knew, including the few Ruidoso leads. He listened eagerly.

150

Rosa interrupted us. "*Señor* Buck, you will have breakfast with us, yes?"

"Thank you. I'd appreciate it. I've been up since day-break. Old habit." I'd already had coffee, but anything to get Chip relaxed and talking.

We sat down at the table to coffee, fruit juice, scrambled eggs with salsa, bacon, and toast. Chip, still striving to tease, said: "Breakfast in bed, this sweet little burro likes to serve me."

"You, man, you brag like big *hacendado*," she scolded, fixing him a vexing smile. "But I would, if you'd eat it. Maybe you brought up on cactus in Chihuahua?" She turned to me, her face as earnest as a small child pleading her cause. "*Señor* Buck, he no eat enough. Just coffee for breakfast. A leetle pinch of sandwich at noon. A leetle more nothing at night. He has bad dreams. He needs to see doctor."

She'd almost come out with it, but would not, I knew, out of respect for her husband. Because it was Chip's place to tell me, and Chip, out of pride or shame, couldn't bring himself to it yet. But it was building up. It would break before long.

"You need to eat something, Chip," I said. "The eggs are great."

He shook his head, no, but managed a smile over his coffee. He looked like hell. "Rosa," he said, "she came into my life when I needed her. She is special little burro."

"I can sure see that," I said. "That's good. Rosa's a fine girl, and you're not so bad yourself."

He broke a little smile at that. I waited, but he had no more to say. We left the table, and, while Rosa cleared the dishes, I sat next to Chip on the divan. "Chip," I said, "there are two things I've never done as long as I've been your agent. I've never preached at you, because I know what it's like to be young and a winner, which you are. And I've never lied to you, and I won't start now. And we've always been honest with each other as agent and jockey."

He couldn't meet my eyes. It was touching how fast Rosa got there beside him, sensing, I knew, what was coming.

I put my left hand on his shoulder. "Chip, you've got to take care of yourself . . . for yourself, for Rosa. Now, do you want to tell me what the problem is?"

He was staring at the floor. He said: "I got a bad test for coke, and the stewards busted me . . . for sixty days, they did."

I didn't say anything. No blaming. This was just the beginning. Let him tell the rest of it his way, this Mexican kid with the God-given hands and horse savvy of a natural rider. His voice seemed to come from a distance. "I remember the first time you sat me down on a bale of hay and tried to straighten me out. You the only one, *Señor* Buck. I was good boy for long time after that . . . When you had to go back to Oklahoma, the parties got bigger. But I met Rosa. She knew *pronto* I was using coke. She'd go to parties with me, but she wouldn't party. I tried hard to get her to. But she was too smart." He shed a grin. "She even married me. I came back here, got some mounts . . . Chip Romero,

152

man, the Chihuahua Kid, he's ridin' good again, they say at the barns. Gonna be lead rider at Ruidoso Downs. Wanna bet? Hey, man, you don't bet against a sure thing. Not against Chip Romero, the Chihuahua Comet . . . There he goes now in his Porsche . . . Was this Chihuahua *hombre* full of himself! I thought I could do anything. Sometimes, before I went to the track, I'd do a coupla lines of coke. Rosa would cry and say . . . 'Go with God,' but she never left me. She tried hard to help me. Even hid the car keys when I wanted to use them late at night. So I'd start walkin' some place I knew about . . . You can get drugs just about anywhere, though it's easier in California, where I started using . . . Then she'd drive by and pick me up and take me back home. Now, Rosa, you tell *Señor* Buck what happened next."

She looked at Chip, her eyes like dark hollows, and then she looked straight at me and said: "I turned Chip in to the stewards. I did because I was afraid for him . . . and afraid what he might do to others . . . But he hurt only himself."

Their eyes bore into me, both hoping for understanding, both hoping Buck Clegg, because he'd been a top jockey and was Chip's most trusted friend, could do something. What they didn't know was that this great Buck Clegg had been close to what Chip had become, a druggie. No cocaine, but plenty of whiskey and amphetamines, that had come near ruining his life forever. You bet Buck Clegg understood.

"I understand," I said, more than they would ever realize. These two Mexican kids. That was all I said. All that needed to be said, to let them know. No preaching. I still waited, because it wasn't finished.

Chip's voice tore at me suddenly. "You've got to help me! You've always been good to me!"

"Yes," Rosa said. Each was near tears.

"It's all right," I said. "It's all right. You're going to the hospital, Chip. We're gonna get you so you can ride clean again. We'll see about it first thing today."

That broke everything loose. We hugged each other. We even wept a little, maybe me the most, because I understood, because I'd been down that one-way road to my own private hell, praying for help as I went, and somehow I'd found it and made my way back.

CHAPTER
ELEVEN

I checked Chip into the local hospital that afternoon, where he met with doctors and a drug abuse counselor, who told him: "People help people stay straight, same as nobody stays sober without AA meetings. Nobody does it alone. You're fortunate you have a good wife and a good friend here. You'll need to stay in the hospital thirty days or so for the course of treatment. I'll visit with you regularly. When you leave the hospital, don't run around with the people who use, and you'll be all right."

Rosa and I left Chip waving at us and looking upbeat. She would see him everyday as long as permitted, and I would see him as often as I could. But I reminded him that might not be everyday because of the case.

"I think I'd better give up the apartment before rent comes due and move into a trailer with a girl I know from El Paso who is waitress at a club," Rosa told me. "I think I better look for waitress job, too. Chip spend too much money on drugs."

"I can help you. No problem."

"Oh, no," she looked embarrassed. "I no mean that, *Señor* Buck. I have money now. I save when Chip not looking. *¡Gracias!*"

"If you need anything, let me know. I'm staying at the Amigo Motel. I'll be in and out. Mostly out. Just leave word."

She drove off in Chip's Porsche, and I thought how lucky he was to have her in his corner. He'd come out of the hospital clean. But then the battle would just be starting. There would always be the urge to break over if he went to a party. Chip's very nature was against him. He was so young and easily influenced, so vulnerable, a babe in a drug-crazy society. Rosa was his only real hope, Rosa and the obvious fact that they truly loved each other. I felt more optimistic for him when I thought about that.

I went out to the track, and, after I'd told the stewards about Chip's decision to go into the hospital, I summed up the Jim Ned situation for them and why I was in Ruidoso. They couldn't see the connection until I brought up Dr. Grubb; even so, they said, it seemed mighty remote. Why bring the horse out here? How would the gang profit here? No way they could run him. I agreed it didn't make easy sense, but it was the only lead I had. No, they said, Grubb hadn't come to the track this season. Although he was free to practice under the court ruling, they would not permit him to do so until he came clear in court.

I spent the next four days visiting and loafing with trainers and jockeys, but doing more listening than talking. In all that time, I picked up not one shred of helpful information — and nobody had seen Grubb. Charlie called once. He thought he'd found a reliable man to run the ranch for a while. Twice I dropped by

156

the hospital to see Chip. Each time, he was sleeping. I left word at the nurses' desk to tell him I'd been there, for them to make certain he knew I'd come to see him. Rosa had been there every day.

Too much time had passed without results, wasted, I felt, except for getting Chip into the hospital. I'd almost lost track of what day it was. Driving along upper Sudderth in a rented car, I came close to getting rear-ended, when I saw the bill-board in front of the Pines nightclub. You couldn't miss it. The same country/western star's blown-up photo featured there until today. Now Lori Beth's in color, looking right at me. While I stared, the damnedest feeling slammed through me.

Behind me, a big-hatted guy in a powder-blue Lincoln rode the horn, blasting me, and shot me a dirty look as he gunned around and I pulled over to the curb to read the bill-board:

STARTING TONIGHT FOR TWO WEEKS ONLY . . . FROM 8 UNTIL 1 . . . THE PINES PROUDLY PRESENTS . . . COUNTRY MUSIC STAR MARGO DRAKE AND THE WILD ONES . . . FRESH FROM LAS VEGAS . . . EVERY NIGHT . . . RESERVED SEATING AVAILABLE . . . COME EARLY.

She looked even more fetching than usual. Her dark hair done casual style, I guess you'd say, while her green eyes seemed to look straight at me with that

157

sweet expression, kind of questioning-like. Well, I suppose I could imagine a little.

I drove into the parking lot and went to the club's office. There was a line already there, because it was afternoon now. When I reached the end and asked about a reserved seat, the young woman said: "Sir, we're sold out. Sorry. All we have left are some general admission tickets. You'll have to stand up."

I bought one. More people were lining up. From there I drove to the hospital. Chip was awake and groggy from medication. I gave him the *abrazo* and asked: "How do you feel?"

"I'd like to get out of here."

"That's a good sign. You look better. But you need to stay the course. The nurses say the beginning is the hardest part. You'll feel better before long."

"That's what Rosa says." He sat up straighter in the bed. "Any news on Jim Ned?"

"Nothing. Charlie Vann will be here in a few days. We'll decide, then, whether to stick it out."

I left there more concerned about Chip than when I'd come in. I sensed something about him that bothered me. A certain unrest in his eyes at times, an evasion as we talked. He wanted to get out of there and use. Would he last the course? I wouldn't bet on it. Rosa could be in for a lot of heartbreak.

A story on the sports page of the afternoon El Paso *Herald-Post* didn't ease my mind when I read that **Jockey Chip Romero, recent winner of several quarter horse stakes races on the West Coast, has been suspended for sixty days by Ruidoso Downs**

158

stewards and admitted to the Ruidoso hospital to undergo a series of drug treatments.

That didn't help a bit. Chip would be humiliated. Who had spilled the story? Well, I guess it had to come out sooner or later. Another thing he would have to face as a top jockey, as a public athlete.

Lori Beth and her Wild Ones were scheduled to kick off the evening's entertainment at eight o'clock. I was there by seven-thirty, and the small bar off from the closed dance hall was packed like a railway cattle car, men shoulder to shoulder at the bar, couples at the few tables. I gave up on even getting a beer, and waited.

There was a rush to get in when the dance hall doors opened shortly before eight. Two doormen checked tickets. I found a chair against the far wall, as excited as a country boy at his first Saturday night picture show, as we used to call 'em. I was also proud of Lori and what she had accomplished. All based on her own talent, I hoped, not through sexual favors with record executives. One in particular, Gavin Scott, while she'd pushed tapes along Nashville's Music Row without success. Promises made that never came through. Both Lori and I knew what was expected of a talented young woman entertainer, sometimes, if she was to move up. You know what I mean? She'd told more than one big-shot she'd get there through talent and not bedroom doors.

While the crowd grew restless waiting for the band to come on, I reviewed some emotions and happenings that I had tried to seal off after our two lives had broken apart, when I was still on top. Though stretched

159

thin, flying from track to track to ride my pick of horses, Lori doing well as a featured singer, but not yet with the record contract she deserved.

It happened when we were both in Ruidoso. I was booked to ride Jim Ned in the Rainbow Derby. Lori was singing with a hot rockabilly outfit called the Stagecoach Five. Then this Gavin Scott, president of Peak Records, shows up unexpectedly in town. Lori was ecstatic.

"I know he's come here to talk contract," she said. "I'm so excited, Buck. I feel this is finally it."

"He could've done that in Nashville," I said. "Why just now?"

"You know it takes time, and there are so many good singers."

True. But I'd never liked the guy, though I'd never met him personally. Maybe I was also a little jealous, like any man with an extra pretty wife.

She introduced us early one evening before she went on at the Win, Place, and Show. I still didn't like the guy, even less now. There he stood, all six feet-two inches and two hundred pounds or so of lean flesh and a smile that looked like piano keys. There wasn't a curly hair out of place. Everything about him perfect, from his silk suit to the sculpted face that showed the magic of plastic surgery. No man could have been born with a face that perfect; well, hell, yes, I was prejudiced. Me with my battered face.

Every evening, when I went to catch Lori and the Stage-coach Five, Gavin Scot was in the audience. He sat there rapt, never taking his eyes off her when I looked his way. As he watched her, his eyes seemed to strip away every inch of clothes she had on, which wasn't much. Naturally, I didn't ask him to have a drink with me, and he didn't ask me. I gathered that he didn't like me any more than I liked him. I felt he was after my wife.

Lori had never been better. She'd just written the love ballad "Let Love Linger," and the way she sang it every night to a packed honky-tonk house and the hand she got, she was fast making it a hit. When the show ended at one o'clock, she and the band always had to play another number before the crowd would leave.

At intermission, this night in particular, I went for a drink at the bar. So did Scott. When we passed in the crowd, neither of us spoke or acknowledged that the other existed, which suited me fine. This had gone on for three days. Lori told me she'd talked to Scott twice about a contract on the afternoons when I was at the track, but they still couldn't agree on the terms.

"But I'm going to get that contract," she said.

"There are other record companies," I reminded her.

"But this is the one I want to be with. It's tops." No second-class outfit for Lori Beth. I had to agree. Earlier, a lesser record company had produced her debut album called "Yours," which had only moderate success because she felt it wasn't pushed enough.

When the show had ended and I started to make my way through the crowd around her dressing room, a fight broke out in the bar. Two cowboys going at it hammer and tongs over a cute little girl in blue blouse and denim skirt while she stood by and screamed falsetto. A heck of a fight. Everybody stopped to watch. They fought from the bar across to a table and back to the bar, throwing punches every step, neither one getting the upper hand, while the girl's screaming never stopped. It was remarkable how she could keep that up. Finally one of the two bartenders, a brawny but tired-looking older man, rushed around the bar and tore the two apart.

"Finish it outside!" he yelled. "Not in here!"

Hacking for wind, they stopped, and so did the screaming. But it wasn't over. The crowd parted to let the three go out. In moments, I could hear the fight starting over while the girl screamed — "Stop it! Stop it!" — without any effect. The meaty thuds carried inside the bar.

I'd expected to find Scott among the watchers. I didn't see him. Not that it mattered. It took a while to work through the crowd around to the entrance of the dressing rooms where a guard blocked the curious. He knew me from other nights when I'd picked up Lori.

"You missed a good fight," I told him. "Two cowboys. Beats what you can see on TV."

"We have some pretty good ones every night," the guard said. "Drunks."

"This was over a girl."

"It's always over a girl or about a horse. I've learned you never want to run down another man's horse. It's like kickin' his dog around."

We shared a chuckle over that keen observation. I was about to say more, when Gavin Scott came out like a man pleased with himself. His look riled me. What had happened in there to make him feel so self-satisfied? He saw me, but would have passed without speaking. That got to me. "Looks like you showed a lot of early foot gettin' here?" I said, holding back what I really felt like saying as I reined in my temper. I wanted Lori to have that contract, hell or high water.

"Oh, you . . . Clegg. In my business, sometimes I have to work odd hours to get the job done." He went on, still with that satisfied look I didn't like.

Lori was all smiles when I entered her dressing room. "Look," she said, pointing to her dressing table. "Flowers. From Gavin. He'd arranged with the manager to have them waiting for me as a surprise when I came in after the show."

"Nice," I said. Only that.

"So thoughtful," she said.

"Thoughtful," I agreed. The bouquet was beautiful. This Gavin Scott had manners. I'd give him that much credit. I didn't recall that I'd ever sent her flowers, but I hadn't forgotten her birthday which is July 7, before and after we'd married, and I'd remembered the one anniversary we'd had, and I'd tried to please and surprise her at Christmas. Guess bouquets don't fit my style. Just wasn't educated to show appreciation that way. A gap in Buck Clegg's no schooling past the eighth grade, compared to Lori's degree in music from Memphis State University. No excuse. A man should have sense enough to learn, whether he's college-bred or not, but my lacking didn't mean I didn't love my wife.

"Did he say anything about the contract?" I asked.

She seemed to hesitate. "I suppose it wasn't the time. He complimented the band and me. Said we were outstanding tonight. However, he did say that he hadn't forgotten the contract. That was all he said about it. Just wasn't the time, I know, and I'm too tired now to talk much, anyway."

"Seems to me," I said, "a record contract should be a simple matter of yes or no."

She smiled at me in understanding. "There are details, honey, and then there are more details. Maybe I need a lawyer, if I could ever stop long enough to hire one."

"I'll get you one."

"I did talk to a lawyer back in Nashville," she said. "So I know what's fair, and I know what I want. I'm going to get that contract before Gavin leaves town. This has gone on too long."

The particular way she said it stuck in my mind and made me pause later when I looked back at that moment and what it led up to.

As we drove up to the motel, I saw Scott's Mercedes already there. The guy always seemed to be one step ahead of me. And he was uncanny when it came to Lori. The day he'd got in, he'd registered where Lori was at the Swiss Chalet. Somehow he knew where she was. Made me wonder a little, but I didn't say anything. Hell, I trusted her, and she trusted me. More than once I'd had to remind myself that in show business people know a lot of people and often they're thrown into close contact. If Scott wanted to talk contract, Lori had the right to tell him where she'd be, so they could

164

parley. Why not in faraway New Mexico, where the band was booked? A spur of the moment thing.

Even now, I can bring back that entire evening and night, step by step, from the first opening number of the Stagecoach Five and Lori singing, to when I woke up a few hours later and she wasn't beside me.

Supposing she was in the bathroom, I went back to sleep. When I woke up again, soon after, she still wasn't in bed. I sat up. No lights in the bathroom, so she wasn't there. I thought about that. My head cleared, and I got up, alarmed this time. Something was wrong. Maybe in getting up, she'd fainted and fallen. I turned on the lights and looked all around the room. No Lori.

I was even more alarmed. I looked at my watch: four-seventeen. We'd gone to bed not long before two. I opened the door and looked up and down the lighted hallway, dreading that I might find her down or wandering in the hallway. However, she was no sleepwalker. The hallway was empty. That left me one alternative, which hit me all at once in a sickening way. I tried to ignore it, but I couldn't. Gavin Scott's room was down the hallway to my left. I knew because I'd seen him enter it. I hated what I thought, but it wouldn't go away.

I was standing there when the door opened to Scott's room and Lori came out, wearing a dressing gown. Scott's face was visible behind her. Just a glimpse. I couldn't catch his expression. He shut the door.

She gave a start when she saw me, hesitated, smiled at me, and came on. I felt like a spying husband, which I didn't want to be.

"Lori . . . ?" I said, when she reached me.

She was still a knockout, despite no make-up and her unkempt hair. She brushed at it nervously, I thought.

"Talking," she said. "I went down there to talk to him . . . to iron this out."

"Talk?" I said. "At this time of night?"

"Yes, talk." She said it with ease, like she expected me to believe her.

"I don't get this at all."

"I couldn't sleep," she explained. "Then I remembered he'd said in the dressing room he was leaving today."

"I still don't get it."

Our voices were rising. I opened the door, and we went inside. I slammed the door, while I tried to tell myself it was just show people — yeah, show people. Crazy hours. Crazy places. But I couldn't make it stay down.

She faced me, green eyes flashing. "I'll admit it was impulsive, even foolish. I know how it looked. But I've worked hard . . . you know that. I couldn't let this chance slip by."

"Chance?" I said. My tone was turning ugly.

"Yes, chance to work something out."

"Why couldn't you wait till the morning?"

"Because he's taking an early plane out."

"Well, did you work out something?"

She avoided my eyes, then looked at me. "He promised to, soon."

"Lori," I said, "Gavin Scott's been in town long enough to work out a slew of contracts. He's just been

166

leading you on . . . and you fell for it. He wants you . . . and maybe he got what he wanted tonight."

I wanted to call back my words the instant I let them go, but it was too late.

Lori grew very still. Great bruises seemed to rise in her eyes. "Buck! How could you say that to me? How could you? How dare you? Yes, how dare you?" She was raging now, deeply hurt, and beginning to cry. "I won't tell you that nothing happened tonight, because you wouldn't believe me, would you? Because you want to believe I went to bed for a contract, don't you?"

I started to deny, but she raged on, cutting me off before I could say a word.

"How about Buck Clegg, the great jockey? Has he always been true to his sweet little wife, when he's away from her? Buck Clegg, who's always flying off somewhere to ride some rich man's horse? No, I won't ask you to answer that, because I wouldn't believe you if you denied it, Buck Clegg!" She stopped, spent, choking, now sobbing, shaking.

I put out a hand to touch her, but she dashed it off and slapped me hard. She drew back, as astonished as I was. I didn't hit her. I didn't want to. For a long count, all we could do was stare at each other, both of us hurt. Suddenly she turned and ran into the bathroom. Her crying through the closed door sounded like some little girl heartbroken over a smashed doll.

I wanted to go in there and take her in my arms, but I couldn't move. We'd both said too much, like a fast horse that takes one wrong step and ends a promising season.

Not another word was said between us that night.

I didn't wait till daylight to leave. In minutes, I packed and moved out to my old bachelor's quarters at the Amigo Motel.

With both of us on the go, it took a couple of months to work out the divorce. Simple as it was. Mutual consent. "Irreconcilable differences." All that stuff. No squabble over property, because there wasn't any, no fight over money. We made the gossip columns. The lawyers did well. Through my attorney, I tried to settle a sizable amount of cash on Lori that I'd put back from stakes races, but she wouldn't take a dime. After that, I didn't know where she was, and she didn't know where I was. The only trace of her was when I read about her in the newspapers.

Yes, Lori got her contract. I read that in the papers, too.

CHAPTER
TWELVE

Now, filled with anticipation, I was about to see Lori Beth for the first time since the break-up night. My feelings got more tangled, while I waited, and looked back at the good times we'd had together, our hopes for the future, including a family, then lightning had struck out of a clear sky. Sometimes it seemed like a bad dream. Or was it, not sensed by either of us, an accident waiting to happen? Both of us here and there, working apart, meeting on the fly. Regrets? Sure, a world of 'em. I felt we'd both been at fault, both too proud to admit it or to make the first move toward reconciliation, each feeling one had let the other down. Still, if just one had swallowed a little pride that night, maybe it wouldn't have happened.

I shook off the stony past to eye the crowd. Tourists, horse people, cowboys, and teen-agers packed the place. Also, a group of punk rockers, shaved heads painted purple on one side, red on the other.

There was a rustle of excitement when the Wild Ones, smiling broadly, the same as saying — "Oh, what we have for you!" — entered quietly and settled in on the stage. Four guys dressed in red, white, and blue. Piano, guitar, violin, drums. The pianist made a motion, and, as they opened up with a playful version of "El Paso," the stage lit up even more, and, suddenly, Lori came on, singing and swaying. Lori in a short, blue skirt and blue jacket trimmed in white, under the jacket a tight-fitting white blouse. Looking leggy in high heels. Now the dancers took the floor.

From then on, I just enjoyed, feeling pride as well. Next, a snappy two-stepper called "Romp and Stomp," then, for a change of pace, the old, haunting "Let Love Linger," her sweet voice hushed and full. She'd come a long way from the little girl who'd first performed for guests in her parents' back yard in Memphis, and who'd started professionally in happy-hour lounges, singing and playing guitar. Before long, the one-nighters, here and there, with a band. Nashville and Las Vegas waiting in the wings. Eventually that had-to-have contract.

She had plenty of backup. The racehorse piano player could ripple the keys, or play it as softly as raindrops falling; the young Mexican on the drums was like an uncaged wild man; while the guys on the violin and guitar shuffled the tempos and shifted keys. Sometimes the band would just improvise and let themselves run, Lori, never at a loss, singing high and low, and dancing along, showing a lot of leg.

I stayed put at intermission, figuring I'd never find my chair again. By now, you couldn't get into the place.

The varied evening charged on without let-up: raunchy rhythm and blues. ballads, bluegrass, and an array of current country stuff, including "Riding the Rough String," the sad tale of a stove-up bronc' twister,

170

and "Catch Me, Cowboy," that caught the crowd's fancy with whoops and yells, joined in by the punk rockers, and, to keep things going, a straight speed dance number, "Tear It Off" — the last two songs which I remembered Lori had written. Now slowing the pace with "I'll Be Waiting." And a never-fail oldie, "Georgia On My Mind," which again allowed her to display her voice to the fullest.

Just before closing time the band tore into a 1920's rip-snorter, "Yes, Sir, That's My Baby," and the place blew wild. The punk rockers started throwing beer on the dancers. A little of that and a cowboy punched a rocker; the other rockers rushed to the aid of their pal; more cowboys and horse guys joined the cowboys; and the dance was over. The band quickly shut off the fast music and began playing, "Good Night, Ladies," while Lori sang and bouncers broke up the fisticuffs. I stayed clear. I wasn't mad at anybody. I'd been in enough barroom brawls.

In a short time, the bouncers, with police, had cleared the hall, and the stragglers were pleading for farewell drinks at the bar, that also was closed. *Sorry, folks. Come back tomorrow night.* The last I saw of the battling revelers was of two punk rockers and a cowboy being escorted to a police cruiser.

I stood outside in the cool night, feeling the let-down of what had been a most enjoyable evening, bittersweet as it was. Now what? I was halfway to my car, my steps slow and thoughtful, before my mind firmed. I'd walked away once, which was wrong. I wasn't going to do it a second time. On that, I turned and swung around to the rear entrance.

"You can't go in," the man said.

I told him who I was. Would he mind asking the lady if I could see her? I passed him a twenty-dollar bill.

"I'll see what I can do."

He was gone a while. Meantime, the band members filed out, laughing and talking about the fight.

The man returned. "Go on in. Can't say she was happy about it."

I thanked him, wondering what I was going to say first to her.

She was seated in an easy chair, still in costume, sipping a canned drink, looking tired but relaxed.

"Hi," I said.

"Hi," she said. No proffered hand.

We looked at each other. Although I saw no forgiveness in her face or eagerness to greet me, neither did I see anger. The rest was elusive. That could be the old hurt lurking behind the wall of the green eyes. In my own, I hoped she saw that I was glad to see her. Inside, I felt ill at ease, still not knowing what to say.

"You might sit down," she said.

I did. "You wowed 'em tonight. I saw the whole show."

"I have a good band. Best I've ever had. They can play anything, and we all get along."

We continued to take inventory of each other. What I saw further was all for the best. A shade more maturity, perhaps. Otherwise, unchanged. She would always be pretty. I let the silence run on. "How've you been?" I asked after a while.

"Oh, fine."

"That's good."

"How've you been?" she asked in turn.

"Mighty fine."

She laughed. "We're playing the same tune. I read that you had to quit riding."

"The last spill at Sunland told me it was time." I wasn't about to say what the doctors had said. I wanted no sympathy, least of all pity.

"I believe," she said, with a direct look, "there was some question about how you checked out physically."

"It was time to hang 'em up . . . that was all. We all come to that." Why say more?

"I wondered," she said, "because I knew what riding meant to you. So now . . . ?"

"I'm a jockey's agent. But that's not why I'm in Ruidoso this time. I've been back in Oklahoma, trying to help Charlie Vann find Jim Ned. He was stolen while standing at Charlie's farm outside Norman. Maybe you read about it?"

"I did in Vegas. I was shocked. But why Ruidoso?"

"We think the case leads back here. There've been some clues. So far, they haven't panned out. It's pretty slim stuff, but all we have to go on. I'm getting discouraged."

A curious look formed in her face. "But why come to me?"

"Two reasons, and you can believe the first one or not. I wanted to see you."

She diverted her eyes. "How am I to take that?"

"As the truth."

"That's good to know . . . I guess." Her tone struck me as uncertain. "And what is the second reason?"

"You may hear something around the club about the horse."

"You don't hear much inside stuff from a stage. Where are you staying?"

"At the Amigo Motel."

"Horses, it's always about horses, isn't it, Buck?" Some bitterness in that, maybe mixed with regrets, and I couldn't blame her. "Always will be."

"That's been my profession, the only one I know, as show business has been yours, and if it wasn't for a stolen horse, I wouldn't be seeing you tonight. Driving down Sudderth, I happened to see the big announcement out front." It was time to go, this was getting nowhere, and twinges of guilt were beginning to punish me. But . . . "You get top billing now, Lori. I'm glad for you. I'm proud, too." I was telling her the truth. She knew it was true, because I could see it strike across her face. She got up and, moving to her dressing table, seemed to wait for me to say something more.

It had to come out, but I sensed it wasn't what she wanted to hear, as I said: "Some time ago, I read where you were going to marry a TV producer. In some Hollywood column." I got that out and waited, dreading what she'd say, but I had to know.

She shook her head. "We went together a while. Didn't work out."

174

I felt relief, but there was yet more. "And Gavin Scott? I know he was smitten with you. Can't say I blame him for that."

She shrugged vaguely, neither yes nor no. I could take that either way. *If she had gone to bed with him to get that contract, whatever happened to forgiveness, Buck Clegg? On the other side of the coin, what about that week-end with the nice Mexican girl in L.A., Buck Clegg? Afterward, you felt guilty as hell, Buck Clegg.*

Suddenly she flared: "What is this, show and tell?"

"I just wanted to know, Lori."

"Well, now you know." She became sarcastic. "Oh, yes, there is one more item, Mister Clegg. I turned down an offer from *Playboy.* What do you have to say about that?"

"Maybe you should have taken it. Improve the magazine. Brains plus beauty. They don't always get both."

It wasn't funny. She said: "What do you have to tell me, Mister Clegg?"

I gave her the same vague shrug. "The girls don't bunch up around me like they used to after them big stakes races."

It still wasn't funny. "It's *those*, not *them*, Buck. Remember?"

"I remember when you remind me."

Still not funny. Apparently, the Gavin Scott thing was still hanging fire. Or was it? She hadn't made that plain. Well, if nothing else, I thought I had cleared the air. By coming here, I'd tried.

"Can I take you to your motel?" I asked.

"I'm staying with friends . . . the Kemps." I remembered the name. A well-heeled Texas oil couple we'd met a few times. "The management is providing me with a car."

"That's nice," I said. It was time to go. "Good night."

"Good night," she said.

No statement by either of us. But I wasn't leaving here without touching her — if I might. I put my arms gently around her and bent to kiss her. She didn't resist. But instead of her lips, she gave me her cheek. As I kissed her, I felt her fingers lightly touch my shoulders, but no body contact. No clinging. For a moment, I thought I sensed the old feeling between us, but for barely a moment. Then it was gone. Maybe I was wrong. Maybe it was only wishful thinking. Maybe I'd lost her forever.

I dropped my hands and turned away. I was leaving, when she said: "I'll call you, if I hear anything about Jim Ned."

"Thanks."

CHAPTER
THIRTEEN

Charlie called next morning to say he was flying in, and that afternoon I met him at the Sierra Blanca airport. He looked anything but the big-time horseman and millionaire banker and car dealer when he got off the plane. Same sweat-stained hat, though brushed clean, same worn boots, though shined this time, but, other than that, the same Charlie, plain and simple, a feller you might take in need of a bank loan to get through till he sold his calf crop. However, he'd had a recent haircut, and he wore a new beige jacket that he'd probably bought on sale at a discount store, and a checked sports shirt I'd seen many times. He'd gained some, but had the racehorse belt buckle cinched up tight, which made him look trim in fresh jeans. The brown eyes in the ruddy face, usually on the melancholy side, shed cheer and anticipation.

We shook hands like long-lost brothers and slapped each other on the back. I couldn't help eyeing him a bit critically. "By the way," I said, "they still sell hats and boots in Ruidoso. Might even find you a little store where they sell shirts."

"Aw, Buck," he said, when we picked up his one bag, "I'se afraid if I put on the dog too much, somebody might try to sell me a sore-legged racehorse or a new condo." He laughed, and I did, too. Charlie wasn't going to change. As a matter of fact, I wasn't sure I wanted him to change, only to be kinder to himself.

As we drove off, before us in the distance, the Mescalero Apaches' massive Sierra Blanca still crowned with snow, Charlie said: "Have you found out anything at all?"

I'd dreaded this. "Not one thing. Got any suggestions?"

"I know you've talked to a lot of people."

"I have . . . mainly at the track. Besides that, I've done a heap of listening. And I'll do a heap more of both."

"I'd better do some on my own tomorrow."

"Anything new back in Oklahoma?"

"I called the FBI before I left. They're still on the lookout. Figure the case is dead back there, else our friends would still be tryin' to trick us for the reward money without givin' up the horse."

"Which is more reason to figure it's shifted out here," I said for Charlie's benefit. It was better to think that, anyway. From there into town, we rode mostly in silence, enjoying the scenery.

I checked Charlie into the Amigo Motel. First thing he did was call the ranch and talk for twenty minutes or so. "My man back there knows about as much about runnin' a horse ranch as I would teachin' Russians to toe dance," he said, hanging up. "But he's honest. Rick Hinton can help. I miss Tom Shelby . . . Tom's judgment. I'll never understand, completely, why Tom did what he did."

After a round of Charlie's Maker's Mark, I brought him up to date on Chip Romero and, hesitating somewhat, told him that Lori Beth was at the Pines.

"You know, Buck," he said, "speaking as a friend, I've always felt bad about you two breaking up."

"Me, too." I hadn't told him how and why it happened.

"It's never too late to mend a broken fence, if just one party will lift the first rail."

I smiled at him. "Who's that from? Abe, the rail-splitter, or your favorite, Bobby Burns?"

"Pure Charles B. Vann," he said, "learned as a bloodied participant, and from observation, from the knockdown arena of city council meetings to two farmers arguing over how the hog broke into Josh's cabbage patch. Most people are too damned hard-headed for their own good."

"Tell you what. Let's see if we can get in at the Pines. We may have to stand. But maybe we can see Lori Beth at first intermission. I know she'll be glad to see you."

"What about Buck Clegg?"

"I did visit with her last night, after closing."

"Don't believe you answered my question."

"Only one trouble with your theory. After one party gets the first rail up, it still takes two to finish fixin' the fence."

"But it's a beginning. See what I mean?"

The entertainment had started. I bought tickets and was told we'd have to wait a while, that is, until the doorman saw the green of a ten dollar bill. The place was packed tighter than opening night. More bouncers

179

on hand tonight. But no punk rockers in the crowd. We stood.

Lori and the band worked through country music to rhythm and blues, rock and roll, bluegrass, and back to country/western.

At intermissions, after another greasing of palms, we found Lori resting in her dressing room. She jumped up when she saw Charlie and greeted him with a kiss on the cheek and a long hug. I got a look.

"Buck asked me to keep my ear to the ground about Jim Ned," she told Charlie. "Why would anyone do such a terrible thing?"

"We haven't quite figured it out yet," he said, with a wry grin. "But a word of caution, Lori. This is a tough bunch. They pack guns. You be careful. Ear to the ground and no more, you understand?"

We left when a band member came to the door and waved at her. Outside, I said: "There's one club in particular I want to take you to. The Finish Line, out near the track. The horse crowd goes there evenings."

We had to park across the street and walk through a swarm of pickups. Going in, I saw a lot of faces I didn't know and glimpsed some I'd known over the years and some new trainers and jocks and grooms I'd met in recent days. Not many women. The horsy guys nodded to the man. Weren't we all members of the same clan, bound by the unpredictable but addictive profession of the how to win a horse race? We had just ordered drinks when Smiley Evans, his election-day smile turned on like a headlight, broke through the outside of the pack

180

at the bar and joined us, pumping hands and slapping backs.

"Keep that up, you could run for sheriff out here," Charlie said.

"Don't think my Okie twang would go over so good, and I don't savvy this rapid-fire Spanish," Smiley drawled. "They'd think I was some bird from a foreign country. Why, sometimes it takes me a minute or more to get a whole sentence spoke. Another thing, first time I ran for sheriff my old daddy told me . . . 'Son, you can't expect to be elected unless you go around and drink coffee with everybody in the county.' I remembered that and got elected. Now, tell me, Charlie, how would an ex-Okie from flat country get over all these big mountains in time to do all that?"

"Start early."

"That's what my daddy said . . . Well, I escorted my little filly Quick Cash in this afternoon and got her all checked in at her suite at the Ruidoso Downs Hilton. Clean straw and everything. They treat you nice here. You're a winner till you lose. Wonder what my feed bill will run? Now the worry starts. Will my filly catch a cold these cool nights, like so many Okie and Texas horses do soon after they get here? Will she get homesick for Cleveland County and her run-down ol' barn at the run-down ol' home place south of town and want to go back? She's a stall-walker. Will I have to buy a goat to keep her company? When she looks up at these great big ol' mountains, and that great big ol' grandstand with thousands of people in it, is she gonna get too scared to run? Y'know, little country filly comes

181

to big-time race track. Worse yet, will she fall in love with one of these handsome young studs and forget all about why she's here?"

"You worry too much," Charlie said, grinning. "Blanket her at night and give her time to adjust. Just walk her around in the sun for a few days. No hard works. She's already in shape to run. Leg her up with slow trots. Maybe one good gallop couple of days before the trials. She'll do all right. She's bred to run. All you need do is to make her feel good . . . and keep her relaxed."

"You ought to know," Smiley said. Suddenly, he looked apologetic. "Here I am goin' on about my filly and I haven't even asked you if there's any news."

"Nothing yet."

"Charlie just got in this afternoon," I said. "I've been here a few days."

More horsemen joined us, men Charlie had known when Jim Ned was running big, and everybody knew your name, as Wildhorse Johnson said. Before long it was like a reunion, something Charlie needed after the frustrations back in Oklahoma. That called for more drinks. Charlie signaled for a waitress.

I was surprised when a smiling Rosa took the orders, looking trim in a short-skirted outfit. With her big eyes and smooth face and clean smile, she caused plenty of heads to turn as she hurried back to the bar.

"Chip Romero's wife," I told Charlie. "A good kid."

"I saw you come in, *Señor* Buck," she said, aside, after serving and collecting for the drinks. "I need to talk to you tonight."

I read worry and urgency in her eyes. "Sure. I'll watch the bar. When you're not busy, I'll come over."

After the first rush of greetings and catching up on the past, talk at the table circled around as it must to Jim Ned. No breaks in the case, Charlie said, and too soon for the insurance company to pay off. After that, straight horse talk.

When there was a lull at the bar and I saw Rosa idle, I went over and asked: "What is it?" It was about Chip, of course.

"That Chihuahua *hombre*," she said, "he worries this burro."

"He's still in the hospital?"

"Yes, but how long I don't know."

"He needs to finish the treatments."

"I know . . . he knows. But he wants to ride . . . ride anywhere."

"I'll go see him tomorrow."

"Please, *Señor* Buck. He worries me. Never like this before. He don't tell me everything."

"Rosa! Drinks!" The bartender calling.

Drifting back to the table, I understood Chip's desire to ride again soon. I could understand his restlessness. He'd gone willingly into the hospital, eager to get clean so he could ride again. Now the tough part — going through the lengthy treatments, the inactivity, no money coming in, while friends kept riding. All about him the hum of Ruidoso's big-purse horse world. But there could be no short-cuts for Chip Romero. His suspension, here, barred him from riding at the northern New Mexico tracks. Same in California. What was left if he went AWOL? Not much. Match races in the Southwest or on bush tracks, a maybe, even there, if they followed American Quarter Horse Association rules. Or Mexico. Anything went in Mexico, in match races between wealthy ranchers, for which insiders believed the well-known Town Policy had been stolen, to stakes races at the *Hipodromo de las Americas* in Mexico City. Sure, they had rules there. So what, *señor?* Maybe I could talk some patience into him tomorrow.

Visiting at the table continued at a genial pace, the conversation ranging from outstanding horses of the past and some hairline finishes to the season's top two-year-olds and favorites for the upcoming Kansas Futurity. Smiley Evans didn't brag, but he let it be known that his filly could "run a little" and had tasted victory back in Oklahoma. He'd need some luck, he knew that. In turn, the listeners had to know her breeding. They all wished him luck.

"Just don't squeeze all the juice out of the lemon," one joked, when Smiley said he'd nominated Quick Cash for all three futurities.

I was content to listen, glad Charlie could enjoy himself, which he sorely needed. He hadn't laughed this much since Jim Ned was taken.

It was late when we all stood up and moseyed to the door. At this hour the place was still fairly crowded. As Charlie's friends sought their pickups and cars, Charlie and Smiley and I stood a while, still talking, enjoying the cool, pine-scented night.

A conference was going on to our right in the parking lot. A heated conference that kept getting louder. Several voices. In the darkness, no faces were visible, just a huddle of dim figures in the out-thrown light from the club. From the tone of the voices it was more than a conference now. Fast building to a parley, marked by hot dickering. The three of us quit talking, drawn that way.

A pickup dashed up from town and crunched gravel turning into the parking lot. It skidded to a stop. In the head-lights I could see four figures bunched, heads bent. The driver turned off the headlights, slammed a door, and rushed up to join the negotiations.

"This is a ripoff!" a tough-sounding voice complained. "It ain't what you quoted earlier."

"Things changed, sonny boy. You have to change." A cool, older man speaking.

"We won't go for that." The first speaker again, a young man's belligerent voice, it seemed.

"You won't get it any cheaper, sonny boy."

"We ain't gonna be held up, either." The young man wanted to fight about it, it seemed, but had no volunteers.

"You want first-rate stuff, you pay first-rate."

"But you changed the price on us."

"The deal changed on us. That's the way it goes sometimes. Take it or leave it, sonny. Grow up or go back to the pool hall and have a light beer. That . . . or maybe you boys had better talk it over."

In the muddy light, three figures drew off to one side to confer. A few moments and they swung around to parley some more.

"You, young gentlemen, must take into consideration all the problems, not forgetting certain risks, of making such merchandise available to you at a somewhat higher cost than usual," a new and older voice said, smooth, unruffled, mediating.

That voice! It dug into me, froze me. I felt myself tracking back, back, back, trying to connect.

"Let's take 'em!"

As the three rushed the other two, the same voice rose. "I say, stand clear. You're just a bunch of inconsiderate young ruffians. Stand clear, I say!"

That dramatic baritone voice. I whipped around to Charlie. He was looking at me. Had he caught it, too?

Before we could speak or move, a shot exploded as the five milled. Another shot. A cry. The group broke apart, running about the parking lot. Nobody went down. Maybe the guy was only firing warning shots. Three motors sounded almost in unison. A pickup snarled down the road that led past the racetrack. Another one, after a short sprint, took the highway to Tularosa. A car bolted up Sudderth Drive toward town.

The crowd was pouring out of the Finish Line. Everybody seemed to be shouting.

Above that, I yelled: "Did you catch that, Charlie? That was Golden Voice himself! I'd know it anywhere!"

"I did, and I was dumbfounded." His voice was far calmer than mine.

"So they're up here. By God, they're here! We're right! Let's go after 'em!"

"What are we waiting for?"

186

We all started off, then pulled up as one. What did we follow?

"The car," Smiley said. "That's likely the pushers. My pickup's right here. Get in."

We took off. Smiley drove like a sheriff, hell-bent, intent. Traffic was light along Sudderth this late, the fleeing car the only vehicle in the right-hand lane. When the road curved ahead and the car's lights disappeared behind a line of trees and store buildings, Smiley kicked the pickup even faster. As we made the curve, I saw that we had gained. Then the car disappeared again around another curve. As we straightened out, we picked him up again.

"He'll probably take the Alto Highway," Smiley yelled. Alto village was some miles to our right from the last traffic light, higher up into the mountains on a winding road. Off it the ski-run road to Sierra Blanca and the road to the airport.

Ahead of us, a police cruiser's lights suddenly lit up the night as the car barreled by. The cruiser pulled out of a parking lot in pursuit, lights flashing, siren going. The car ignored the red signal light at the Alto turn, headed for the upper cañon. At the nearby traffic circle, the car cut right, hardly pausing, the cruiser beginning to close the gap.

"Do you have a gun?" Charlie yelled at Smiley as we roared along.

"I always pack a gun, but I hate to use it."

"You may have to. I figure that's Dapper Thompson with Golden Voice, whatever the hell his name is."

187

Now Smiley wheeled right from the traffic circle. "You and Buck both better start packin' guns till this case is over," he said.

The car and the cruiser picked up speed after the turn as the road angled into a gentle curve. We'd lost some ground. Smiley forced the pickup faster. Ahead, we saw lights turning. Without warning, before us all at once, a narrow little bridge loomed, and we crossed the rushing Río Ruidoso.

At that point the car's driver either became confused or lost heart. He suddenly slowed. When he did, the police officer shot the cruiser up alongside and around and expertly blocked him off. Smiley breathed hard, our headlights like bold daylight on the scene. In my mind's eye, I could see Golden Voice and Thompson coming out of the car, shooting.

"Wait," Smiley said. "Let's see what the officer's gonna do. We can furnish backup."

When the officer bulged around the rear of the cruiser, revolver drawn, we all left the pickup, Smiley with handgun out, Charlie and I watching from the right side.

"Come out of there," the officer called.

I heard the driver shut off the car's motor. A long pause. Still, he didn't show.

"I said to come out of there." The officer stayed posted by the rear of the cruiser, playing it cautiously.

"I'm coming." The voice was indistinct. Somehow it didn't fit.

Another moment and a skinny, teen-age boy, straw-colored hair standing up like porcupine quills,

188

pale and shaking with fright, stepped from the car. He wasn't armed.

The officer read him his rights, ordered him against the car, and shook him down. Nothing. A check of the car showed no drugs. When he checked the boy's driver's license, the boy said: "It's my dad's car."

"And you get tickets for running a red light, speeding, and evading an officer. Plus the rest of the night in jail."

We had some tall explaining to do ourselves, accepted with skepticism until we willingly gave our names, showed our driver's licenses, Smiley his sheriff's badge and credentials, and posted the officer on what had just happened at the Finish Line, which he then called in to headquarters.

On the way back to town, Smiley drawled: "Kinda looks like the ol' super sleuth from Cleveland County made the wrong pick on the car. Guess a pickup is a better cover vehicle for a drug pusher to drive than a big, expensive-looking Lincoln like the boy was driving, about which I imagine his daddy will have a little visit with him tomorrow." He wasn't finished. "Another item. Charlie, I want you and Buck to get gun permits and handguns tomorrow. I'll go with you. And hope you don't have to use 'em. Final item. Just count ourselves lucky tonight that wasn't Golden Voice, as you call 'im, and Dapper Thompson in the car. We'd have been at one helluva disadvantage. Outgunned two to one."

"The main thing is they're here," Charlie said. "So Jim Ned is around here, somewhere, I hope. Unless they murdered the horse when they couldn't sleaze the reward money out of us."

"I don't figure it that way a-tall," Smiley said, speaking even slower, "if they turned down the fifty thousand, which they could've had easy by givin' up the horse, there has to be something bigger at stake than any of us know. It's here, locked up somewhere in these great big ol' mountains. You betcha it is."

I agreed in silence, glad he'd said it, instead of me. It was more convincing coming from the sheriff.

"Tomorrow," Charlie said, "I think we'd better talk to the local authorities."

CHAPTER
FOURTEEN

"Yes, our department has noticed a decided increase in local drug traffic within the past week or so. I don't mean crack and marijuana, which are always around . . . the cheap fixes . . . I mean cocaine. We're getting the so-called pure stuff in here, virtually uncut, which requires more than a kid's spending money or what he can make at a fast-food place. Naturally, they want to try what they think is the best, which calls for a furtive ransacking of dad's wallet or mother's purse. Suddenly, there's been a flood of it. With it, an increase in burglaries to keep up the habit. It's a vicious cycle. More kids messed up, now that school's out. Also, more of it along the back stretch at the Downs. So the track people tell us. They run a pretty tight check there, too. Of course, you can get drugs anywhere, if you know the right people. What happened last night at the Finish Line not only increases our concern, but tells us that the pushers are getting bolder. More open. Shots fired, done to scare off the kids. Fortunately, no foolish youngsters injured. Unfortunately, no pushers apprehended." He tried to smile, but it was wan. "You could say it was a drug deal that went sour when the pushers tried to jack up the already high price."

The speaker was J. C. "Jud" Ivy, the Ruidoso chief of police. A serious-minded young man in his early thirties, obviously a product of training and early dedication. Black hair cut short, clean-shaven, gray eyes somber with the gravity of duty.

"All we ask," Charlie said, nodding, "is that your department get out a description of the horse to other law enforcement agencies. I'm thinking of the sheriff's office, the Highway Patrol, the El Paso FBI office, even the Drug Enforcement Administration, now that we know two of the suspects in the case are dealing drugs in Ruidoso. Also, let it be known that Mister Clegg, who rode Jim Ned in all his big stakes races, and I, the owner, are here from Oklahoma, aiding in the investigation. Also, that we can be reached at the Amigo Motel. Also, that there is a fifty-thousand-dollar reward out for the safe return of Jim Ned. Also, another fifty thousand will be paid for information leading to the arrest and conviction of those responsible for the theft."

"Oh, we'll do that, Mister Vann." Ivy actually smiled now. "But do you realize, sir, that the description you've given me . . . a big bay stallion, standing sixteen hands, weighing in the neighborhood of twelve hundred pounds, with a small star on his forehead, and wearing a bar shoe on his right front hoof . . . could . . . with the exception of the bar shoe . . . fit many of the hundreds of horses in this area?"

Charlie smiled, too. "I do. But, at least, you know not to look for a gray horse. Or a blaze-faced bay, or a blue roan, or a black or a brown, or a buckskin, or a dark chestnut, or a bright chestnut, or a light sorrel."

192

Ivy lifted both hands and feigned abject surrender. "You've made your point, Mister Vann."

We got our .38s and shoulder holsters later that morning. My weapon felt awkward to me. I've never been much of a hand for guns. All I knew was how the damned thing worked.

At the Amigo, with the holsters in place, Charlie said: "I'd rather have my shotgun in a pinch, but you can't go around packing a double-barreled cannon in public." — and set to work practicing his draw. He was slow, but I was slower. After a while, we got faster, just a shade.

Toward the middle of the afternoon, we dropped in on Chip Romero. I could see the change in him from the last time. Although he appeared calmer, much calmer, and had picked up some needed pounds on an extremely skinny frame that had allowed him to make weight without starving or going to the steam room, his face told me a different story, soon confirmed while we talked.

"How you doin'?" I asked him, after making the introductions.

"Tired of this place."

"After a month you'll be out of here."

"Yeah." He wasn't happy, even if the place was good for him.

Charlie couldn't have been nicer. "I want Buck to book you aboard the next two-year-old I ship out here. I'm high on a yearling colt that's the spittin' image of his daddy, Jim Ned. In fact, I've nominated him for next year's All-American. How does that strike you?"

"*Gracias, Señor* Vann." Little enthusiasm in his voice. Next year was too far away. Now was what counted to a druggie.

I couldn't be certain, but I had a feeling that somehow Chip was still using on the side. How, in the hospital? If so, someone was bringing it to him. But who? One of his friends at the track. Had to be. It sure as hell wasn't Rosa. I still questioned myself because I hoped I was wrong. But how could a man use and go through the program at the same time? Punish himself that way? Furthermore, why would he do it? Well, he could, and say he was clean when he came out, and everybody would believe him, including the proud stewards, and he could get by till the next drug test. Who knew the devious thinking of a druggie? I thought I did.

We visited on, Chip tight-lipped and even guarded, which wasn't the old Chip, yet always courteous. I guess the closest description would be to say that he was uncommunicative, even a little angry the way things had gone for him. Spoiled, maybe, by early success, he thought the world owed him something.

I didn't want to leave him like this. I felt responsible, in a way, because I'd virtually hand-raised him as a jockey, when he showed up at Ruidoso Downs, a kid fresh out of Chihuahua, shy and hungry, his English worse than my Spanish. Something about him had impressed me. I liked him at once. I fed him, got him a place to stay in the stable area, vouching for his honesty, and he never let me down. I found him a job, mucking out stalls. Good-natured, willing to work, a natural around horses, he was soon a hot walker and

194

a groom. Then very soon an exercise rider. Then an apprentice rider. Now, observing him in the hospital room, I remembered his first win aboard an unknown Thoroughbred filly named Wild-flower owned by an Oklahoma cotton farmer. That day, as Chip slipped her between horses as the field turned for home, she flat daylighted the co-favorites and paid seventy-four dollars on a two-dollar win ticket. When he brought her back to the winner's circle, he was a boy on air, hardly touching the saddle. I'll never forget his expression. He was on a cloud, in another world. That race launched him. Trainers took note. But it was too much, too soon.

To cheer him up, I started telling how I'd made my start on the bush tracks, and how tough it was.

"I lived in a tack room and got by muckin' out stables and rubbin' horses, the way you did. After a while, a kind-hearted trainer let me exercise his cheapest claimers. Boy, was I proud! I even developed a swagger around the stables."

That produced a faint grin. I hoped he didn't think I was preaching — which I was, round-about.

"*Señor* Buck," Chip said, "he always tell a good story."

"That's just the beginning," I said. "Now came my first ride. It was at Manor Downs in Texas. Why, there must've been three or four hundred people in the stands. Naturally, they'd come out to see Buck Clegg ride his first winner."

The grin was stronger this time.

"I was aboard a sorrel colt that had yet to break his maiden. He'd been out four times, but something always seemed to go wrong. He'd either get bumped at the break. Or had his head turned when the gates opened. Or he'd stumble or the ground would break out from under 'im just as he broke. His name was Lightning. In the saddling paddock, the trainer told me . . . 'Lightning has a tendency to break to the left. Be ready for that.' I found out I needed that, and more. What made it worse was that we'd drawn the one hole. At the break, Lightning headed straight for the rail. I pulled right, but couldn't stop 'im. He was cold-jawed. I had his head turned almost to his withers, and he still went over it."

I paused for any dramatic effect.

"What happened then?" Charlie asked, when Chip didn't.

"I was so green I didn't know I was supposed to jump off my horse when he went down. I thought you had to be brave and stick with your mount all the way. Like a captain goin' down with his ship. Otherwise, they'd call you a coward. I wound up with a broken right leg in two places, some busted ribs, a collapsed kidney, and a concussion. Lightning got up, but I couldn't, though I was conscious all the time . . . After a while . . . it seemed like a long time . . . meanwhile, I could hear people hollerin' . . . some guys picked me up and put me in an old pickup. That was bush track for ambulance. No stretcher or doctor, either, unless you wanted to use the vet."

"I never knew that," Charlie said.

"I never told you," I said.

Chip smiled in understanding.

"They had to operate and put in a bunch of pins," I said, determined he'd hear the whole story. "I was grounded for three months . . . But I learned a valuable lesson from that spill, and it helped me more than once when I went down again later. A jockey has to know where he is in the air when a horse breaks down. He has to know how to hit the ground. In short, he has to know how to handle his body, like a gymnast, you might say." I looked at Chip. "You learned that early, too, didn't you, at Sunland?"

He nodded. But his grin was already fading. Maybe he was thinking of the glad-handing past, when he'd won big, and everybody knew Chip Romero's name.

"But that's not the end of the story. I rode Lightning to his first victory at Manor Downs. Thanks to a trainer who had patience, he'd learned to run straight."

A nurse entered the room. She didn't speak, but the sweeping look she laid on us said it was time to leave. We said so long, told Chip to hang in there, that he was doing fine, and we'd be back soon to see him. Chip nodded, but his attention seemed on distant places. When our eyes met, he looked away, which told me that Buck Clegg was no longer his closest friend.

At the car, I said to Charlie: "I'm afraid he won't last the route. He still hasn't come to terms with his problem." I was also thinking of Rosa.

"It's a shame, a young man with his ability."

We killed time to finish out the day, driving over Ruidoso, noting its growth since the heady days of Jim Ned, just talking and projecting. After a drink at the Amigo, Charlie called the ranch. Everything seemed to be going well. Any business calls to the ranch were being directed to the bank. If any leads on the case came in, the ranch manager was to call the Amigo. Nobody had called about the horse. The case was flat dead, back there.

After dinner that evening, we squeezed in at the Pines. The Wild Ones and the whooping, stomping crowd were lively as before. Charlie wondered if the mountain air was an energy factor. Lori Beth was singing and swaying, in another short-skirted outfit, this time with gold sequins that set off her dark hair.

At intermission the guard, after checking, let us in to see Lori.

"I haven't heard a thing," she said, waving us in. "I've also asked the bartenders and bouncers to keep their ears tuned."

Charlie thanked her. "Well, we do have some news, Lori. The kidnappers are here in Ruidoso."

Her eyes became enormous. "You've seen them?"

"Yes, but we don't know what they look like."

"Then how would you know?" She frowned in disbelief.

"We know one man's voice. The main guy, we think he is. The mastermind. The negotiator. The big-time operator he fancies himself. His voice is very distinctive. Oh, it's good. A rich baritone. One you might hear and remember in a Broadway musical or on TV. Buck calls him Golden Voice. We recognized it last night in the dark outside the Finish Line, when a dope deal went wrong with some kids and a fight started. Golden Voice shouted, and everybody took off."

"This is incredible, Charlie."

"Incredible, but true, and the first lead we have here. We've heard this bird on the phone back in Oklahoma enough times when he was trying to set us up for the reward money and not deliver the horse. Another time at an attempted hold-up that backfired on him. I'd know his voice in a roaring snowstorm." Charlie let out a breath and sketched in the chase and the wrong car. "That's all," he said.

"That's quite a great deal," she said, impressed.

"Now it's a waiting game, maybe a long one. We've checked in with the local authorities. Maybe it'll break fast. You stay out of it. You hear, Lori?"

"I have to go now," she said, giving him a hug and me a brief glance. Sometimes the unspoken and eyes that place you at a distance, maybe *paced distance* is more correct, like in a duel, tell more than words. As we turned to leave, I sensed nothing left between Lori and me but empty space. I felt like a mere bystander, a complete stranger.

"Sorry," Charlie said, when we'd passed the door. "I didn't give you a chance to visit with her. I should've let you tell it."

"Now, Charlie, Jim Ned's your horse. Your place to tell it."

"You need to talk to her alone."

"I have."

After another day, I saw that Charlie and I were fast settling into the same unavoidable but frustrating routine that had worn us down back in Oklahoma — more waiting, more restless inaction.

I took us to lunch at *Señor* Pete's. As we started to leave, I bought a copy of the Ruidoso *News*. A black headline caught my eye:

NATIONWIDE SEARCH FOR WONDER RUNNER SHIFTS TO RUIDOSO

The nationwide search for Triple Crown Champion Jim Ned has shifted to Ruidoso and vicinity with the arrival of the famed bay sprinter's owner, Charles B. Vann, of Norman, Oklahoma, and the horse's former jockey, Buck Clegg.

Jim Ned, termed the world's fastest quarter horse after he broke Truckle Feature's record of :21.01 in 21 flat, was stolen recently from his pad-dock at the Vann ranch near Norman. No trace of the horse has been reported since.

Vann has posted a $50,000 reward for the stallion's safe return, plus an additional $50,000 for the arrest and conviction of the kidnappers.

Vann and Clegg, while taking active roles in the investigation, are staying at the Amigo Motel. In recent years since his retirement as a leading rider, Clegg has become a jockey's agent here and in California.

Aiding in the investigation are the Ruidoso Police Department, the Sheriff's Office, the FBI, the Highway Patrol, and the Drug Enforcement Administration.

200

Jim Ned, described by local horsemen as a big, strapping horse with a gentle disposition weighing about 1,200 pounds, is a son of the great Easy Jet. Jim Ned had been returned to training at the Vann Ranch when taken. His first crop of two-year-olds will reach the tracks next year.

Authorities have been silent about progress in the case since it opened. A strict watch also has been in effect along the Mexican border.

I smacked the paper in disgust as I finished reading and handed it to Charlie. "Authorities, it says! Who gave them the authority to break this?"

Charlie scanned it rapidly, looked up, and said: "A clerk was busy taking notes when we talked to Police Chief Ivy."

"But it tears away any cover we had. Even says where we're staying at the Amigo."

I expected him to join in anger, instead, he said thought-fully: "I know. That was my first impulse. Sure, and maybe the police department wants local people to know it's on the ball. In there with the FBI and the DEA . . . But this could have a very positive result. It could smoke out Golden Voice and his bunch. Make 'em come out of the brush . . . come to us . . . if they think we're closing in."

I could only nod maybe.

I guessed there could be days like this in the sleuthing game, when nothing happened, when you felt as useless as a one-legged man at a butt-kicking contest, as my father used to say during hard times. Could Buck Clegg, the great detective, formerly the great jockey, have a near case of occupational burn-out? I was full of self-mockery, I think they call it, and boredom, when Charlie suggested that we not sit around at the Amigo all afternoon and watch old movies on TV. Why not go out to the track and nose about? Might pick up something. I didn't want to tell him that, based on my experience, it was most unlikely that any clue to the whereabouts of Golden Voice would be found there, but I went.

We found Smiley Evans at rest on a bale of hay outside Quick Cash's stall. "My filly just loves these big ol' mountains," he said, ever the optimist. "She stands and gazes at 'em by the hour when I put her on the walker." As he spoke, a blazed face watched from over the stall door. Of course, we had to pet her.

"Smiley," Charlie said, in a guying tone, "I hope you haven't misinterpreted that. You don't want her standing flat-footed, looking off, when the gates open in the trials."

"My God, that never occurred to me."

"Naw. What it means is, she's getting adjusted and feels good. Don't rush her with hard works. Just keep her loose."

Smiley bowed. "The oracle has spoken again. I am follerin' your advice. No cold yet. I sprayed her stall with disinfectant before I ever let her step foot in it. And she seems relaxed. So far, I haven't had to buy a goat . . . By the way, anything new?"

"We made the local paper today. Now Golden Voice knows we're on the scene."

"Hmm. You figure that's good or bad?"

"Guess we have to say it's good . . . if it brings the kidnappers out in the open."

"You mean if they'd make themselves known to *you*." Smiley's funning vanished. He sounded like an officer of the law now.

"Like what, for instance?"

"Like if they figure you're a threat. Like if they come gunnin' for you two. Or if they set you up, like they tried to across the river that night."

"We wouldn't fall for that."

"You don't know what you might do if you thought you had a gambler's chance to get your horse back. Could be a setup in another guise. I think you and Buck had better stay on the look-out for trouble from now on. Pack your guns, wherever you go."

"Will do."

We'd started to drift on, when Smiley, in a remembering voice, said: "Now you tell me something, Charlie. Word along the back stretch was, this morning, that a well-dressed Mexican has been looking around for somebody to ride match races in Mexico. How do you figure that?"

"I don't. They have jockeys in Mexico."

"Man'll go anywhere if the money is big enough."

"How big was it?"

"They didn't get that far. Nobody was interested. The guy was just scouting the territory, I guess. See who might be interested. He was talkin' to top jocks. Not apprentice riders."

"You mean, do I see a possible connection between that and Jim Ned? It's possible, if the horse is in Mexico. But I can't see that, when we know Golden Voice and probably Dapper Thompson are here."

"Which means Jim Ned is still on this side of the border."

"If my calculations are correct."

"You always could calculate pretty good, when I came in for a loan and we got down to the interest," Smiley said, breaking a grin. "Meantime, you boys know where I am if you need me."

We drove back to the Amigo and, following a coupled of leisurely drinks, ate dinner at a drive-in barbecue, which Charlie didn't need, but liked. As we moved through thickening traffic, Charlie observed: "This town draws everything from millionaires to deadbeats on the make, when the season gets into full swing. I just know my horse is around somewhere." He was trying to convince himself all over again.

It was an old question we had chewed over many times, and each time we came up against the same dead-end. Where was the profit with a horse that couldn't be run here? They could breed him for a high figure somewhere, but wouldn't most horsemen shy away once they knew who the stud was? No way to make big bucks fast.

We caught a half hour of TV news in my room and watched a game show, followed by a sitcom. Charlie was nodding, when the phone rang. I expected a call from the ranch, or maybe Smiley wanting us to go out with him for a late dinner.

I picked up the phone, said hello, and a voice said: "Mister Buck Clegg, the eminent jockey, I presume?"

It was Golden Voice. I almost dropped the phone. "This is Clegg," I said, and punched Charlie awake.

"That isn't much of a greeting after all this time."

"Enough. Where you been?" That bastard.

"Around."

"I've missed seein' you on TV and all them movies you claimed you starred in."

"You don't know what I look like."

"But you have that rich baritone voice, which helps fill out the picture. By now I know pretty well what you look like."

"You lie, Clegg! You have no idea what I look like."

"Let's say it's more like a police profile. Or similar to what you see on the wall at the post office. Them mug shots."

"Too bad they didn't run your battered countenance in the paper with the story."

"Yeah, I hated that. My public, y'know."

"You're just a broken-down jock, Clegg."

"About like some busted actor I know who took up horse-stealing because he couldn't make it on the stage or in 'B' pictures. Which reminds me . . . what is the occasion for this chummy call? Last time I saw you was back in Oklahoma, when you and Dapper Thompson tried to hijack us for the reward money."

"Dapper Thompson? How'd you get that name?"

I'd caught him off guard there. He couldn't mask his surprise.

"I didn't. The police did. He's wanted for two murders. He could turn on you, if things didn't go to suit 'im. Might pay you to keep that in mind. I must say, you travel in select company."

"All right, Clegg, I've had enough of your back-stretch blarney. I've called to deliver you and Charles Vann an ultimatum. Lay off . . . drop the investigation . . . or the horse will be shot."

"So the horse is here?"

"I didn't say."

"I don't figure you left him in Oklahoma."

"Pray tell, how did you arrive at that astute conclusion?" He was off on his theatrical bent now, relishing the sound of that dramatic voice. I could just see the bastard posing. Who'd he think he was, Barrymore? At least.

"Because Jim Ned is the most valuable quarter horse in the world, and he has the potency to pass on his speed and soundness to his progeny. Mister Vann has some yearlings to prove it. Sound as he is, he could run for several more years, barring injury."

"You consider yourself an authority, I see?"

"As a matter of fact, I do."

"All the more reason for you to heed my warning. Think of the loss, Clegg."

"Would be your loss as well, whatever you have in mind for profit. I know you're not a horseman."

"As a matter of fact, as you say, I happen to have a high regard for outstanding horses."

"Same as you had the other night for them teen-agers?"

"What teen-agers?"

"The ones outside the Finish Line, when your drug deal soured and the Dapper fired shots to warn 'em off, and everybody took off."

"Curse you, Clegg! You know so much!"

I started to bring up the chase, to rub it in how we'd recognized his voice, and how lucky he was that we'd chased the wrong vehicle. But no, he was riled up enough. Let him guess how we knew about the teenagers. So I said: "The fifty-thousand-dollar reward still stands . . . cash. All you have to do is hand over the horse. Be the easiest money you ever made. Beats selling dope to kids."

"Fifty thousand is peanuts."

"Before you turn down an easy fifty thousand, let me ask Mister Vann if he wants to talk to you." I cupped my hand over the phone.

Charlie shook his head, no. "You've said it all. Just tell him to take the fifty thousand."

"He says he'll shoot the horse, if we don't drop the case."

"Tell him, if he'll turn the horse over for fifty thousand, I will drop it."

I blinked on that and told Golden Voice: "Mister Vann says, if you'll take the fifty thousand, he'll drop the case. How's that?"

"It's still peanuts, Clegg. I said *peanuts*. In addition to my first ultimatum, I add this . . . make a public announcement that you are dropping the investigation. Do it, if you both value your lives. Show further proof by returning to Oklahoma."

"You're gettin' kinda personal. You mean you'd shoot us, if we don't drop the case and get out?"

"Precisely. And with ease. We have the means." He hung up.

I turned to Charlie. "He gave us two ultimatums. First, he threatened to shoot the horse, if we don't drop the investigation. You heard the second one. We'll be shot, if we don't."

Charlie didn't look scared. In fact, a little smile was working at the corners of his mouth. "We know they won't shoot the horse. They won't because they've got another deal cooking . . . big money, though God knows what it is. That's been it all along. Why they wouldn't give up the horse back in Oklahoma and won't now."

"Meantime, we could get shot."

"But the point is they're here, and the horse is here." He kept smiling. He actually looked happy, which was better than I felt.

CHAPTER
FIFTEEN

Quick Cash was scheduled to run in the third race the first day of the Kansas Futurity trials. Charlie and I dropped by her stall to wish Smiley Evans and his filly good luck. He was all dressed up like it was election day back in Cleveland County, and as nervous as a country boy at his first pie supper.

"How's she looking?" Charlie asked.

"Fine. She's relaxed. Just hope she breaks clean and gets out where she can run. We're in the three hole. That's better than one. I'm always afraid she'll get knocked into the rail." Stepping to the stall door, he looked in on his charge, ran a calming hand over her neck and face, and came back. "She's got a bad habit of jumpin' truck tracks, so I put a shadow roll on her. Think that'll help?"

"Should. It can't hurt."

We visited a while, and every little bit Smiley would get up to see about his filly. "I just wish I'se as calm as she is now," he said. "But the moment I saddle her, she'll tighten up like a ball of twine."

"That's all right," Charlie said. "Just means she's psyching herself up to run . . . Thought I should tell you that Buck and I had a phone call from our old friend, Golden Voice."

"And . . . ?"

"He threatened to shoot the horse, if we don't drop the case, which I don't believe, and then threatened Buck and me."

"When I get my little filly through these trials, one way or the other, good luck or bad, I think you'd better swear me in as a member of your posse. This thing is buildin' to a head."

"Looks that way. Well, we don't want to distract from the race. Good luck."

We all shook hands.

In the packed stands, the governor of New Mexico couldn't have found a seat. Earlier, Charlie had managed for a table high up at the extreme east end, which put the finish line far to our right. Across the track, in the infield, we had a good view of the paddock as Smiley saddled his mahogany bay filly.

The Kansas Futurity, I thought, recalling races and faces, the first leg of the Triple Crown for two-year-old quarter horses. Two-year-old babies, really, but it's the honey that draws the bees, and the short horse division for juveniles is no exception, ending with the million-dollar All-American Futurity. Tail winds and head winds. Bumps and slips. High hopes and broken dreams.

Shortly before post time, I went below for cold drinks. Charlie was busy over a daily racing form. I was coming up the ramp, easing through the crowd, juggling the drinks, when a man, apparently waiting at the head of the ramp, turned and looked directly at me. I would have paid only passing attention, but his eyes followed me till I went by. A nondescript-looking man except for the bull shoulders and strong, pockmarked face. At the last instant, he stepped back for me to pass. I climbed the high steps to our seats and put down the drinks. Glancing down, I noticed the man still at the head of the ramp. He was watching us, it seemed. Or he could be looking for someone or trying to locate a reserved seat like other late-comers.

I forgot him when the horses filed out on the track for the post parade. Smiley rode with obvious pride as he ponied his filly by the stands. She was on the smallish side, but she moved with balance and sass. Good shoulder and good depth. A refined head. A real beauty with that blazed face and bay coat. The racing form said she'd been out four times and had never finished off the board in Oklahoma at Blue Ribbon Downs or Remington. Two wins, a place and a show. Today's board had her at nine-to-two odds. Apparently, she was being ignored. But Dash for Cash's girl hadn't come out here just to look at the mountains. I would bet on her to win and for good luck. She could be the sleeper.

Yet, I couldn't ignore a certain sadness while I studied her and thought of her potential. *Chip, I could've had you on that nice filly. If you had only learned to say no, Chip. If you had only learned that much.* Like thinking of a person whose life had ended.

According to the racing form, Quick Cash's main competition would come from Bold Bug, in the four hole, a blocky, muscular gray colt with three wins and a show in Texas, and Cherokee Gal, who would break from the seven position, runner-up in the recent Sun Country Futurity at Sunland. Before that, a place and show in Texas. A rangy chestnut filly. Maybe a long-striding late closer. The Judge, a black colt from Arizona wearing No. 1, impressed me because of his balance and powerful conformation. Likely a pure sprinter. His record tallied up to two wins and a place over the same distance as today's race, a power blast at three hundred and fifty yards. The top ten qualifiers in the two-day trials would go for the $500,000 purse late in May, after about three weeks of rest.

Having eyeballed the field, I hurried below and bet $10 on Quick Cash to win. At the top of the ramp, the pockmarked man was bent over a program. He glanced up at me, looked me fully in the face without expression, and turned his attention back to the program. A deadpan expression, I thought.

"Think I'll bet Quick Cash across the board," Charlie said, passing me on the way down to bet. "There's a tail wind. It'll be a fast heat."

"I put a little win money on her," I said.

The horses were nearing the gates when he puffed up the stairs by the railing. "Lines are long," he said. "Almost waited too long, but I wanted another look at the four horse."

The stands stilled. The announcer, in a matter-of-fact voice, said: "The flag is up." Then: "There they go."

At the break, Bold Bug took it all, and he was running straight. Quick Cash, also quick out of the gate, was just a step behind. The crowd was shrieking already. Every horse seemed to have a rooting section. Everybody standing around us.

Bold Bug had the first call, Quick Cash dogging him. Along the rail The Judge picking up steam. Cherokee Gal, left at the break, beginning to stretch out, eating up ground in leaps. Bold Bug showed daylight now, but Quick Cash's rider tapped her left-handed, and she closed the gap. A game little filly.

Suddenly the field tightened as Cherokee Gal rolled up on the outside and The Judge made up ground. The two horse also showing run. The ten horse spooked at something along the outside wall, and banged into the nine horse, both runners out of it right there, but nobody down. More broken dreams.

It was bedlam around us. Fans above us on the aisle rushed down to the railing opposite us. In order to see, I wedged into the railing.

I could see Quick Cash, running gamely at gray Bold Bug's saddle girth, refusing to quit. And long-striding Cherokee Gal up close. The Judge and the two horse going head to head.

That was my last glimpse of the race before I felt myself suddenly and powerfully seized from behind and lifted toward the top of the railing. A woman beside me screamed and fell back. I heard Charlie shout my name. Twisting around, I grabbed the top railing with my left hand. Below me, I saw the pockmarked man, on his face the same deadpan expression, his mouth set like a steel trap.

There seemed no end to his strength. He broke my hold with an ease that terrified me. As he lifted me higher, I saw the concrete many feet below. I grabbed for the railing with my left hand, caught it, and kicked. My right boot took him in the face. Blood flew like race track mud. But he merely broke my left-handed hold and lifted me higher and higher. His vacant, bloodied stare didn't change. I was helpless now, near the peak of his lift. In another split second, he'd hurl me down to the concrete.

I was shouting and struggling all the while, as helpless as a child. I could see faces turning away from the race, horrified to see me dangling in mid-air. I could see men in the crowded aisle struggling to reach me.

It was over, then it wasn't, as I saw Charlie making a path and grabbing for me with his left hand and striking with his right at the same time. I felt Charlie grab my belt buckle, and yank. I was tumbling down against bodies in the aisle. I heard Charlie shout: "Stop that man!" Others took up the cry.

A man and woman helped me to my feet with wondering looks.

"You all right? You all right?"

I tried to nod. I was all right, I discovered, except for both sore-muscled arms that felt they'd been pulled from their sockets.

The woman said: "That terrible man was trying to throw you over the railing."

I nodded.

"Did you know him?"

"No, ma'am."

"Some nut," the man said.

I stood up and looked toward the finish line.

The race was over. The tote board was flashing the photo signal. There seemed to be some confusion in the winner's circle. Horses and people milling. Smiley was there, holding his filly's bridle. My vision blurred. I shook my head. In doubt, I turned to a man at a table and asked: "What happened?"

"It looked like a dead heat between the three and four horses. The time was fast, seventeen point sixty-four. The filly caught Bold Bug in the last jump."

Good. With that time, even if she ran second, she had a good chance to make the big money finale.

As my head cleared, I saw Charlie talking to a uniformed security officer down below. Charlie kept pointing to the runaway.

On unsteady steps, I eased down there.

"He plunged into the crowd," Charlie was telling the officer. "I didn't see much of his face."

"I did," I said, "but I'd never seen him before."

"You fellows come to the office so I can fill out a report on this," the security man said. "That is, if you don't mind missing a few races."

There was little to add to the report. We left out the obvious connection between the pockmarked man and Golden Voice. What could track security do about that? Nothing.

"All I can say," Charlie said, walking to the parking lot, "it's a damn' good thing you wear big belt buckles."

"And," I said, "that you've got a quick left hand and a stout arm."

"But how did that guy know you?"

"I wondered, too. Guess he was watching the motel and followed us to the track. Tailed us to our seats."

We passed an uneventful evening. I was still awake around midnight, kept so by a sore body, when my phone rang. I figured I knew who it was before I answered.

"Mister Buck Clegg, the eminently lucky jockey."

"You ought to know my voice by now. I know yours. That great baritone wasted on horse-stealing and attempted murder."

"I'm afraid you brought it on yourself when you and Charlie Vann failed to publish the public announcement."

"We can't return to Oklahoma and expect to get the horse back."

"Your chances are even less by staying here."

"How should we take that?"

"We know your every move."

"For the last time, why don't you take that easy fifty thousand and return the horse?"

"You are speaking of mere peanuts." His voice, reeking of swollen ego, struck that dramatic tone that I'd grown to despise. The bastard! But it told me for certain there had to be another deal hanging fire. Big bucks. Mighty big bucks.

"What if I got Mister Vann to raise the ante . . . say another fifty?"

216

"More peanuts."

"Peanuts, hell! It's more good money than you ever made playing them minor roles on TV and in the 'B' flicks. What'd you do, hold a spear or open a car door?"

Had I ever struck a sensitive spot! He roared back at me: "Next time we'll do a complete job! I pledge that, Buck Clegg, you knave! Cæsar speaks!" He hung up. So maybe the bastard had played some Shakespeare. At least, I took it for Shakespeare. In her well-meant efforts to improve her unlettered husband, Lori had exposed me to some of the tragedies, read and explained them to me. I felt amused at his high-sounding outburst until I realized he meant bigger trouble. The last was close enough, which made my sleep no easier.

I saw more trouble looming next morning when Rosa dashed up in the Porsche just as we left our rooms for breakfast. She came to us on the run, her big eyes filled with alarm and fear.

"*Señor* Buck! Chip's gone!"

"He left the hospital?"

"Yes!"

"Where'd he go?"

"He called me late last night. Said he was going where he could ride again for big money."

"But he didn't say where?"

"He no say. Said he'd get in touch later. Said he's sorry. Knows we need money. Couldn't wait longer. I told him not to worry about money till he's well. I work. I take care of us."

She was beginning to cry. If anything shakes me up, it's a woman crying. Charlie, too. We patted her on the shoulder.

"It has to be Mexico," I said. "He can't ride this side of the border. He knows that, Rosa."

She could hardly nod.

"But he didn't say Mexico?"

"He just say he ride again soon for big money. He get in touch."

"Then he will get in touch." I believed that. I wanted her to believe it.

There was nothing more to be said, but still she hesitated. "More bad thing," she said, biting her lower lip and crying again. "Chip, he's using again. I know. I tell by the way he talk. His voice . . . He make everything sound too big. Too much. Everything so good, when it's no good . . . I know from before."

"Sorry, Rosa. You've done all you can do now. Go on about your work and let us know when Chip calls. If he's still on this side, we'll get him right back into the hospital. He can start over. It will be all right."

When she'd gone, I said: "The hospital should be able to tell us more. If he was using at the hospital, who was providing the drugs?"

After some looking and asking, I was directed to the nurse who'd virtually chased us out of Chip's room. A gray, militant, efficient type. A Mrs. O. C. Burns, head nurse, in fact.

"Who are you?" she asked suspiciously.

"I'm Chip Romero's agent, Buck Clegg. His wife just told me he's jumped ship. When was that?"

"I still don't know why I have to tell you anything."

"You're miffed because he broke treatment. Don't blame you. Well, I checked him in here. If you need proof, ask the drug counselor."

"He walked out yesterday afternoon," she said, balky about it.

"Do patients, particularly drug patients, just sashay in and out when they please?"

"They absolutely do not. He sneaked out. A nurse looked in his room, and he was gone. He was not under twenty-four hour lock and key. We treat patients humanely here. He came in voluntarily."

"His wife said he's using again. She could tell by the way he talked over the phone. How could that happen?"

"Listen, if you're suggesting that somebody here . . . ?"

"I'm not. But the point is he *is* back on the stuff. I want to know how. Maybe somebody from the track was slipping it to him. He must've left with somebody. He had no car. His wife has it."

She stood up and marched from the room. Back in seconds, she said: "As I stated to you previously, Mister Clegg, nobody saw him leave. But, earlier in the afternoon, a white man came to see him."

"What did he look like, this white man?"

"You're just full of questions, aren't you, Mister Clegg?"

"Yes, ma'am."

She swished out again, and was back promptly. "This white man . . . I believe the Mexicans call them Anglos out here . . . was rather tall. Of middle age. Slightly stooped. He wore a Western hat, but almost every man in Ruidoso does." Meaning the hat was of no use as a clue, but true to her duty she'd pass it on, anyway. A picture was beginning to form in my mind, when she stopped and seemed to search for a missing item. "Oh, yes," she said, "he also had a black beard. I believe you'd call it a spade beard. That's all we know."

I felt like whooping. Instead, I said: "Thank you very much, Missus Burns. You're a peach."

She blushed.

I was leaving, when her voice caught me. "There is also the matter of the unpaid balance which Mister Romero left."

"Send me a statement at the Amigo Motel, and I'll take care of it."

She cracked a smile.

I left with troubled thought, trying to piece things together. The spade beard. Grubb. Emil Grubb. None other.

How had he known Chip was in the hospital? Easy. It had been in the paper. Was Grubb recruiting for a rich Mexican rancher or ranchers, seeking a top jockey to ride match races in Mexico? Where else? That made sense, though none for Chip Romero, who obviously was getting drugs from the suspended vet. And Grubb connected to Jim Ned and the bar shoe in the barn back in Oklahoma, and to Golden Voice and others and the pockmarked man. Now what?

CHAPTER
SIXTEEN

I was tired of the drawn-out not knowing, tired of more waiting for a decisive turn in the case, tired of always being on the defensive, instead of acting, because we had no visible target and didn't know what course of action to take — wouldn't until we located Jim Ned in a vicinity where there were already many hundreds of running horses. To add to the confusion, horses were being shipped in and horses were being shipped out by trailer.

I was wearing down, and, beginning to brood a little, I thought of Lori Beth. Neither of us would ever plead for the other to reconcile — that was out of the question. Pride, again. Each had hurt the other too much. But I needed a change from the never-ending inaction of the waiting game.

Next morning, I called Lori at the Kemps. Would she like to go for lunch down the Hondo Valley to a nice place we both remembered?

The line was silent for a hanging moment. I could tell that she was surprised at my voice. I pictured her frowning over her decision. Should she go or not? Would it be a sign of wanting to reconcile on her part, even of weakness, if she accepted? Was Buck angling to make up? That could never be.

I'd decided she was going to refuse, when, in a formal voice detached from any audible warmth, she said: "That would be nice. But I'd have to be back by four o'clock for re-hearsal. We're working on some new numbers."

"I'll get you back in plenty of time."

Mrs. Barbara Kemp, a mannered Texas blonde with the good looks that generally seem to go with big-bucks Texas oil money, let me in the stylish condo. Although I'd seen her and Del only a few times socially in the past, I thought her eyes were particularly intimate and prying as she looked me up and down. Like, what's going on here? Is a romance brewing? Old fires about to be rekindled? Had Buck Clegg aged? Did he look more battered than usual? No doubt, she knew the major part of what had happened between Lori and me, because the break-up had made the public prints, but there was much she didn't know and which I gathered she ached to know.

Lori, it seemed, was a long time getting ready. Meantime, Barbara and I chatted about the lovely weather, upcoming races, and Lori's band playing to packed houses every night at the Pines.

When Lori did show, I felt like giving her a wolf whistle. She looked great in a navy blue, tailored dress and a light jacket to match, legged in high heels, her dark hair pulled down around her face. Southern girls dress up when they're going someplace, anyplace. Nice. Makes you proud to escort 'em.

To Mrs. Kemp's disappointment, I sensed there was to be no greeting kiss between us, not even a peck on the cheek, not even a light hug. Just an informal — "Well, I'm finally ready." — and a — "Hi." — from me.

We walked out to the rented car, a pace or two apart. I opened the door for her, and, when I came around to the driver's side, I caught Mrs. Kemp peeking from the window. *Sorry, Barbara. Now don't try to read too much into a little drive downvalley and a simple luncheon.*

I'd started the car and looked to back out, when I noticed that Lori hadn't buckled her seat belt. "It's the law in New Mexico," I said, reaching across her for the belt.

Her firm hand stopped me. "I can do it," she said, which she did with a click. Nevertheless, I got the light, pleasant scent of her cologne, the same she'd always favored, but the name eluded me at the moment. I also saw that she sat as far away from me as possible.

"You look mighty nice," I said as we drove away.

"Thank you."

As formal as we were starting off, I thought wryly, maybe I should have put on a suit instead of neat tan slacks, shined boots, tan shirt, turquoise-and-silver bola for a tie, and a tan jacket to hide my shoulder holster and handgun.

May in southern New Mexico is unbeatable. Today was cool and bright, the air sweet after an early morning shower. We drove in awkward silence. I couldn't think of what to say except to comment on the beautiful weather.

"Mighty nice day," I said.

"Yes, indeed."

As the town fell behind us, then Ruidoso Downs, and we neared an apple orchard along the winding course of the river, I said: "Looks like there's gonna be plenty apples this fall in the Hondo Valley."

"Yes," she said, gazing off.

"Sure make some great apple pies."

"Or apple sauce."

Suddenly, she burst out laughing. "Buck, if we aren't careful, we'll be conversing in monosyllables."

"Or in sign language," I said, laughing in turn.

That broke the ice-jam between us. Not that we both started talking in flurries — we didn't. But I felt the tension between us fall away. However, the hurt would always be there like a bad scar. I sensed it in her quietness. So we drove on in wordless silence, enjoying the scenery, me even her mute company.

After a while, she turned and looked at me directly for the first time since we'd left the condo. "I see you're wearing a gun."

"Just a precaution."

"A precaution since that man tried to throw you over the railing at the track?"

She startled me. "I had it on then, but there wasn't time to use it. And couldn't have in that crowd. How did you know?"

"One of the band members had a seat not far away. You were recognized by others. Racegoers remember you."

224

"Oh, yeah, Buck Clegg, the great jockey, who rode Jim Ned to the two-year-old Triple Crown. Anyway, the guy got away."

"But why did he do that?"

I hadn't wanted to bring it up, even mention it, for fear she'd think I was after sympathy. Now that she knew, I might as well air the whole thing. "The man was hired by the gang that stole Jim Ned. The other night the ringleader called. Threatened Charlie and me, if Charlie didn't call off the investigation. Of course, Charlie's not about to do that. Then that happened at the track."

"I understand it was a close call for you."

"Close enough. Charlie grabbed at me and knocked the guy down."

"What can you do?"

"Keep looking. We think Jim Ned is in the area, and we think some kind of deal is in the making, involving the horse. That's why the gang is getting edgy about the case."

"A deal? How do you mean?"

"Back in Oklahoma, they tried to take the reward money and not turn over the horse, which indicated they had more profitable things in mind. Now they've shifted base out here, which means the horse, also, is out here . . . we think and hope. Last night, when Golden Voice called again and threatened us, I brought up the fifty-thousand-dollar reward again . . . that it was his, if he'd just return the horse. He laughed at me. Said fifty thousand was peanuts. When I said Charlie might raise the ante, which I'm sure Charlie would do, the guy said more peanuts."

"This is scary. But what sort of deal could they have in mind?"

I shrugged.

"Meanwhile," she said, "they've threatened and resorted to violence at the track, for fear you and Charlie will find the horse before they can complete the deal, whatever it is."

I looked at her. Pleased. "Lori, it couldn't be stated better."

We fell silent. Lori seemed extra thoughtful. Maybe pensive was the word. When the twisting highway took us around a curve and a busy horse ranch lay between us and the river, I spotted a band of yearlings.

"Look at them young horses . . . I mean *those* young horses," I said fast.

She glanced at me and smiled. "You're doing better, Buck Clegg."

"Not much. It's hard for a man to break set, old ways. Like tryin' to break a horse of a bad habit."

"Why, between us, does it always seem to come back to horses?"

"Because about all I know is horses."

"And about all I know is music."

I wanted to say that she was much more than that, but dared not. In her guarded state of mind, she would take it as flattery leading up to something. I grasped now for the first time that she'd felt an unspoken neglect back there when I was riding four days a week, you name the track, and had my pick of top mounts. I was too busy to realize it then, but should have. So much for the past, which was etched in stone, as they say. Between us now — her hurt, stiffened by Southern pride, of which there is no other, and my macho pride, considerably watered down.

We drove the remaining distance to the roadside restaurant without speaking a word. When we squeezed into the overflowing parking lot, the sound of piano music and the voices of people having a good time greeted us, come, I thought, like us, to get away from the crowded streets and racing frenzy of Ruidoso.

After some delay, we found a table for two. Would Lori like a Margarita?

"I'd like one, but it would make me sleepy. You have one."

"Guess not. I don't drink alone any more."

"You used to say a Margarita was no good unless you could taste the tequila through the mix."

So she remembered that. "I still do. But today I'll pass."

I caught the question in her eyes as legible as printed words. "And I've passed on amphetamines," I said. "Did, before I quit riding."

"I'm glad," she said, and I believed her.

So we had iced tea. We both ordered salads, mine from habit to make weight.

The luncheon crowd was thinning fast, and there was no one near us, when she said: "There's something I've been wanting to tell you and Charlie, after what he said about this Golden Voice person. I wasn't sure it meant anything at first, and it may not yet." She glanced around before going on. "Several nights ago a drunk tried to sing with the band. The place was so crowded. I was taking a little break while the boys played 'Honky Tonk Woman.' They said, before they knew it, he was on the bandstand, facing the dancers and singing. A real show-off. At the same time, he was making all sorts of lewd gestures. Just as quick, the bouncers hustled him out. He resisted them and sang all the way out. Of what I could hear at the tail end of his solo, I thought what a good voice he had. Of course, he was drunk and somewhat off key and too loud."

"What kind of voice?"

"His range was that of a rich baritone."

"There's a lot of baritones."

"Yes, but this man was quite good. Exceptional, I'd say, when sober."

"Golden Voice has a baritone you remember on the phone. Did you get a look at his face?"

"Not much. I was just coming back on the stand when it happened. By then the bouncers were taking him away."

"What little could you tell?"

"The little bit you could make out of a person's back and the side of his face as he's being forcibly ejected? He was well-dressed. Looked like a man of medium build. Brown or dark brown, wavy hair. He had quite a head of hair. The brief side view glimpse I got, he was clean-shaven. Oh, yes. He had a rather haughty way of carrying himself, as if he was aloof from all around him, and how dare the bouncers touch him. I remember that. He was very puffed up about himself."

228

"That's Golden Voice. He's got enough ego for two actors."

"Now, I'm getting mash notes from him."

"Oh? How do you know they're from him?"

"In the first one, he said he was the man who was unfairly ejected from the club the other night. Always signs the notes, 'Admirer.' Says he wants to meet me. All that old stuff women entertainers get from sloppy drunks and weirdos. Say he's there every night."

"I have to give him credit for good taste."

"Not funny, Buck Clegg."

I took everything in, weighing it in my mind, before I said: "He could be our man." But I held back, saying how I thought we might find out.

She seemed to sense that and said it for me. "He said when I'm ready for him to formally introduce himself in my dressing room some night after the show . . . he didn't say *if*, which shows the ego of the man . . . I could let him know by dedicating a number to Sam, an out-of-town guest."

"Careful, wasn't he, not to tell you to leave a note for him at the bar, where he could be identified? Possibly he could be the man, but I don't want you to get involved in this."

"Can you think of a better way of finding out? You and Charlie could be nearby, with the police, and you'd know when you heard his voice. Don't you see?"

"I see it all too well, with you involved. On the other hand, you can't arrest a man on the basis of his voice. Yet, the police might hold him on suspicion for twenty-four hours. After that, who knows?"

The piano player returned at that moment, and, when he rippled the keys, I saw an opportune time to switch the discussion. Would Lori care to dance?

She hesitated, and I thought I could see the same reluctance I'd sensed over the phone when I'd asked her to lunch.

"Let's do," she said all at once. I would've appreciated more enthusiasm.

It was strange, even startling, feeling her in my arms again while she moved like a piece of silk. I wanted to say that, but knew she would instantly reply that's what I used to say about some extra nice racehorses blessed with balance, speed, and power, and there we'd be again, back on the stalemate of the old battleground.

Whereas I was awkward and out of synch, like a clod with two left feet at a country dance.

"I thought you wanted to dance?" she said.

"I do. It just takes me a while to get started. The track's a mite cuppy today."

I hoped she'd grin at my funny remark, but she didn't. I took a grip on myself then, and we did better, gliding away, but formally. I'm not a bad dancer, when I'm organized. However, Lori maintained a very careful distance between us, which I respected. Her left hand resting very lightly on my shoulder, hardly touching. Man sure wouldn't read anything into that. Everything as proper and above board as a high school prom, with hawk-eyed chaperones eyeballing every step and clench. But how could I know? I never went to high school.

230

The music changed, and I couldn't even name the number, but it sounded a lot like "Just One of Those Things." Forget about the *those* and that Mel Torme. Hell, we didn't need a vocalist. The talented gray-haired gent at the piano, who should've been anywhere but the lower end of the Hondo Valley, was really bearing down, when I noticed that Lori's left hand was no longer lightly on my shoulder, but pressing a bit, and that my right hand, formerly barely touching the small of her back, had tightened and she hadn't complained or moved away from me.

Then, suddenly, the music ended, and Lori stepped away, and we went back to our table. We had another iced tea and watched other couples when the music started again. I knew by now that she wouldn't dance with me again, because she'd let her Southern guard slip a notch during the first round.

"If I ever need another pianist, I know where to get one," she said, listening.

"He shore can tickle the ivories," I said.

"I believe that's an original critique," she said, entertained.

"Oh, no. It comes down in my family from my father's daddy, who was an old-time cowhand and as a boy went up the trail on the drives to the northern pastures. The boys used to say that, when they heard a good piano player in the saloons. Just about anything sounded good to young fellows starved for entertainment. I think they generally called the musician, professor."

"What did they call the girls?"

"I don't recall that was ever said. Some cowboys were too bashful to even speak to a girl."

Our talk seemed to dwindle to mutual silence, and I didn't ask her to dance again. We just watched the dancers and listened to the music, letting our thoughts run back to other good times, maybe? Untroubled times. Nashville, Vegas, Sunland, Los Alamitos, Ruidoso. Well-wishers. Voices. Acclaim. "I bet the jockey today, Buck. Good luck tomorrow . . ." "Where'd you learn to sing like that, Margo? Would you and the boys play a request for my wife?"

Time hadn't passed, I realized, looking at my watch, it had fled with the speed of light. "Lori, I guess we'd better go for you to make the rehearsal. It's after three."

She was gazing off. "Oh . . . yes." Hurriedly: "Well, it's been nice." Southern girls are even mannerly to ex-husbands.

I didn't say anything like: "Let's do it again." I just nodded and left matters there, better unsaid. *If it ain't broke, don't fix it and break it.* As we went out, couples were still arriving. The bar was having a banner day, and the guy at the piano was gifted and tireless. What was his problem? Booze, drugs, women? I felt for him. I also wanted to thank him for a lovely, one-dance afternoon, and a bounty of thoughtful listening.

This time she buckled up without a reminder from me. Before us some twenty-five miles of scenic, winding river road to Ruidoso, high cliffs flanking us on the right, on our left sleek running horses grazing green bottomland pastures, and towering cottonwoods, leaves like shiny sequins turning in the breeze, which now and

232

then allowed teasing peaks of the shining river. The sight further inspired me, as the afternoon had. *Keep this up, Buck Clegg, and someday you might be able to pen a line or two of poetry.* Maybe.

I could have been in Charlie's "family car," the way I settled down to forty-five miles an hour. No word was spoken, but I knew Lori was also enjoying the scenery.

"The best kept secret in New Mexico," she said. "It's lovely along here."

"It is. When it's all over, this is where I'm comin' back to. This and around Ruidoso."

"What do you mean, when it's all over?"

"After we find Jim Ned, and I'm through as a jockey's agent."

"You really think Charlie will get him back?"

I didn't want to use the word *gut,* but it was the only one that fit. "My gut feeling is, Lori, that we will, and before long . . . because the gang is around here close . . . but there'll be a price for it, just as there's a price for all good life in this world that needs protection. I want this horse back as much as Charlie does, believe me . . . I can't quite explain it. It's a kind of visceral feeling between a rider and his horse. I broke Jim Ned. I was aboard the first time he ran, back at Blue Ribbon Downs in Oklahoma. And believe me, he was a handful . . . Later, Jim Ned brought me fame and fortune. Because I understood him and knew how to ride him, he won the Triple Crown . . . We'd come out of the gates like a bat out of hell, and he'd hit full stride. Then sometimes he'd hear the roar of the crowd and prick his ears and start to hang a little bit, distracted. Then I'd

233

holler in his ears to cut down the road, and he'd take off like a hoop rolling, as old-time horsemen used to say." I looked at her and tapped my forehead. "My, I really gave a speech, didn't I? Sorry."

"You just spoke from the heart, Buck. It needed to come out."

"I've never said that, even to Charlie. I reckon people need to communicate more."

Not meaning to, I'd touched a sensitive issue between us. Glancing down, I saw her left hand resting on the car seat between us. I placed my hand over her hand, then, looking in the rear view mirror, I saw the car come up behind us and seem to take position there.

Old warnings chilled me. I kept looking. The car was about a hundred yards behind us. There it stayed, like a hawk watching a rabbit., I wasn't driving fast, far slower than the few cars and trucks swishing by us from Ruidoso, so the driver could have passed us with ease. Traffic was light.

I drove on for another half minute, constantly watching. When I lifted my hand from hers and looked again, she said: "What is it?"

"I think we're being followed."

"Followed?" Wide-eyed, she looked through the back window. "Two men," she said. "They're coming closer now."

I saw that as well and picked up speed. They did the same, but keeping about the same distance.

"Can you tell what make of car it is?" I asked her.

"I believe . . . it's a Camaro."

A Camaro. Shades of Oklahoma and John Brown, alias one Dapper Thompson.

"They're coming closer now." She wasn't panicking, but her voice sounded dry.

"Hold on, Lori, and get down. We're goin' for a ride."

Something *pinged* against the car. Another *ping*.

She was still looking back. I yelled at her. "Get down! They're shooting at us!"

She was slow obeying, had to steal a last look. I grabbed her shoulder and forced her down. "You've got to stay down!"

There was another *ping*.

They were really on the charge now, with the idea to pull up alongside and let us have it, or force us into the cañon wall. The same scenario tried on the country road that night Charlie almost pitched fifty thousand dollars out the window.

But, for the moment, the narrow road was to our advantage. As they started to come around, I cut left, blocking them off. They dropped back, and I drove faster, gaining ground.

"You all right, Lori?"

"Yes. What can we do?"

"Just ride the race. You stay down."

"Can you drive any faster?"

"Not much. I think there's a governor on this car."

I'd forgotten I packed a gun. I pressed the power button that lowered the driver's window. Then I drew the .38, and leaned out the window, steering with my left hand.

Two gorilla-masked faces leered at me from the Camaro. Lori was disobeying and looking, too, because she yelled: "Those faces . . . they look like gorillas!"

"Scare tactics," I said. "Used that back in Oklahoma."

I fired two quick shots, aiming at the windshield. I saw no effect, but the Camaro eased off.

My car was swerving. When I turned to right it, Lori yelled — "Look out!" — and an eastbound car sliced by, the driver's mouth working as he glared at me.

"Next time you shoot," Lori said, "give me the wheel. I'm not helpless, you know."

A car and a truck headed east forced the Camaro to hold off. When the road cleared, it bulled after us again.

"Take the wheel, Lori."

The Camaro's driver began weaving back and forth when he saw me lean out the window. I snapped two shots, leaving two for when they came even with us, if nothing changed, and nothing changed. Unfortunately, I'm no great hand with a gun. They still tracked us, even closer now.

I had the rental car running all out, but it wasn't enough. We tore around a curve, tires screaming. Ahead, traveling our way, a big truck filled the lane. I intended to pass him, but the highway narrowed and a oncoming truck loomed, bulging toward us. In a few more seconds, the trucks would pass each other.

I didn't ease up.

"Buck . . . don't!" Lori yelled. "There's a truck coming!"

"Hold on. We're goin' through!"

236

I waited till the Camaro was closing on our tail. I floorboarded the car, and we shot up to the truck on our right, the oncoming trucker blowing his horn and burning rubber. All the time the narrowing road was forcing him inward. I kept going. Like staying on the rail and waiting a hole to open. I needed racing room.

As the trucks passed, I felt and heard our left rear fender scrape. For just a flick of time, it seemed to catch. We swayed, and then we broke free. Behind us, I heard a louder scrape, next a crunch. We tore ahead, the road clearing like a straight-away.

Looking back, I saw the eastbound truck slowing to a smoking stop. The sideswiped Camaro was limping along. It stopped near the westbound truck.

"You can look back now," I said.

Looking, she said: "Those terrible men . . . their hideous gorilla masks." She shuddered.

I didn't ease up much till we reached town. "You want to go to the club or home?" I asked her. "Then I'd better report this."

"Home."

At the condo, we stood by the car. "Sorry the afternoon turned out so rough," I said.

"But it came out OK."

"With luck." I wouldn't tell her what had flashed through my mind at the last moment: of cutting to the rail and waiting for a hole to open, which it did. Sometimes they don't. No, that would take us back to racehorses. Also, I wanted to embrace her by way of apology; however, she might think I was taking advantage of two people being brought together in what had been a touch-and-go situation. The last was an understatement, if there ever was one, when it was murder all the way. *I bet on the jockey today, Buck Clegg.*

"After what happened this afternoon," she said, "I have all the more reason to dedicate a number tonight to Sam. I wouldn't know Golden Voice, if I saw him face to face. This way you and Charlie and the police can find out."

"It's chancy. I don't want you involved."

"But you have nothing to say about it, do you, really?"

My smile was dry. "None at all. But I don't like it."

"I hope you will all be waiting for him tonight when he comes to the dressing room?"

"Guess we don't have a choice. You bet, we'll be there."

"Good luck." Not even a hug, not even a handshake between us after what we'd been through. When she turned to leave, I rebuked myself for thinking we'd made a fresh beginning this afternoon. How I had sensed it, in the touching and the long silences, I could never be quite sure, and I was less sure now. I was merely hoping. *Was she supposed to fall into your arms, Buck Clegg, just because you'd been nice to her? That's not the way it happens in real life.* The moment, whatever promise I thought it held, was gone.

She turned to go inside the condo, paused instead, and, looking back, said: "You drive a car the same way you ride a racehorse . . . hell-bent."

"It's the only way, if you're gonna get there first."

"Not bad."

I thought she smiled, just a little, as she went in. But I wasn't sure.

CHAPTER
SEVENTEEN

Would Police Chief Jud Ivy beat around the bush and say it was out of his jurisdiction, which it was, when I suggested we rush downvalley to the disabled Camaro and take into custody two men who had not only attempted to murder Lori and me, but also were prime suspects as Jim Ned's captors?

"I've got the bullet holes in my rental car to prove it," I said. "Margo Drake will back my story."

He was out of his chair as I finished. "Attempted murder is every officer's concern," he said seriously. "And horses and tourists are the lifeblood of this town. There isn't time to go through channels and wait for the county. Let's go."

Behind his clean-shaven, official show of duty, I caught the desire to score a beat on the county and other agencies. He called another officer, told a desk sergeant to notify the county of our mission, and we three took off with shotguns and sidearms in a squad car, the chief driving.

"I don't have the opportunity to get out like this very often," he said relishingly, as he broke the speed limit through town, siren wailing, lights flashing. But once outside the city limits, he turned everything off — "So we can make a silent approach."

When we spotted the Camaro pulled off against the cliff side of the highway not many miles from town, I realized that in our mad dash Lori and I had covered far more ground than I'd thought at the time. The westbound truck had gone on, but the eastbound, which had burned rubber trying to avoid a crash, lay like a stranded whale on the very edge of the road overlooking the valley. The driver was down under his vehicle, inspecting. About forty-five minutes had elapsed since the climax. On second glance, the Camaro looked ominously quiet.

Ivy headed straight for it, drew up in front, and we all piled out, weapons ready — the chief, left, the other officer right, me with him. We stalked around the car and halted. Suddenly I felt very foolish.

There was nobody inside or around the car.

I walked back, curious, and found a bullet hole near the center of the windshield, not a vital shot, because it had gone between the seats. The radiator also was leaking from a bullet hole. Buck Clegg was a better shot than he thought, but no Kewpie doll.

Ivy hollered at the truck driver, who crawled out.

"Where'd the people in the car go?" Ivy asked.

"A motorist stopped to help, and would you believe it, they took his car at gunpoint?"

"Where is the motorist?"

"Would you believe it, he caught a ride with another motorist? I've never seen a crazier day. I blow the tires, tryin' to prevent a wreck, when some fool drives

241

between me and another trucker. The two guys in the coupe there are chasin' the first guy and get squashed, but nobody hurt. I can just see my outfit gettin' sued over this, and it was their fault. Me, with two busted tires."

"Want me to send out a wrecker?"

"Yeah, will you?"

"Sure."

In the crash, the Camaro had taken a smashed rear end and a crumpled left rear wheel and tire. Ivy jotted down the Texas license, searched the car inside, and said: "We'll look in the trunk when we get it towed in. I anticipate finding some extra nice goodies. And we'll go over it for prints. Meantime, we'll see what Texas can tell us from the tag."

Driving back, I dropped word to Ivy about tonight, when Lori Beth would dedicate the number to "Sam." Would the chief care to join Charlie and me on a stake-out? I believed that was the proper word.

"You're assuming Sam is this guy, Golden Voice, as you call him. That's not much to go on."

"Is . . . but it's all we have. I think he's our man. The club closes at one o'clock. She'll be waiting in her dressing room for him to show."

"Wouldn't miss it for the world. You fellows come to the station around midnight, and we'll set this up. Additionally, when we get in, I expect I'll have another customer waiting, the Good Samaritan motorist who got his car snatched. I expect we'll find it shortly, abandoned on some off-trail mountain road.

242

Charlie just groaned as I told him the afternoon's happenings. "Nothing surprises me any more," he said. "Absolutely nothing." Just as quickly his face relaxed. "I have some good news. Smiley's filly made it into the finale. She's not big, but she's compact and muscular. Horse doesn't have to be big to be fast. Look at Northern Dancer. On that, let's have a drink and go to dinner."

After dinner we rested in Charlie's room, reading the papers, watching some TV. A continuation of the waiting game. When the phone rang after nine o'clock, Charlie answered. He nodded and nodded and showed no surprise, just accepting what was being said, asking a few questions. He might have been talking to the Norman bank about a luncheon meeting, or about some farmer's loan. He hung up. "Chief Ivy . . . The Texas license tag was stolen, which figures. But in the trunk they found an Oklahoma tag with C L letters and the numbers four four zero eight. If my memory doesn't fault me, isn't that the number that traced back to C. D. Cole, the bird we ran over who checked into the Norman Hospital as Earl Smith?"

"It does. He also has other aliases . . . C. D. Reese and C. B. Blaine . . . that we know of."

"It sure hooks up," Charlie said. "That's not all the police found in the trunk. There was some hundred thousand dollars' worth of marijuana and cocaine. A pretty good indication of the new source of drugs in town. Chief Ivy can't wait to dig into this further."

"Guess it's too early for anything on the prints?"

"They'll check on 'em."

"No matter. The Camaro has to be the one used to try to run us down that night west of town, when we put Cole in the hospital. Too, the wild way that guy chased us today fits that night's driver and the John Brown who had the Camaro fixed in the Norman body shop, better known as Dapper Thompson. I figure he's the logical man to have been driving today, instead of Cole, who might be too crippled up, or Golden Voice, who strikes me as more of a planner than a fast car driver. But I think he was in the Camaro."

Charlie made a wry face. "Looks like all the old gang's here, which they wouldn't be unless there's something big in the wind."

"I get cold all over when I look back and figure that Thompson and Golden Voice probably watched Lori and me from the bar. Golden Voice knows me from Elk City, remember? But I don't know him. It was likely from the bar, because only couples were in the dine and dance area. It was our tough luck to run into 'em out there. They didn't follow us from town, because they'd have jumped us on the road."

Charlie suddenly snapped to attention. "And why was the pair way out there? Not to dine and dance. That restaurant could be a supply point for drugs. Or a safe, out-of-the-way place for 'em to meet. It's something to pass on to Chief Ivy."

We drove to the police station before midnight. Chief Ivy knew all about the Pines and how it was laid out, since it had been burglarized several times and the department often received calls from there to pick up

244

unruly drunks and break up fights in the parking lot. He outlined the position each man would take back from the rear entrance which led to the dressing rooms. He'd alerted the guard, an older man and a former policeman, on what was coming.

"I thought at first we might post a man or two across from Miss Drake's dressing room . . . there's a small storage room there . . . but that might endanger her. Letting the suspect get that far, or if there'd be a scuffle. If this suspect is our man, he'll be armed. So we'll nab him when he states his business at the door. The guard will ask him what he wants, and so on. We'll be close by."

"What then?" Charlie asked.

"We'll hold him for questioning."

"How long can you do that?"

"Depends."

The band was playing "Honky Tonk Woman" when four of us posted ourselves behind the club. A single bulb over the rear entrance and light from the street laid a sallow glow over the area, this under a quarter moon and drifting clouds. Lori's car was parked nearby. The band played two more numbers, then I recognized "Let Love Linger." Even from here, muted, Lori's voice reached me clear and sweet. I guess it was her favorite, though she'd never said. It was the way she sang it. Maybe some contradiction there, maybe some regret, or was I being cynical, or was Buck Clegg, the great jockey, reading meanings that didn't exist? Probably.

Now the music died, and I could hear the rise of voices leaving the club, the crunch of gravel, and cars starting. No fights yet.

A figure came reeling up to the guard. "Hey, there, frien'. I'm here to see Margo Drake. She told me to come aroun' after the show."

"Better go on."

"She told me to be here."

"She didn't leave word with me. You go on."

"I'm goin' in there."

"No. You're not."

"I am."

Expertly, the guard grabbed the drunk, spun him around. A hand at the drunk's collar and belt, he marched him toward the corner of the building. The drunk kept going.

Not our man. Main thing, he didn't sound like Golden Voice. Another understanding worked out at the police station, thought of at the last moment before we left. I was to make the first move toward the suspect because I knew his voice. I guess we all felt embarrassed at almost having forgotten the only means of identification. For that reason, the guard was to let callers have their way.

Noise out front was fast thinning, when two men approached. One said: "We want to talk personal with Margo Drake . . . we do . . . about playin' a special request tomorrow night." The guy's voice was so low and rambling it was hard to make out.

We hadn't counted on two men. Could this be Thompson and Golden Voice?

Drawing him on, the guard said: "What's the request?"

" 'Singin' the Blues' . . . that's what, by God," came the tetchy drawl.

I felt my tenseness drop. Not our man.

"Believe that's a yodel number," the guard said.

"Part of it."

"Miss Drake don't yodel. She's all singer."

"Yodel is singin', too. We'll explain when we see her."

"You can't see her tonight. You can make your request in person tomorrow night when she comes on stage."

"We aim to see her now."

"You boys want me to call the cops?" The guard drew his blackjack, and whapped it against his left hand.

They looked in doubt at each other. "Fine one you are," said the second man, with a drunk's indignation, who also wasn't Golden Voice, and they staggered back toward the front of the club. The first guy began yodeling, and it was worse than bad.

Some twenty minutes passed. I saw Lori come to the entrance and gaze around and go back. None of us spoke or moved.

It wasn't far from two o'clock when Ivy left the shadows. "He's not coming tonight. Mister Vann, you call us tomorrow, if anything pops."

Charlie thanked him.

I went to Lori's dressing room. She was dressed, waiting. "I wonder what scared him off?"

"Who knows? Maybe he won't bother you any more." I gave her a full report on what we'd found at the wreck and learned from the truck driver, and how the police had planned tonight's vigil. I had to add with a twisted grin as I said: "They must have taken off their gorilla masks when they seized the car, because the trucker would've mentioned that."

She stood very still, clasping her hands, and sighed: "If I'd only seen his face full-on the night he tried to sing with the band, I could identify him for you. The boys didn't get much of a look at him, either. Too, the lights are rather dim. The customers prefer it that way . . . Now, I believe, it's time to go home."

"Charlie and I will follow you."

"I don't think it's necessary."

"We will, anyway."

As I walked her out to her car, my guilt felt heavy. "I'm sorry you got dragged into this. And to think it all started with an innocent invitation to lunch."

Her laugh was short but forgiving. "At least the luncheon was nice and the ride with Buck Clegg was truly exciting, one I won't forget." She unlocked the door and stepped in. Instead of starting the motor immediately, she looked up at me, and I thought she was going to say something. She seemed to hesitate.

"What is it?" I asked.

"Oh . . . just a thought. I'd better go."

"Good night," I said.

"Good night."

Charlie and I followed her to the condo, and didn't drive off until we saw her go in.

248

"Do you think this bird will bother her again?" Charlie asked.

"I'd bet on it."

CHAPTER
EIGHTEEN

Restless as ever, balked at every step, it seemed, when we took the initiative, Charlie and I made a swing next day through the little mountain villages of Lincoln and Capitan, stopping now and then to visit with horsemen Charlie knew, inquiring as we went, stating the reason for our search, in no hurry, listening and observing. A fruitless journey, but we felt we had to do something.

It was getting dark when we drove into town. Dinner took an hour and a half, most of that time waiting for a table, which is not unusual at the top eating places in Ruidoso during the height of the racing season.

Afterward, I considered going to the Pines, but it was late, and I opted to stay in and went to bed early.

My phone's ringing jarred me out of a deep sleep. I listened a bit longer, reluctant to move. The ringing didn't stop. I turned on the bedside lamp and picked up the receiver, slow about it. My watch read: one thirty-three.

"Hello," I said. You get a lot of wrong-number calls when the races are going, friends trying to locate friends, friends saying come over and join the party, or some guy calling for tips on tomorrow's program. Tips I don't have.

"Buck . . ."

"Yes. Who is it?"

"Lori . . ." Her voice sounded strained, not like her at all. I sat up, wide awake now. "Are you all right?"

"Well . . . yes and no."

"Are you hurt?"

"Not physically . . . just frightened. My car stalled after I left the club. I was chased. I ran."

"Where are you?" I remembered the Pines closed at one o'clock and the club furnished her a car.

"At a little all-night store on Mechum Drive. It's . . . it's . . . Tom's Country Store. That's it."

"You're all right there?"

"Yes."

"I'll be there as fast as I can. You stay inside."

"I will."

The harried tone of her voice still worried me while I dressed, mindful to strap on the handgun.

From the Amigo to where Mechum Drive intersects Sudderth Drive, coming down from the high country, is several miles. I made it at breakneck speed and turned. Soon the highway was climbing. After about half a mile, my headlights picked up a car pulled off on the right shoulder, lights still on. Not far from there I saw a well-lighted store. It was the place. A pickup was parked in front, but no passenger cars, so the car I'd passed was Lori's.

I ran inside. A young man was stocking items on shelves.

"Where is she?"

He smiled and pointed to a table at the rear of the store. Lori sat there, before her a cup of coffee. Her hair

251

was unkempt, and she looked spent, but in control. I saw her quick relief when she saw me. She stood, and I put my arms around her and kissed her cheek and patted the back of her head. She didn't return my kiss, but held on to me until a voice said: "You'd better have some coffee, too."

"This young man has been very nice to me," she said, freeing herself. "I left my purse in the car. I didn't have any money, and he let me use the store phone and insisted I have some coffee."

He put down a cup of coffee. "I thought you needed help."

She gave him a thankful smile. "I did, indeed."

"Thanks very much," I said, and held out my hand.

Over the coffee, I said: "Tell me what happened."

"The club closed at one o'clock, but I was later than usual leaving. Had some little things to do. The guard saw me out to the car, and I started off OK. By then the parking lot was empty. I drove out to the street and saw no one behind me . . . But as I turned up Mechum, I saw a car's lights come on, and I soon knew I was being followed. The driver didn't try to pass, but stayed a short way back . . . as if he were sending me a threatening message . . . Well, it worked. I began to get scared. I hadn't gone far when the motor started to miss and labor. That did frighten me! I felt so helpless. I went on a way . . . then the car just quit. I pulled off as far as I could, but left the lights on."

"That was good. Go on."

"I got out. Up ahead, I could see the lights of the store. Not far, really. But they seemed a long way off."

"What did he do then?"

"He pulled in behind me and stopped . . . left the motor running. When he got out, I was already shaking. Then I saw his face in the lights and was terrified." She swallowed. "He wore a gorilla mask. I was petrified . . . I couldn't move. He came slowly toward me and paused . . . It was almost as if he were playing a rôle."

"Did he say anything?"

"Oh, yes. He said . . . 'I am Sam, your most ardent admirer. I've been wanting to meet you, Miss Drake.' His voice was so formal, so resonant, so theatrical, and affected and stagy . . . and he held himself just so, as if in costume. Everything seemed so unreal . . . and even more terrifying. I couldn't move. And then he said . . . 'I believe it's time we got together on a more intimate basis, my fair lady.' I'm sure it was the same voice I heard at the club that night, when the man tried to sing with the band and was taken out."

"Golden Voice," I said.

She had to catch her breath again. "Then he bowed from the waist and said . . . 'I'm sure you'll find my company entertaining in more ways than one,' and he made a lewd gesture with his fingers . . . That made me mad. Broke my trance. I started running."

In her eyes, I could see her reliving the scene again, shutting it out.

"Go on," I said to help. "What did he do?"

"He started chasing me on foot. But when a car came by and slowed down, he ran back to his car. He must have turned around and gone back the other way, because I didn't see his car again. It was terrible." She wiped at her eyes with a knuckle and sniffed. "I guess I'm just a weak sister."

"Weak sister, hell," I said. "You couldn't have done better. The point is you're all right." I patted her shoulder, though I wanted to do more.

"But he may follow me again."

"From now on, you don't drive home alone from the club. I'll see to that. You left your purse in the car. Let's go get it."

We thanked the young man, and drove downhill to her car.

"You sprinted a good two hundred yards to the store," I said. "Not bad for a city girl in high heels."

She punched my shoulder.

We found her purse intact in the car, took the keys, turned off the lights, and struck out for the condo. I told her I'd drop by the police station on the way back. "I think something was put in your gas tank, or the motor wouldn't have acted like that. Unless you were short on gas?"

"I glanced at the gauge, when I stopped. It was a quarter full."

"What time did the guard come on?"

"Around nine o'clock. He's always there when I take my first break about then."

"That left plenty of time to do something."

That was the extent of our conversation. She leaned back against the seat, and in seconds I saw her head droop. Seconds more, and she was fast asleep. No seat belt. But this was no time for observing the state law. I drove with slow care.

When we reached the condo, a low light was on inside. I turned off the motor and the headlights. I was reluctant to wake her, remembering how I used to let her sleep longer after she'd been performing late and needed the rest, stolen, priceless times when I could fly in to be with her a few days.

I think she could have slept on and on. At last, I said: "Lori, we're here."

She woke up with a terrific start. She fisted her hands, moving her arms to defend herself. Bad dreams, I thought. Hearing the resonant voice, seeing the gorilla mask coming toward her in the buff light, the lewd fingers busy.

"You're all right," I said as gently as I could. "You're at the condo."

She seemed to emerge from a dense fog. She relaxed her hands and sat up.

"You're at the condo," I said again. "You're all right. You had a little nap on the way."

She shook her head in a clearing way. "I'd better hurry in. Barbara will think something happened. She always waits up for me. Baptist ladies do that for young women guests."

"I think the Baptists have something."

She slid out before I could get around to the door, going independently up the walk with a heel-clicking stride. I caught up with her at the door.

There she turned and very properly looked up at me and said: "Thank you, Buck, for coming to my rescue." No touching. No embrace by either of us.

"You just needed a lift was all. You'd already made your escape."

"Most of all, I needed somebody to be with me."

"Glad I was available."

"I don't know what else I could've done."

"You could have called the police. Or had the young man do it."

"Somehow I never thought of that."

Inside, a brighter light came on like a signal.

"I have to go now . . . and thank you again."

She kissed me lightly on the cheek, I kissed her lightly on the cheek, and then she went in.

It seemed like a long ride back to the police station and the motel.

The day after Lori's frightful experience, with Charlie invited to lunch by old friends, I went on a solitary mission of hunger to *Señor* Pete's, my favorite Mexican restaurant in Ruidoso, where I'd gone only infrequently when I was riding. Just one meal there could add glue-like pounds to a jockey's thin frame, which meant hours of self-reproach, if not repentance, in steam and hot rooms and whirlpools to pay for half an hour of voracious indulgence. I filled up on my old addiction: a combination plate of one cheese enchilada, one beef enchilada, one beef taco, one tamale, everything but the taco loaded with chili con carne, backed up with mounds of refried beans and rice, and Mexican beer served in a frosted glass. Not forgetting the appetizer of hot salsa and tortilla chips. To live in the Hispanic Southwest is to live.

I was feeling my jockey's usual conflict of satisfaction and remorse when I paid the cashier. Turning to leave, I found Gavin Scott, the president of Peak Records, behind me in the line of gorged customers.

He was as surprised and filled with dislike for me as I was instantly of him. He literally inspected me up and down, inch by inch, Mr. Perfect, all two hundred pounds of him in a silk suit of summer-sky blue, and tie and shirt to match. Not one hair out of place on his wavy brown head. Bared teeth like rows of piano keys. I didn't look at his shoes. Light-brown beard neatly trimmed. I could even smell his Eastern establishment cologne. The big-time executive, I thought, biased, come West to take in gullible country/western performers who wouldn't know a good contract from one that took everything down to last Saturday's pair of dirty socks to tonight's guitar strings. I was biased, but I didn't care. Scott felt the same, by the way the pale blue eyes tried to put me down. He moved in a step, towering over me, his manner pure, undisguised intimidation. I didn't give an inch. My head came up.

He said: "You again . . . Clegg." That superior tone, giving me that satisfied look of old, that ridicule and scorn. "Still hanging around, I see."

That did it. The cause leading to the break-up that night at the motel flashed through me. I launched a roundhouse swing from the general direction of the parking lot. If I do say so, I have the strong upper body strength and hands that a jockey needs.

The blow took him on the point of his splendid, sculpted chin. It sent him reeling and flying across a laden table that two college boys occupied. Food flew like mud on an off track. Dishes crashed. Tableware clattered.

The boys yelled with indignation and jerked back from the table. Women screamed. Somebody was shouting in out-raged Spanish from the kitchen. The place was suddenly roaring.

Scott rose, his dignity collected. With meticulous care, he brushed a splatter of con carne off his sleeve and came at me in a trained weave. So the guy'd had boxing. So what? I didn't wait. We met like two bulls in a pasture. I slugged him on the jaw, in his middle. His head rocked back, but he didn't go down. His belly was sports-club hard. I kept throwing punches, landing and missing. In my eagerness, my hay-maker was wild. I wanted blood and busted bones. He had to have a soft spot somewhere. I kept swinging.

He feinted with his left and out of nowhere, fast, a fist caught me on the side of the jaw. So the guy *could* box a little. I fell, sprawling, in my ears a rising storm of screams and shouts. Somebody hollered for the police. That guy still shouting in stout Spanish had to be Pete.

I got up and charged Scott again. I knocked him against the long counter and sent customers scrambling, more dishes falling as the counter shook. He feinted with that clever left hand and slugged me right-handed under the ribs. More boxing. He hurt me, and my wind got short, but damned if I'd let him know. I just grunted and went for his jaw again, left and right, left and right, taking blows as I swung. No fancy stuff. I ached for contact. I pounded that flat, hard-muscled middle again. He gave ground, but he didn't go down. He tied me up. I broke free and rushed him again. His long arms punished me, but I refused to back up or let up. I kept punching, driven by all my pent-up feelings since the break-up. There seemed no limit to my will to fight. I'd never felt so good, bruises and all.

We were slugging away, in a virtual stand-off, when two cops burst into the place. We didn't stop then. I felt myself wrestled to the messy floor and handcuffed. When I got up, I saw that Scott was likewise in cuffs. His face was bloody, and his nice blue suit wasn't pretty any more. Too bad. My ribs ached, and I knew my face resembled a chunk of broiled steak, rare if you please.

Around us *Señor* Pete — I felt sorry for the friendly little guy with the Pancho Villa mustache for all the wreckage we'd caused — was raving and pointing at us. I couldn't blame him. We'd also ruined his luncheon business for the day.

I didn't say a word as the cops hustled us out to the squad car. But Scott, on his dignity, said: "I can explain everything, officer. This man attacked me. There are witnesses back there."

"Tell it to the judge."

"I want a good lawyer."

"You can find one in the phone directory, when we book you. I'm taking it you aren't local."

"You are quite correct."

The two cops shared a look, unimpressed.

When they booked us at the station, the desk sergeant seemed to write on and on, listing the charges, as he listened to the arresting officer.

"I want to talk to an attorney," Scott said.

"Use the phone."

He was still talking, when I was ushered into a cell, in need of bail money, unable to locate Charlie at the motel on another phone. I left word for the girl on the Amigo switchboard to tell Charlie where I was, no explanation till then, but nobody shot, nobody hurt. Mr. Vann, she said, had called to tell me that he would be late, still visiting friends. *Of all times!*

Scott looked sorely imposed on, when an officer walked him past my cell. We glared at each other. He halted. "You certainly created an embarrassing public spectacle," he said. "Typical, I'd say of you, Clegg."

"I was going to finish it, when we got interrupted."

His lordship strode on. The son-of-a-gun could box. Good punch, too.

It was seven o'clock before Charlie showed up. "What happened? Though I can pretty well tell by looking at your face. Did more than one jump you?"

I told him as briefly as I could, while leaving out the real issues: Lori's trip to Scott's room that night and his beating around the bush about the record contract. I just said we'd had a scuffle at the restaurant that went back to some nasty business when Lori was just starting out. Charlie accepted that with more than usual understanding and no questions asked. Charlie, my friend, then bailed me out.

I spent the remainder of the day nursing my bruises, feeling that each one was for a worthy cause.

There was a backlog of cases, and it was eleven o'clock in the morning before Gavin Scott, again

260

impeccably attired, this time in light gray, and I stood before the magistrate, a dour little Anglo whose forbidding expression said we could expect no clemency from him. An attorney in cowboy boots, loud shirt, and jeans stood with Scott. Charlie sided me.

First, the magistrate read our names, identifying us to himself as we nodded. "You are both charged with creating a public disturbance on Sudderth Drive and damaging private property, to wit the well-known business establishment of *Señor* Pedro Escobar, among this city's leading citizens, whose restaurant is known as *Señor* Pete's. Further to wit . . . two broken tables, three broken chairs imported from Juárez, numerous broken dishes and glasses. In addition, virtually the entire loss of *Señor* Escobar's noontime business, a loss which carried over into the evening because of a shortage of tables and chairs and dishes and glasses . . . You understand, I hope, that Ruidoso business people must make their money, if any, during the racing season? Otherwise, they go bankrupt."

Just then Escobar, arriving late, rushed in waving a long sheet of paper that he shoved at the magistrate, who scanned it and said: "In addition to the aforestated losses, *Señor* Escobar lists, to wit . . . one damaged lunch counter, which is now out of line and will have to be repaired. A coffee-maker broken by flying glasses, and four bent counter stools, plus an extensive cleaning of his business establishment that required him to hire additional help."

He looked up. "How do you plead, Mister Clegg?"

"Guilty, Your Honor."

"How do you plead, Mister Scott?"

"Not guilty, Your Honor."

The magistrate scowled. "On what grounds?"

"I didn't start the fight. Mister Clegg did. He attacked me."

"Hmm. Do you wish to go to trial on this matter?"

"I do, Your Honor."

Scott's attorney spoke up. "Your Honor, counsel asks to confer with his client at this juncture."

"Go right ahead."

The attorney took Scott aside, and they began to talk in low, earnest tones. From the attorney's gestures, he was trying to make a point. After a minute, Scott seemed to nod against his will.

Coming back, the attorney said: "Your Honor, in view of the difficulty of rounding up witnesses for his case, as justified as he feels his stand is, my client wishes to change his plea from innocent to guilty."

"Very well."

The magistrate made some quick notations and looked at us. "Each defendant is hereby fined one hundred dollars for disturbing the peace, each defendant six hundred dollars for damages to the business establishment of *Señor* Escobar, each defendant two hundred dollars for loss of business revenue caused by the disturbance and the damages, each defendant fifty dollars for cleaning costs of the aforesaid damaged establishment, and each defendant court costs of fifty dollars each." Another quick tabulation, and he smiled for the first time. "Which comes to an even thousand dollars each."

I was thinking that the price of rickety wooden chairs at *Señor* Pete's — "imported from Juárez" — had taken an astronomical jump in market value. My face must have reflected that reasoning, because he said: "Do you wish to question the court's ruling on this matter, Mister Clegg?"

"I do not, Your Honor." *Lord, just get me out of here before I go broke.*

"You, Mister Scott?"

"No questions, Your Honor."

"That's it, gentlemen."

We trailed out. Since the court, I immediately learned, would not accept my personal check, Charlie had to make arrangements. I would give him my check later. I waited outside while Charlie and the attorney lingered behind, talking horses and the Kansas Futurity, Charlie high on Smiley's filly.

Scott came out. He started to go on, but I said: "It was worth every cent of it as far as I'm concerned."

He leveled me that nasty look, but didn't speak. Like he had more important matters to tend to.

I wasn't finished. "I thought you had it coming to you after the night, here, in the motel, when Lori went to your room. That broke up our marriage."

He wheeled on me. "You're a flat damn' fool, Clegg! You lost a fine woman because you thought she'd cheated on you. Well, she never did with me, as much as I would've welcomed it. Indeed, I would have. She's earned all her honors, including that very profitable contract, on her singing and musical talents alone. No trade-outs. It's time you knew that, Clegg."

I suddenly felt numb.

"In case you wonder why I'm here, and I know you are, I've come to ask Lori Beth to be my wife."

He turned and walked away, full of himself.

I could only stand there, struck speechless, unable to move, my mind locked.

CHAPTER
NINETEEN

I was silent all the way to the motel, while at the same time Charlie was talkative. "I'd say that Gavin Scott had it coming, after what you told me. He's an uppity so-and-so. A cold fish."

"He is. I thought he had had it coming, too, but sometimes a man can jump to conclusions and be wrong."

He cut me a puzzled look, but I offered no explanation.

I needed to get away for a while by myself and think. At the motel, on the excuse that I had to go to town, I took the road toward Alto. I wasn't collected enough to call her yet. How was I going to make amends? What could I say? *Sorry* sounded mighty inadequate. Was it past that? I was proud of her and thankful that I'd been wrong. Now I was left with a burden of shame and guilt because I hadn't trusted her under suspicious circumstances. *Whatever happened to trust in people, Buck Clegg? Trust that goes beyond surface assurance?* Looking back, I tried to put together events leading to the break-up, playing it over, step by step. Scott had been in the picture for some time. He'd unfairly delayed and delayed on her contract. We rubbed each other wrong. I didn't like him as a man. He didn't like me, partly, I guess, because I came from a different world, but, mainly, because I was Lori's husband. It takes just one little match to start a forest fire, and the motel episode had furnished the needed spark.

I turned around and headed back. It was past one o'clock when I stopped at a pay phone and called the condo. Barbara Kemp answered: "Lori isn't in, Mister Clegg. May I take a message?"

"Guess not. Did she say when she'd be back?"

"No. She left with someone in a green Mercedes. Perhaps you know the party?" She was fishing. Ex-husband calls when former wife is out with another man.

"I'll call her later. Thank you."

The *later* turned out to be six o'clock, and Lori had gone out again. I'd missed her, which meant dinner for two, candlelight and wine. I had a drink with Charlie, and we went to dinner at his favorite barbecue joint and had a pitcher of beer.

But what I had to do couldn't be put off till tomorrow. By nine o'clock I had a far-back seat in the Pines, listening to the Wild Ones dig into "Just Like a Woman," Lori singing it just like a woman. It was going to be a long evening, but I could wait. Looking around, I spotted Gavin Scott at a table near the dance floor. He never took his eyes off the vocalist. I went to the bar for a beer.

So the evening dragged by. A minute before closing time at one, I noticed that Scott was gone. That hurried me, until I heard a voice from the crowd say: "Hey, Buck. Remember me?"

In the dim light, I had to look at him for a moment. It was Turner — Rod Turner, a jock friend I'd known in El Paso some years back. "Sure, Rod. How are you?" We shook hands. I knew that he'd had a lot of tough luck.

I heard the band sign off. I'd better hurry.

"I just got out of the hospital in Albuquerque," he said. "Been a long haul. You still a jockey's agent?"

"I am, but I've got two boys, and I'm working on another thing right now."

"I was hoping."

"I'll sure do what I can for you, Rod. Where are you staying?"

"With friends. I'd better call you from time to time. Where are you?"

"The Amigo." Time was getting away from me. I excused myself. "Rod, it's important that I catch somebody in the next few minutes. Tomorrow you go out to the track and talk to Mike Peterson. OK?"

It took another minute or two to work my way through the crowd to the club entrance, but a two-man shoving argument was going on. The pair blocked the doorway. A bouncer arrived and tried persuasion. "You guys go outside, so everybody can leave." When they insisted on continuing the argument there, the bouncer grabbed an arm. At which the pair jumped the bouncer. He was getting the worst of it, when another bouncer, pawing a path through the crowd, joined the fray. In a short time, the two bouncers cleared the doorway.

I hurried out and around to the rear of the building. By now the guard knew me and why I was there.

"You're late. Miss Drake just left with another guy in a Mercedes."

I bit my lower lip. Tomorrow, I thought, and tomorrow may be too late for Buck Clegg.

The light was on in Charlie's room, which struck me as unusual this late. I knocked. "This is Buck."

He let me in, and I could tell that something was up. Charlie looked grim. His eyes glinted. "That son-of-a-bitch called about eleven o'clock. He said it was his last call. I tried to carry him along . . . you know? Told him there was still an easy fifty thousand waiting for him . . . just return the horse. And, if he was nice, I might sweeten the pot up to seventy-five, or so. Maybe a hundred thousand, if the horse was sound. And guess what he said?"

"Believe I can," I said, remembering.

"He said that would just be peanuts. A hundred thousand would be peanuts. He was gloating! I can hear his voice yet. 'Peanuts, Charles B. Vann, peanuts.' Then the son-of-a-bitch hung up. He just called to rub it in. His last call. What does it mean, Buck?"

"You've said before, they had another deal cooking for the horse. This proves it's gone through."

"But what kind of a deal?"

"Biggest money is in drugs."

"Or Arab oil money? A deal to sell the horse out of the country?" He sat down and hung his head. "I keep thinking about the Shergar case. If this is gonna end the

268

same way . . . The horse never found." He had that doleful look. He went over to his duffel bag and pulled out a bridle. "It's not good to look back too much on sentimental things, but I brought Jim Ned's bridle along for luck."

"We can use some. Now let's get some rest. Maybe we better call Chief Ivy in the morning."

I was dressed and thinking about breakfast, when the phone rang. A faint, careful sounding, but unmistakable, voice, said: "*Señor* Buck?"

"Chip! You OK?"

"Listen. They're flying Jim Ned to Mexico at nine this morning."

I gulped. "Who is and from where?"

"The *gringo* gang." He talked faster, his voice still low. "From Sierra Blanca Airport. Nine o'clock. Big plane from Mexico. Drugs. Be careful, *amigo*."

The line went dead.

I felt a great lift. The old Chip I knew had called. The kid from Chihuahua with the guts, and the judgment, when to take a horse through a hole along the rail.

I roused Charlie and told him the news.

"Let's get Chief Ivy, have him call the county and the DEA, and we'll all be waiting when they bring the horse in," Charlie said, dressing fast, slapping his handgun.

"One thing bothers me," I said, turning it over in my mind. "If everybody goes busting in there too early . . . and the gang has a look-out at the airport, they might spook and not come in at all. We'd be back where we are now . . . no Jim Ned."

Charlie turned to me. "You mean . . . let them bring the horse in before we make our move?"

"Well . . . yes. Why don't I drive to the airport? When they trailer the horse in, I'll call back to the police station. There's an RV park about seven or eight miles this side of the airport. You and Ivy and the rest could hold there till you get word from the station to come on."

"I agree on the chance there'd be a look-out," he said. "We know these bastards are slick. But as for you going up there *à la* Buck Clegg . . . that's out. No more Elk City stuff. Been enough gettin' chased and shot at, and some strong man tryin' to throw you over high railings. We've come this far together, and we'll go on together."

Enough said.

He got Chief Ivy on the phone. They worked it out except for one change. If a phone call wasn't available when needed, one of us would rush back to the RV park as a backup messenger.

"Now," Charlie said worriedly, "what happens to Jim Ned when we jump the kidnappers? They'll come in before the plane lands. So there's no plane to load him on . . . the big drug deal's off. What will they do? Sure as hell, they'll gun him down on the spot just to spite us."

"We'll have something to say about that."

"Sure wish I had my old shotgun."

★ ★ ★

270

It was after seven o'clock when we left the motel, Charlie mindful to bring Jim Ned's bridle. Like a kid holding onto something dear. I understood.

There wasn't a cloud in the sky or plane on the wing as we drove up to the Sierra Blanca Regional Airport and parked. With no major airline connection, the facility depended mostly on private planes during the racing season. Charlie had hired a plane out of Albuquerque.

As we left our car, my eyes caught a green Nissan pickup. Curious, I went over. My breath took a leap when I saw an Oklahoma tag.

"What is it?" Charlie asked.

"The guys who followed me to Elk City drove a green Nissan pickup, remember?"

"Maybe it's a coincidence."

"Not with an Oklahoma tag. I think the look-out is here."

The office was at one end of a building which, I remembered, also housed a hangar. A large hangar lay to the west. We looked. No horse trailer drawn up there. We entered the one-clerk office and nodded. "Just waiting," we said. We walked on past other offices to check the smaller hangar. No trailer in front there. My watch read seven forty-two.

We strolled past two light planes to the far corner of the building, away from the office section. I suddenly checked myself, surprised to see a man watching the road to Fort Stanton, about four miles to the northeast. From where he stood he could also watch the Ruidoso road. He kept rubbing his chin and shifting his feet. He

271

took a few limping steps, sun-shading his eyes from the eastern sun. When he did, I got a partial view of his face, but that was enough. Recognition shot through me, hooking up with the Nissan. In the Norman Hospital room. A hard-featured, long, thin face. Underslung jaw. Sandy hair. Still limping from being run over. He'd seen us drive up. He'd seen me look at the pickup. Why hadn't he taken alarm? Well, he couldn't see my face at close range from there, and I'd been casual in my looking. But he would know me close-up as I knew him. I'd come that near, maybe, to nixing the whole thing.

I moved back to Charlie, muttering: "The look-out."

Out of sight, around at the front of the hangar, he asked: "Did you get a good look at him?"

"It's none other than the Norman Hospital Earl Smith, alias C. D. Cole, and others. We could take him. Knock him out?"

"Nothing I'd like more. But that would cause a commotion." He inclined his head toward a man who looked like a mechanic, crossing from the main hangar. "Let the look-out give us the signal when he spots the bunch coming with the horse. Use him. He can't hurt us."

"Better," I said, thinking bankers are used to a waiting game, whereas jockeys aren't.

We strolled back to the lobby of the office and discovered that we could see the look-out from here, which we couldn't before, because he had positioned himself closer to the road.

"May I help you?" the Hispanic girl at the desk inquired.

"Just waiting for some friends to come in," Charlie said, and thanked her.

I took him out of her hearing. "Chip didn't say which way they'd come in with the horse. Only two ways they can . . . the Fort Stanton road or the Alto road. In our hurry, I didn't think of it, either. Occurs to me just now they might bring the horse right by the RV camp."

Charlie grinned. "If they do, I'm sure Chief Ivy would stop *any* horse trailer . . . only with a bay horse, in particular, after I schooled him on the color of horses."

"That would be too easy a break. I can't see 'em hiding a horse around Alto or off the Ruidoso road. Too many people. Too congested. This has been an uphill fight all the way, Charlie, and I don't think it will change at the last minute."

"I'm afraid I have to agree."

We settled down to waiting and watching the look-out, who was showing nervousness. Pacing back and forth, he checked his watch frequently. I looked at mine. It was seven fifty-nine. Charlie sat down and folded his arms. I watched the road. Time seemed to inch by.

I heard a distant drone. Too early for the drug plane? I gave a mental shrug. We exchanged glances and drifted outside. The look-out appeared at the far corner of the hangar to look.

It wasn't the drug plane — it wasn't big enough to transport a racehorse. Instead, a light plane gliding in.

Two couples got out, chatting as they passed us into the lobby. We resumed out watch. The time: eight ten.

One of the women, middle-aged, white hair wind-blown, dressed in pink slacks and a pink blouse, put in a call at the pay phone. "Hi, Janey. This is Liz. Yeah, we just got in from Dallas. Great flight. Great weather out here. Couldn't wait to get away from the humidity . . . Did you get the tickets?" She listened a while. "Hey, that's great. Box seats, you say? Can't beat that. You sure went to bat for your old sorority sister and her new running mate . . . You'll be crazy about my Sylvester . . . I call 'im Sy . . . he's a peach and so devoted . . . Did we go to Sally Sue's wedding? Well, did we ever! And believe me, those hardboots back in Lexington know how to throw parties. Aged bourbon that you don't get out here. I slept every morning till eleven. I won't tell you how much I picked up . . . One afternoon, we went out to Calumet Farm and saw the great Alydar . . . Sy's promised me one of his colts . . . if the price is right."

As the woman continued to chat, with no indication of a let-up, her companions fidgeted. A gray-haired man beyond middle age, apparently her husband, kept a patient look as he carried on a courteous conversation.

His wife was still on the phone, when the look-out quit pacing, eyes on the Fort Stanton road. A blue sedan was approaching. Behind it a jeep, and behind the jeep a pickup pulling a white horse trailer.

Charlie sprang to the window. "Here they come!" He darted me a look of triumph, followed by a frustrated

274

fury. His ruddy face grim, his clamped mouth a slit. For a flash, I thought he'd head for the door.

"Let them come in," I said. "Let's see how many there are."

The look-out jumped to the road, waving them on.

At this distance I recognized two faces: the pockmarked man driving the lead vehicle, the spade-bearded Dr. Grubb driving the pickup pulling the horse trailer. I felt the grip of a powerful emotion as the trailer passed and I glimpsed strips of bay hide through the panels. Charlie was rigid, jaw set, hands knotted.

The faces I saw all wore big hats, pulled down low. The jeep's side curtains were up, so I couldn't make out who rode there, but it had to be Dapper Thompson and Golden Voice aboard, with only two people in the sedan. That looked like a woman riding with the pockmarked strongman. The woman at the farmhouse east of Chickasha? Everything was coming full circle. Where was Chip? In the pickup, I hoped.

They swung into the airport and drove across the tarmac near the main hangar and parked, the look-out limping fast to catch up.

Charlie stood riveted, eyes fixed on the trailer. It was eight twenty-five, time to call. I glanced at Charlie, but the Dallas woman was still gabbing and the Hispanic girl was busy on the office phone.

"Charlie," I said, "one of us has to go fast to the RV park."

"I'll go. Meanwhile, you stay put, hear me? No more à la Buck Clegg." He handed me the bridle. "Take care of this for me till I get back."

275

A late caution spoke to me as he stepped away. "Don't tear ass out of here all at once when you start off. Go a way before you do. They're on edge. They might spook on us."

I watched him leave, driving leisurely. *Good, Charlie, good.* A man beside the horse trailer was watching, also. It was Grubb. He soon faced around, apparently satisfied, and lit a cigarette. Pockmark and the woman stayed in the car. The pair in the jeep did the same. Waiting. Waiting. I saw no sign of Chip, which worried me. Had they caught him calling me? I didn't want to think past that.

It was eight thirty-two. I could feel my tension tightening, more than before any stakes race I remembered. *Get along, Charlie, pardner, get along.*

The mechanic Charlie had noticed walked across the tarmac to the main hangar, paying no attention to the vehicles or the horse trailer. Nothing new about horses flying in or out.

Pockmark left the sedan and crossed over to the jeep. The driver opened the door. They huddled to talk. A short parley and Pockmark turned back, an evident swagger in his walk. The look-out spoke to him, but he ignored the man and went on. A display of strong man self-importance, I'd say.

The gabby woman was finally off the phone. Janey was coming to pick up everybody, she said, and started enthusing about "what an absolutely gorgeous view Janey has from her condo. Goes great with Margaritas, Sy."

276

Charlie had been gone but a very short time, not enough time to reach the RV park, when I heard the roar of a big plane, coming hard from the southwest. I went outside. This could be it.

The pilot made a fast turn around the airport, wagged his wings in signal, and set the big bird down. A twin-engined job providing plenty of cargo space to hold a racehorse. The pilot taxied back and stopped about a hundred yards from the vehicles, but the motors continued to run.

The jeep rushed up to the plane, and two men got out. The driver, the short one with the banty-rooster strut, would be Dapper Thompson, the other one, slender, taller, very erect — Golden Voice.

Time was beginning to press. I kept glancing at the Alto road, hoping for what wasn't in sight.

There was an air of haste as a group of armed men quickly left the plane, looking all about as they did, and joined the pair from the jeep. They talked; they gestured. Golden Voice seemed to point to the horse trailer in affirmation, then back at the plane. There was a pause. The two groups appeared to disagree. The men from the plane drew apart and conferred. One stood out from the others. A tall Mexican wearing a broad white hat. He kept waving his rifle. When they turned around, he seemed to be doing most of the parleying. Golden Voice gestured at the trailer again, then the plane in a haggling manner.

Over by the trailer, Grubb was lighting another cigarette while he watched the proceedings. Pockmark watched beside the sedan, the woman still inside.

The Mexican spokesman, facing the plane, signaled, and a man tossed down a wrapped package. The spokesman tore open one end and motioned for Golden Voice to inspect it. He bent down to do so, but after some seconds, when he stood up, he seemed indifferent. The Mexican eyed him and spoke. Evidently Golden Voice was a sharp bargainer. I guessed he wanted more. The Mexican signaled again, and a second package came down.

The empty Alto road seemed to mock me.

I grew very still, feeling all hollow inside, suddenly knowing that I'd run out of time. When Golden Voice had finished examining the second package, and the deal was agreed on and the rest of the packages were unloaded, the gang would bring the horse up fast to be led aboard.

Strained, I glanced around me. Inside the hangar, next to the office, was a low, four-wheeled cart, on it an opened box of oil cans. Nearby, a tall, drawered tool chest. I was moving on instinct. I chose a long-handled, heavy wrench from the chest and laid it with the bridle behind the box. I found myself pushing the cart toward the trailer. Not too fast, but at a steady walk, my head lowered, hoping I attracted no attention. But what was a guy in a Western hat doing pushing a cart across the tarmac? Out of character, for certain.

Grubb was still facing the plane as I neared the rear of the trailer. No Chip, anywhere. I refused to think beyond that. Inside the pickup, for a flash I caught sight of a face. Chip? I couldn't tell. Could be another gang member.

From the corner of my eye, I caught that the bargaining at the plane seemed about to come to a close.

I saw Grubb's eyes slant around suspiciously as I reached the rear of the trailer. He threw down his cigarette and moved toward me. I stopped and picked up the wrench and hid it against my right thigh. When he came around the corner of the trailer, I brought the wrench down across his head. His eyes flew wide. He gave a little cry, staggered, and tried to grab me. I smashed him again. This time he buckled and stayed down. I kicked him under the rear wheels.

A shape ran up to me from the other side of the trailer. It was Chip. I scarcely recognized him. They'd beat hell out of him, but for some reason they needed a top jockey. Maybe part of the big deal from this side.

I shoved the bridle at him. "Quick," I said. "Bridle the horse. Back him out. Be quick!"

Chip was gone with the words.

At the plane, I saw both parties standing back. Packages being tossed out and stacked. The deal was done. Even the look-out man was there now.

I heard hoof clatter. Chip backed the big horse out. He looked way underweight, but there was fire in his bulging eyes, and he was kicking to go.

Before I could mount, I saw Pockmark lumbering toward us, shouting the alarm, waving an ugly handgun. I pulled my gun, and my snapped first shot only slowed down his bull rush. I steadied, and my second shot found him full in the chest. It lifted him up a little and knocked him back, a startled look showing on the pitted dead pan. He sprawled face down.

"Give me a leg up!" I yelled at Chip. It wasn't easy; the horse was dancing and rearing. On the second boost, Chip lifted me to the bare back. I clutched black mane. He hurried me the reins. I said: "Run! Anywhere! Be fast! Get away! Now!"

He hesitated.

"Run!" I yelled. "Over there!"

He ducked away, sprinting for the open main hangar, where two mechanics watched.

Under me, I could feel the big horse trembling to run. He broke with a terrific rush as he always had. A hard horse for a jockey to stay with, they used to say, but an easy horse to ride. Like hell! It was all I could do to hang on bareback.

As I headed him west around the hangar, toward the juniper trees flanking the Alto highway, I saw Thompson and Golden Voice running for the jeep. The race was on. Ahead, mainly unfenced, open country.

I slowed him down after the first couple hundred yards. We began to fight each other. He hated me. He wanted to kill me. He started buckjumping in a circle. I brought him around. He tried straight ahead sunfishing, but he wasn't a professional rodeo bucking horse. I yanked his head up. He still fought me — hated me even more. He wanted the freedom the man on his back denied him. Tearing at the bit, he lunged for a juniper to rake me off sideways. We missed the tree by a foot. I yelled at him. I straightened him. I held him in. I cussed him to myself. *You big bastard. You'd run*

280

yourself out in half a mile or less. You've got a distance to go, and, by God, you're gonna do it! My arms were just hanging extensions of lead. A little more and I felt he'd jerk them out of their sockets. I hunched over, elbows tight, legs slipping against sweat-greased hide.

We rode on at a gallop. He seemed to like that, temporarily, then he tried to run away again. I fought him, rode him like a leech, sometimes thrown clutching on his neck.

He seemed to settle down again, some of his hellish spirit burned up. I had no idea how far we'd gone. That was when I caught the high-speed whine of a car on the highway. I looked. But it wasn't my bunch coming from the RV park. It was coming from the airport — the jeep. They'd caught up. The horse was still valuable to them, still their big swap for the drugs.

I heard the whiz of a bullet glancing off wood behind us and the blast of the gun. I turned the galloping big horse away from the highway, into the scattered junipers. Too scattered — I soon saw — more open country.

When I looked again, the jeep was off the highway, circling in fast to cut us off. It vanished below a grassy fold. I decided to cut back closer to the highway, toward thicker cover. Maybe slip between them. We ran weaving through more junipers, the big horse blowing hard.

Now a new roar on the road. More than one car. Coming from Alto — it was — coming fast.

We ran through the cover.

281

I almost pulled up at sight of the parked jeep straight ahead. Thompson with rifle raised, leaning this way and that to get a shot at me, Golden Voice ready to grab reins. They still wanted the horse.

Desperation took me. I stayed low. Instead of veering off, I kept my horse running at them. At the final instant, they tried to jump aside. We plowed between them, split them. I heard and felt horseflesh strike bodies. Screams. My last glimpse, as we broke clear, was of a face falling away. Thin, haughty, full of arrogance and hate — Golden Voice.

We kept running. I asked the big horse for more, and he gave me all he had. Free, now. Across on the highway cars had stopped. Men running this way, shouting.

I didn't see the deep wash till it was suddenly before us. Jim Ned tried to jump it. He couldn't. His front quarters dropped. I went flying over his head, still grasping the reins.

Old survival reflexes took over. Roll. Keep rolling. I was going to hit on my left shoulder and side. I struck and kept rolling, but pain shot up through my back and legs. I knew I was blacking out. The last I remembered was holding onto the reins and Jim Ned dragging me. Then, oddly, the big horse stopped.

CHAPTER
TWENTY

The hospital smells were all too familiar. They took me back to my last race. The fast Thoroughbred filly on the lead in the six-furlong stakes at Sunland. The field in the turn now, me tucked in along the rail, waiting to make my move on a tough colt called Gila Gold. The filly suddenly snapping a foreleg and breaking down sideways. My horse crashing into her. I saw where I was going to hit and rolled as I did. But the apprentice rider behind me didn't seem to know what to do, or was blocked off and couldn't go outside. He galloped right through us.

Buck Clegg had a broken right femur, fancy name for the thigh, and a broken ulna in my left forearm. Nasty breaks. To that add two broken ribs, a punctured lung, and damaged vertebrae.

But hold on. The smells were the same, all right, but that wasn't my last race. Besides, I didn't have a broken femur or ulna — at least, I didn't think so. My pain seemed localized in my lower back and legs. So my clearing head informed me. I moved with a groan and looked into the concerned brown eyes of Charlie, bending over my bed. I saw his relief, but the concern didn't go away.

"You two had a nasty spill," he said. "Happened not long after you broke into the clear."

"Jim Ned?" I said, dreading to ask. When he didn't answer at once, I feared the worst. "You didn't have to . . ."

"Didn't have to put him down. But he'll never run again. Garbaged one knee and a cannon bone. But he's still a horse. I'll take him home, and he can stand there the rest of his days, passing on his good traits. Thanks to Buck Clegg and Chip Romero."

"We all tried," I said, and I told him what Chip had done at the airport. "Now tell me what day this is."

He smiled. "The morning after the biggest race Jim Ned ever ran and the biggest you ever rode. I've got a lot to bring you up to date on. But, first, I want you to do something for me."

"What's that?"

"Show me you can move your legs. You've had us all worried around here. One more bad fall like at Sunland . . ."

I threw back the covers, and slowly, inch by inch, hurting, I lifted my right leg.

"Good," he said. "Now the other one."

I repeated the move, the left leg a little easier. I was puffing when I finished.

"You see," he said, "you hardly moved at all till this morning." He sighed and literally flopped into a chair by the window. "The gang kept the horse up around Fort Stanton. Don't ask me for details. I'll know more later . . . Golden Voice, as you call him, known as James Bernard Madison . . . ex-TV actor, ex-would-be

Shakespearean actor, ex-two-bit Western actor and freeloader who used to hang around Ruidoso, is down the hall from you badly bunged up and under guard . . .

"Dapper Thompson tried to make a run for it in the jeep. He's being held for the FBI, a guest at Chief Ivy's Cross-Bar Hotel . . . Doctor Grubb is also here under guard, with a skull fracture. We've got more cops than patients. This place looks like an armed camp. Chip filled me in on how you stopped Grubb . . . The pockmarked muscle man died at the scene. Chief Ivy is still checking his identification . . . figures he's out of the Dallas-Fort Worth area. An enforcer type."

"He was that," I agreed.

"That leaves alias Earl Smith, the look-out, who was picked up at the airport without a fight."

"There was a woman riding with the muscle man."

"Just a camp follower. They'll probably release her, after they've had time to question her at length. She wasn't armed. Didn't do anything . . . That accounts for all the gang, except for a fringe character or two back in Oklahoma . . . The DEA made a big haul at the airport, but they had to go in shooting. Some five million dollars' worth of marijuana and cocaine and the plane."

"There seemed to be some bargaining going on between Golden Voice and the head trafficker."

"That head honcho is a prominent Mexican rancher and horseman. He must have wanted Jim Ned in a big way for match racing to bring in five million in drugs . . . This thing is snowballing, gets bigger by the hour

. . . There's a Medellin connection . . . the plane is registered in Colombia."

A sad expression moved into his face, growing deeper. "Now this will shock you as much as it did me. Golden Voice is singing like a canary, eager to tell everything." In a hurting voice, he said: "It was Tom Shelby who led Jim Ned from the paddock out to the highway that night. That was one thing that always troubled me . . . how a total stranger could lead out a big stallion, even one with a nice disposition, and put him in a trailer he didn't like without makin' a ruckus?"

I was shocked into silence.

"But why," Charlie said, shaking his head, still trying to deny it, "why would Tom do that to himself and his family and his friends?"

We both knew. We just didn't want to say it.

"Tom needed money desperately," Charlie went on. "Big gambling losses. Wilma told us that, but said Tom had done better lately. That was after the payoff, of course. Golden Voice paid Tom five thousand dollars in cash to lead the horse out. But it didn't end there."

"How do you mean?"

"After the gang involved Tom, they not only threatened him . . . they threatened to harm his family, if he told me or went to the authorities. He must have carried around one hell of a burden. He just couldn't go on."

"But how did they get to know Tom?"

"After they had the idea to steal the horse, they cased the ranch. Watched our comings and goings. Learned our schedule. Even came in with visitors a few times to

286

learn the lay-out and see what we looked like. Found out who worked there. Who was the ranch manager. They trailed Tom around and soon found out that he gambled big on week-ends at Remington . . . and lost big . . . One thing for sure, Wilma will never learn one word of this from me. I want her to remember Tom as a good man."

I nodded to that.

Charlie got up. "I've burned your ears long enough. Get some rest." At the door, he turned and said with a half grin: "We found two gorilla masks in the jeep. Golden Voice just has to be a play actor. No better at this than he was on the stage. Sometimes, as the poet said . . . 'the best-laid schemes o' mice and men gang aft agley.'"

I dozed till the door opened. Chip Romero and Rosa stood there, undecided about entering. I sat up and waved them in.

Chip, his eyes mere bright chinks in the swollen face, gave me a light *abrazo*. From Rosa a gentle pat on the my head.

"How you feelin', *amigo?*" he asked.

"First rate . . . and lucky. Here, because some *hombre* from Chihuahua bridled a horse lightning fast for me. This *hombre* is a great friend. Before that, he called me on the phone at great danger to himself."

He shrugged it off.

"Sit down," I said.

They seemed embarrassed, yet determined.

Rosa looked at Chip before she turned to me. "Chip wants to tell you what happened, *Señor* Buck."

"Tell me whatever you want, Chip. I'll listen."

"Doctor Grubb came to see me. Said he'd read in newspaper I was in the hospital. Said he was sorry I was in there . . . couldn't ride for a while. Easy talker, that man . . . Next time he asked me if I wanted a fix. I guess he could see my need. I said, yes. Next time he slipped me a couple lines of coke. Said he knew I was a good jockey. Said again he was sorry I couldn't ride in New Mexico. But he knew a place where I could . . . for big money . . . in Mexico . . . Before I did, he wanted me to see this fast horse. If I liked him, I'd be the horse's groom till he was shipped to Mexico. There I'd ride him in big match races for big *hacendado*. Meantime, I could have all the drugs I wanted . . . He was waitin' when I left the hospital. All smiles, that man. But when I got in his car, something strange happen to me. His beard, his face — 'Chip cupped his hands close to his cheeks,' — made me think of the devil. I was afraid. I thought of my Rosa. Would I ever see her again? He took me to some buildings at Fort Stanton . . . That night I got real high, *Señor* Buck. I did. I was afraid." He seemed to look at me for understanding.

"Go on," I said.

"Next morning the doctor show me this big bay stud. Man, he fill my eye. His weight was down. They no feed that horse right. That day I feed him and groom him good . . . he like that. When I thought they no look, I walk him around outside. But the doctor he see. He get real mad. 'Never take that horse outside again,' he tell me."

Chip looked at Rosa for assurance. She smiled.

He continued: "Next day I ask doctor who this big horse is. He get mad again. 'Just do as you told, you greaser kid,' he say. Pretty soon this man with the bad face come in and beat me up. I know then this big horse is Jim Ned . . . But I say nothing . . . I hear the *gringos* talk at night. How rich they gonna be when they sell Jim Ned for big drug shipment. They laugh big. I was usin' again. I seemed to lose track of time . . . One night, I hear them say the time had come. Big plane with drugs from Mexico be in next morning at nine o'clock. *Gringos* on big drunk. When they slow gettin' up next morning, I slip away and call you."

"Where in the world did you find a phone?"

"In little office. Same phone they use talkin' to Mexico. I slip back fast. I know if they see me, they kill me quick."

I studied his battered face. "If you hadn't called, Jim Ned would be in Mexico. You, too . . . maybe . . . or worse."

He stood up, finished, free of his burden.

"In a way," I said, proud of him, "it was like a race. You knew when to wait, when to make your move. And you did."

He shrugged. "I'm goin' back into hospital. This time I'll stay."

"I believe you will."

They left with warm, backward glances.

Down the stretch, I thought, class tells in people, same as it does in good horses. Chip knows he'll never be cured, but he has a strong support system in Rosa, a good drug counselor, his race riding, and he still has his old friend, *Señor* Buck, who believed in him from the start.

I must have drifted off again, because I didn't know anyone was in the room until I felt a touch and Lori said: "I just heard this morning what happened. It's been on the news. Charlie says you are feeling much better. Before long you'll walk out of here."

I blinked. "I'm fine." No sympathy, please.

"I'm very glad."

"Did Charlie tell you about Jim Ned?"

"He just told me about you. He's so relieved. So am I."

"Jim Ned will never run again. Injured himself when we went down. But he can stand back at Charlie's farm. His breeding won't be lost."

"That's good."

My attempt at a small laugh hurt my ribs. "Seems like it always comes around to horses, doesn't it?"

"Well, Jim Ned is a much loved, famous horse. I understand people wept when Secretariat died."

"Yeah. I did a little."

"You're impossible, Buck Clegg."

"Guess so." I looked up at her, feeling guilty as hell. "Did you know that Gavin Scott and I had a knock-down, drag-out fight? Just about wrecked a restaurant, and we got fined big in court?"

"Yes. He told me. I could see that he'd been in a fight."

"Did he tell you what he told me?"

"Yes."

"I'll say this . . . he's an honest man. Since then, I've tried to see you. But he was always there ahead of me . . . Then this happened. I was wrong. I made a terrible mistake. I can't put into words how I feel."

"I was wrong, too, that night . . . I've also come to tell you that the band is flying back to Vegas this afternoon. The Pines can book another group. That was the agreement when we came, if our plans worked out in Vegas. They did. Bigger prospects are in the offing."

"I sure wish you luck."

"You, too."

"I've already had mine."

"There is something else . . . I sent Gavin away. Now, when you get back on your feet, could you come to Vegas?"

"I imagine I could work that into my social calendar."

She kissed me, none of that cheek stuff — and then she was gone, the scent of her still lingering in the room. *No high-sounding promises between us, no demands. Just come. Sometimes people get a second chance when they least expect it. Not all luck is on the race track, Buck Clegg.*